MATT JENSEN:
THE LAST MOUNTAIN MAN
MASSACRE AT POWDER RIVER

This Large Print Book carries the
Seal of Approval of N.A.V.H.

MATT JENSEN:
THE LAST MOUNTAIN MAN
MASSACRE AT
POWDER RIVER

WILLIAM W. JOHNSTONE
WITH J. A. JOHNSTONE

WHEELER PUBLISHING
A part of Gale, Cengage Learning

GALE
CENGAGE Learning®

Detroit • New York • San Francisco • New Haven, Conn • Waterville, Maine • London

GALE
CENGAGE Learning®

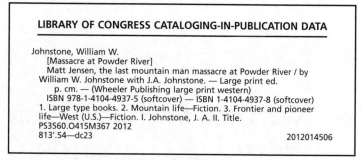

LIBRARY OF CONGRESS CATALOGING-IN-PUBLICATION DATA

Johnstone, William W.
  [Massacre at Powder River]
  Matt Jensen, the last mountain man massacre at Powder River / by William W. Johnstone with J.A. Johnstone. — Large print ed.
    p. cm. — (Wheeler Publishing large print western)
  ISBN 978-1-4104-4937-5 (softcover) — ISBN 1-4104-4937-8 (softcover)
  1. Large type books. 2. Mountain life—Fiction. 3. Frontier and pioneer life—West (U.S.)—Fiction. I. Johnstone, J. A. II. Title.
PS3560.O415M367 2012
813'.54—dc23
                                                      2012014506

Published in 2012 by arrangement with Pinnacle Books, an imprint of Kensington Publishing Corp.

Printed in the United States of America
1 2 3 4 5 6 7 16 15 14 13 12

Matt Jensen:
The Last Mountain Man
Massacre at Powder River

PROLOGUE

20 Grosvenor Square, London, England
June 23, 1944

Overhead, the distinctive buzzing sound of the approaching V-1 bomb grew silent and the guards around General Eisenhower's headquarters looked up to the east to watch a small, pulse-jet-powered, square-winged flying bomb tumble from the sky. It was followed by a heavy, stomach-shaking blast as the missile exploded, sending a huge column of smoke roiling into the air.

A few moments later an olive-drab Packard glided to a stop in front of the American Headquarters. The car was festooned with three small flags attached to the hood ornament: a U.S. flag, a British flag, and the four star flag denoting it to be the car of General Dwight D. Eisenhower. Captain Kay Summersby, the general's female driver, hurried around to open the back door as the general came out of headquarters. Before Eisenhower got into the car his chief of staff stepped outside.

"We just got the all clear, General," General Walter Bedell Smith said. "No more buzz bombs are headed this way."

"Thanks, Beetle," Eisenhower said as he climbed into the backseat.

General Smith and the guards saluted as the car drove away.

Fifteen minutes later the Packard drew to a stop in front of Number 10 Downing Street, and Kay Summersby hurried around to open the door for General Eisenhower.

"Thank you, Kay."

He was met at the curb by Phyllis Moir, Winston Churchill's private secretary. "This way, General. The PM is in the cabinet room."

General Eisenhower followed the secretary through the labyrinthine halls of the residence of the Prime Minister of Britain, and past the two pairs of Corinthian columns that led into the cabinet room. Churchill, with the ever-present cigar protruding from his mouth, was standing at a small bar, pouring whiskey.

"Tennessee mash for you, right, General?" Churchill said. "I prefer Mortlach, which is an excellent single-malt Scotch."

He handed Eisenhower a glass. The whiskey in the glass caught a beam of light that passed through one of the enormous windows, causing the liquor to glow as if lit from within.

"Please," Churchill said when he had his own glass. "Have a seat." He indicated a small seating area which consisted of an ox-blood leather couch and two facing saddle-leather chairs. Eisenhower chose the couch. A coffee table separated the sofa and chairs. Churchill flicked the long white ash from the end of his cigar into the crystal ashtray on the table before he settled his rather large frame into one of the chairs.

"Any word on the buzz bomb attack?" Eisenhower asked.

"Six killed at the Waterloo Station," Churchill said.

"That's a shame."

"Better than last weekend, when we lost two hundred to the attacks. What's our status with the invasion?"

"We're advancing toward Cherbourg," Eisenhower said. "I expect we will have it within a few days."

"Good, good, that's wonderful news. Oh, by the way, I want to thank you for that pile of Western novels you sent over last week."

"I'm glad I had them."

"You enjoy reading Western novels, do you?"

"Yes, sir, I do. I keep a stack of them on my bedside table, and probably read about three a week."

"Outstanding," Churchill said. "I'm a fan of the American Western novel as well. Who is your favorite Western author?"

"I'm fairly eclectic. I like Zane Grey of course, Owen Wister, Max Brand, and Andy Adams."

"Wonderful," Churchill replied enthusiastically. "I like them as well." He held out his glass. "Shall we drink to the American West?"

"It would be an honor." General Eisenhower held his glass to Churchill's. The men drank; Eisenhower took but a sip, while Churchill took a large swallow.

"Tell me, General" — Churchill wiped his lips with the back of his hand — "have you ever read anything about a Western hero named Matt Jensen?"

"Yes, of course." Eisenhower smiled. "In fact, I even know a bit of trivial information about him. His real name wasn't Jensen, it was . . ." Eisenhower paused for a moment, as if trying to recall.

"Cavanaugh," Churchill said, supplying the name. "Matthew Cavanaugh, but after he was orphaned, he took on the name of his mentor, Smoke Jensen."

"Whose real name was Kirby Jensen," Eisenhower said. "And he was quite a hero himself. But, tell me, Mr. Prime Minister, how is it that you know so much about Matt Jensen?"

"I have what you might call a vested interest in that gentleman," Churchill replied.

"All right, now you have me hooked. Why do you have a vested interest in one of America's Old West heroes?"

Churchill took another swallow of his scotch. "I have piqued your interest, have I?"

"I must confess that you have," Eisenhower replied.

"If it had not been for Matt Jensen I would not be the Prime Minister of Great Britain, and I would not be sitting here before you, discussing the greatest invasion in the history of warfare."

"How is that so?"

"Matt Jensen saved my life."

CHAPTER ONE

Livermore, Colorado
Late March 1884

When Jarvis Winslow returned home from the city council meeting, he wondered why the house was dark. His wife and daughter should be there, and supper should be on the table.

"Julie?" he called. "Julie, are you here?"

Winslow walked over to a nearby table, then lit a lantern. Light filled the room as he turned it up. "Julie?"

"Hello, Mr. Winslow," a man said, stepping into the living room from the hallway. He was a smallish man, with black hair and a large, hooked nose. He had a big red spot on his cheek and a gun in his hand.

"What?" Winslow gasped. "Who are you? What's going on here?"

"Who I am doesn't matter," the gunman said. "And what is going on is a bank robbery."

13

"A bank robbery? Are you insane? I'm the president of the bank, but I don't keep any money in my house. Wait a minute, I know who you are. You are Red Plummer, aren't you?"

Two other men came into the room then.

"If you know who I am, then you know I am someone you had better listen to. Let me introduce my associates, Manny Sullivan and Paddy McCoy. You don't want to get them angry, either."

"Where is my wife? Where is my daughter?" Winslow asked.

"They are safe. For the time being," Plummer said. "Would you like to see them?"

"Yes."

"They are back in the bedroom. Bring your lantern."

"Julie?" Winslow called, grabbing the lantern and hurrying into the bedroom. When he stepped through the door he saw his wife and his daughter, both stripped absolutely naked and tied to the bed. They had gags in their mouths, and terror in their eyes.

"What the hell have you done to them?" Winslow shouted angrily.

"We ain't done nothin' yet." Plummer looked over at the other two men. "But I have to tell you, I'm havin' a hard time

14

keepin' Sullivan and McCoy off of 'em."

"I want the young one," Sullivan said, rubbing his crotch.

"You bastard! She is only twelve years old!" Winslow said.

"Maybe so, but she's comin' along real good."

"You see what I'm having to deal with?" Winslow said. "Now, the only way I'm goin' to be able to keep them away from your women is if you do exactly what I tell you to do."

"What do you want?" Winslow asked. "I'll do it."

"I want you to go to the bank, get every dollar the bank has, then bring it here. Once we have the money, we'll be on our way."

"I'll get the money. Just — just don't do anything to hurt my wife and daughter."

Plummer smiled, showing a mouth full of crooked and broken teeth. "I thought we might be able to work something out."

Winslow took one last look at his wife and daughter, then hurried out of the house and over to the bank, which was just one block away. Inside the bank he emptied the safe, taking out twenty-three thousand dollars, and stuffing the money into a bag. He started to leave, but before he did, he scribbled a quick note.

When he got back to the house, he hurried into the bedroom. "I got the money. Let them go."

Then, looking toward the bed, he gasped. Their throats had been cut and blood was all over the bed. His wife and daughter were looking up with glazed, sightless eyes.

"You bastards!" he shouted, throwing the money bag toward Plummer.

"Really now, Winslow, you didn't think we were going to let you live after you knew our names, did you?"

So shocked by the sight of his wife and daughter, Winslow didn't realize McCoy was behind him until he felt the knife thrust into his back.

One week later
Matt Jensen walked into the Gold Nugget Saloon in Fort Collins, twenty miles south of Livermore. On the wall was a sign:

Card cheats will not be allowed
in this establishment.
Please report any cheating to the
Management.

In addition to the sign cautioning gam-

16

blers against cheating, the walls were decorated with game-heads and pictures, including one of a reclining nude woman. Three bullet holes strategically placed had augmented the painting, though one shot was slightly off, giving her left breast two nipples. Below the painting was a mirror which reflected back the long glass shelf of whiskey bottles. At each end of the bar was a large jar of pickled eggs as well as pickled pigs' feet.

The saloon was also a first-class brothel and Matt saw one of the girls taking a cowboy up the stairs at the back of the room.

The upstairs area didn't extend all the way to the front. The main room, or saloon, was big, with exposed rafters below the high, peaked ceiling. There were a score or more customers present, sitting at tables or standing at the bar talking with the girls, drinking or playing cards.

Matt was one of those standing at the bar when a woman known as Magnificent Maggie went over to him and put her arm through his. She got her name, not from her beauty, but from her size. Weighing over three hundred pounds, she was the owner of the Gold Nugget.

"Welcome, Mr. Jensen. It has been a while

since you have graced us with your presence. What brings you to Fort Collins?"

"You know me, Maggie. I follow the tumbleweed." Matt looked around the saloon. "You seem to be doing a pretty good business today."

"Some days are better than others. Could I get you something to drink, Mr. Jensen?"

"Yes."

"Wine, beer, or whiskey?"

"Whiskey."

At the back of the saloon a piano player with a pipe clenched in his teeth, wearing a round derby hat and garter belts around his shirt sleeves, was playing "The Gal I Left Behind Me," though few were listening.

"Oh my, still alone? You haven't found a girl to keep you company?" Maggie asked when she returned with Matt's whiskey.

Matt put his arm around her shoulders. "Maggie, do you think I could settle for anyone but you?"

Magnificent Maggie laughed out loud. "My, my, Mr. Jensen you do have a gift for the blarney. But what would you do if I thought you were serious and took you up on it?"

"I don't know. I'd do my best, I guess," Matt replied.

She laughed again, a loud cackle that rose

over the piano music and all the conversation in the room. "Oh, damn! You just made me laugh so hard that I peed in my drawers."

Matt had just taken a swallow and at her pronouncement he laughed, spewing out some whiskey.

She hurried off to take care of the situation, leaving Matt standing alone at the bar, smiling and drinking his whiskey.

One of the customers got up and walked over to Matt, carrying his beer with him. "Hello, Matt. It's been a while."

"Hello, Bart," Matt replied.

"What are you doing in Fort Collins?"

"A man's got to be somewhere. You still deputying?"

"No, I'm working as a messenger for Wells Fargo now. It pays some better. Oh, by the way, I suppose you heard what happened in Livermore last week?"

"No, what?"

"Bart, there's an open chair. You in or not?" someone called from one of the tables.

"Ah, I've been waiting to get into the card game." Bart held up his beer. "It was good seeing you again."

"What happened in Livermore?" Matt asked.

"Someone killed the bank president and

his wife and daughter. There's a paper down at the end of the bar. You can read all about it."

Matt moved down to the end of the counter where newspapers were stacked. He put a nickel in the bowl and took one, then found an empty table where he sat down to read.

Gruesome Find!

In what may be the most gruesome event in the history of Livermore, Jarvis Winslow and his wife and daughter were found murdered in their home.

Mr. Winslow was president of the bank and many will tell you there was no finer man for the job, as he always showed a willingness to work with people who needed loans.

Mrs. Winslow and her young daughter were discovered tied to a bed, their throats cut and their clothes removed, giving evidence of ravages being visited upon them. Mr. Winslow was on the floor with a knife wound in his back.

The murder seems to be connected to the bank robbery, for over twenty-three thousand dollars is missing. In what must be considered a clue, a paper was found in the bank bearing the names Red Plummer, Manny Sullivan and Paddy McCoy.

The funeral of the three slain was attended by nearly all residents of the city.

Jarvis Winslow, like Matt Jensen, had been an orphan in the Soda Creek Home for Wayward Boys and Girls. They were there at the same time, and a friendship had developed between them. Though they had not maintained steady contact, Matt considered Winslow a brother of sort, and he took it personally when Jarvis and his family were killed in such a way.

Matt was too late for the funeral, but he went out to the cemetery where he found three fresh mounds of dirt, side by side. There was only one tombstone set in the middle of the three graves.

JARVIS WINSLOW
His Wife JULIE
His Daughter CYNTHIA

*Plucked from this earthly abode
by a deed so foul as to
defy all understanding*

Two years older than Matt, Jarvis had

21

helped him adjust to life in an orphanage. Matt remembered a moment he had shared with Jarvis.

"You don't have any brothers?" Jarvis asked.

"No. I had a sister, but I don't anymore."

"I don't have any brothers either. You want to be my brother?"

"Sure, why not?"

Jarvis stuck a pin in the end of his thumb bringing up a drop of blood. Matt did the same thing, and they held their thumbs together.

"Now we are blood brothers," Jarvis said. "And that is as real as real brothers."

"Jarvis," Matt said, speaking quietly over the three graves. "I don't know if your spirit is still hanging around here or not. I reckon that's a mystery we only find out after we're dead. But in case your spirit is here, and you can hear me, I'm going to make you this promise. I intend to find the lowlife sons of bitches who did this to you and your wife and daughter, and I am going to send their sorry asses to hell."

Matt left the cemetery, then rode across town to the sheriff's office. When he went inside he saw Sheriff Garrison and two of his deputies looking at Wanted posters.

"Matt Jensen," the sheriff said, smiling

broadly as he walked around his desk with his hand extended. "What brings you to Livermore?"

"The murder of Jarvis Winslow."

The smile left the sheriff's face. "Yes. That was a terrible thing. The woman and the girl." He shook his head. "I've been in the law business for a long time and I've seen some grizzly things, but I tell you the truth, Matt, that is about the worst I have ever seen. I don't know what kind of animal could do such a thing. They had both been raped, Matt. Then their throats were cut and they bled to death. Not only that, we found 'em both naked. The sons of bitches didn't even have the decency to cover 'em up."

"Jarvis Winslow was a personal friend of mine," Matt said.

"Oh, I'm sorry," the sheriff replied.

"Sheriff, I intend to hunt down the men who did this, if you don't mind the help."

"Of course I'm glad to have your help. I can even deputize you if you'd like. That would make it legal, as long as you catch up with them in Larimer County. Once they get out of the county, your badge wouldn't do you much good."

"That's all right," Matt said. "I've got my own badge."

Over the years, he had done investigative work for the railroad, for which he had a railroad detective's badge. Even though the badge had no actual legal authority, a detective for one railroad was recognized on a reciprocal arrangement by all other railroads. It was also given a courtesy recognition by the states served by the railroads. He showed the badge to Sheriff Garrison.

"I don't see how that is going to help. This crime had nothing to do with the railroad."

"I read in the paper that Plummer, Jenkens, and McCoy got away with twenty-three thousand dollars. Is that right?"

"I'm afraid it is right," Sheriff Garrison said.

"Sheriff, are you going to try and tell me that not one single dollar of that money was ever on a train?"

Sheriff Garrison chuckled. "That's sort of stretching the intent, isn't it?"

"Yeah," Matt replied, his answer almost a challenge.

Garrison threw up his hands. "Well, you'll get no argument from me. Go after them."

"Oh, I intend to."

CHAPTER TWO

Moreton Frewen was an unquenchable optimist, prolific in ideas, and skilled in persuading his friends to invest in his schemes. Although he owned the Powder River Cattle Company, his personal field of operations covered America, England, India, Australia, Kenya, and Canada. He had crossed the Atlantic almost one hundred times.

A brilliant man who urged the building of a canal across the Isthmus of Panama, as well as a means of connecting the Great Lakes to the sea, he was, despite his intellect and creativity, a man who had failed in nearly every business enterprise he undertook. Frewen had the build of an athlete with long legs, a flat abdomen, a high forehead, bright blue eyes and a baroque mustache. An avid hunter and sportsman, he had attended Cambridge University in England as a gentlemen, spending his days

25

betting on horse races and his evenings in the university drinking club.

After graduation he continued the life of a country gentleman, fox hunting and wenching in the shires through the winter, and horse racing and wenching in London during the summer. Living in such a way as to show no interest in a career, he ran through his rather sizeable inheritance within three years. Shortly thereafter, he came to America, married Clara Jerome, daughter of the very wealthy Leonard Jerome and sister of Lady Randolph Churchill, and set himself up as a rancher in northern Wyoming.

Along the Powder River was a stretch of prairie with grasslands watered by summer rains and winter snows. A large open area, it was impressive in its very loneliness, but good cattle country, and it was there that Moreton Frewen built his ranch.

Two of the Powder River Cattle Company cowboys, Max Coleman and Lonnie Snead, were at the north end of the twenty-thousand-acre spread, just south of where William's Creek branched off the Powder River. They were keeping watch over the fifteen hundred cattle gathered at a place providing them with shade and water, and were engaged in a discussion about Lily

26

Langtry.

"They say she is the most beautiful woman in the world," Snead said.

"That's a load of bull. I've seen pictures of her, and she ain't half as good-lookin' as Mrs. Frewen is."

"Yeah, well, Mrs. Frewen is the wife of our boss. We can't really talk about her like that."

"Hell, I ain't sayin' nothin' about her that ever'body else don't say," Coleman said. "All I'm talkin' about is that she is a real good-lookin' woman. You ain't a' doubtin' that, are you?"

"No, I ain' doubtin' that. But she's our wife's boss, so I don't think about her like that. But now, Miss Langtry, why I can think any way about her that I want to, 'cause she's a single woman, and besides which, she goes around the country singin' up on the stage, so she's used to people lookin' at her."

"Yeah, but with her, lookin' is all you can do," Coleman said.

"And day dreamin'," Snead said. "Sometimes I get to day dreamin' about her and I think maybe she's been captured by Injuns, or maybe the Yellow Kerchief Gang or someone like that, and I come along and save her."

Coleman laughed. "Snead, you're fuller of shit than a Christmas goose. Ha, as if you would —" He interrupted his own comment mid-sentence, then pointed. "Hey, wait a minute. Look over there. Do you see that?"

Looking in the direction Coleman pointed, Snead saw someone cutting cattle from the herd.

"Who the hell is that over there?" Coleman asked. "We ain't got anyone out here but us, have we?"

"No, we ain't got anybody over there. So whoever it is, he must be rustlin' cows," Snead said.

"He's got some nerve, comin' out here all by his lonesome to steal cows."

"Maybe he thought there wouldn't be anybody out here."

"Let's run him off," Coleman proposed.

The two started riding toward the rustler. Pulling their pistols, they shot into the air, hoping to scare away the rustler.

"You!" Coleman shouted. "What are you doing here?"

Coleman and Snead continued to ride hard toward the rustler. A single rustler, being accosted by two armed men, should be running but he wasn't. Coleman began to get an uneasy feeling about it when the rustler stood his ground.

"Snead, hold up!" Coleman called. "There's somethin' ain't right about this!"

Suddenly Coleman and Snead saw why the rustler they were advancing toward was so brazen. He wasn't alone. At least six others were wearing a patch of yellow at their necks.

"Damn!" The challenge in Snead's voice was replaced by a tone of apprehension. "It's the Yellow Kerchief Gang!"

"Let's get the hell out of here!" Coleman shouted.

The two cowboys wheeled their horses about, and the hunters became the hunted. The seven outlaws started after them, firing as they rode hard across the open distance separating Coleman and Snead from the rustlers.

The two men galloped away, pursued by the rustlers. Hitting William's Creek in full stride, sand and silver bubbles flew up in a sheet of spray sustained by the churning action of the horses' hooves until huge drops began falling back like rain.

Coleman pointed to an island in the middle of the stream. "Snead, they're goin' to run us down! Let's try and make a stand there. It's our only chance!" Fear gave enough volume to his voice so he was easily heard.

The two cowboys brought their steeds to a halt. Dismounting, they took what shelter they could find behind the large rock that dominated the island. The rustlers held up at the edge of the creek.

"How many bullets you got?" Coleman asked.

"Four," Snead said.

"Just four? You got 'ny in your belt?"

"No, just these four is all I got. How many you got?"

"Five."

"That ain't very many," Snead said.

"It'll have to do."

"Son of a bitch! Here they come!"

The countryside exploded with the sound of gunfire when the Yellow Kerchief riders opened up on the two Frewen cowboys. The first several bullets whizzed harmlessly over their heads or raised sparks as they hit the rocky ground, then careened off into empty space, echoing and reechoing in a cacophony of whines and shrieks.

At first, Coleman and Snead entertained a hope that the rustlers, who had missed so far, would become frustrated and ride away, leaving them unharmed. Then, three more men wearing yellow scarves rode up to join the other seven. A furious gunfight broke out between the rustlers and the cowboys, but the rustlers were expending bullets at a ratio of twenty to one over the two cowboys. The odds, not only in terms of men, but of available bullets were just too great. Within a matter of minutes, the two cowboys had been killed and the rustlers returned to their task of stealing cattle.

Frewen had two dozen cowboys working for him, living in two bunkhouses behind the big house. Called Frewen Castle, it was a huge, two-story edifice constructed of logs. The cowboys ate in the cookhouse and when everyone gathered for the supper meal that evening, they noticed Coleman and Snead had not returned.

"They weren't plannin' on stayin' out there all night, were they?" Jeff Singleton asked.

"No, they were comin' back," Burt Rawlings said. "Me 'n Snead was goin' to ride into town tonight after supper."

"Well, where are they?"

"I think something must have happened to 'em," Burt said.

Burt and Jeff went to see Myron Morrison to tell him of their concern. The foreman agreed to send several cowboys out to look for Coleman and Snead.

When the cowboys reached the range the

first thing they noticed was that there were no cattle.

"Whoa, this ain't right," Burt said. "There's supposed to cattle here. I know, 'cause we moved at least fifteen hundred head up here last week. Where are they?"

"You don't think —" One of the other cowboys paused in mid-sentence.

"Don't think what?" Burt asked.

"You don't think Coleman and Snead run off with the cows, do you?"

"Maybe you could tell me just where in the hell they would go with them?"

"To Logan and the Yellow Kerchief Gang, maybe?"

"No," Burt insisted. "They wouldn't do that."

"Well somethin' has happened to the cattle."

"Right now I'm more concerned about what happened to Coleman and Snead than I am about what happened to the cows. I don't have a good feeling about this."

"Look! Ain't that Snead's horse?"

The four cowboys hurried over to the horse, which made no attempt to run from them. When they got closer they saw that the horse had been shot.

"Damn! Look at this," Jeff said.

"Looks like he come from that way,

from the crick." Burt pointed toward the creek.

Jeff took the wounded horse's reins and led it as they rode toward William's Creek. They saw Coleman's horse standing on the island in the middle of the creek. Hurrying to it, they saw what all were beginning to suspect, but no one wanted to see.

Coleman and Snead were lying dead on the island. Both men were holding pistols. Burt picked up Snead's weapon and checked it, announcing what he found. "Empty."

One of the other cowboys picked up Coleman's gun. "This one is empty, too."

"Looks like they were in one hell of a gun battle," Burt said.

"Injuns? They ain't come this far north, have they?" Jeff asked.

"It wasn't Injuns," one of the other cowboys said.

"How do you know?"

"Look over there." The cowboy called attention to a stake in the ground, to which was tied a yellow scarf.

"Son of a bitch, the bastards is braggin' about it," Burt said. "They left us a sign just so's we'd know who done it."

"Wasn't no doubt about who done it, was there?" another asked. "Who the hell else could it be, if it wasn't the Yellow Kerchief Gang?"

At a small cabin located at the head of a long, deep ravine carved into a butte at the end of Nine Mile Creek, the ten men who had killed Coleman and Snead and stolen the cattle were celebrating their success. The men ranged in age from twenty-one to forty-five years old. Every one of them had a record from burglary to murder. They had been operating in Johnson County for the last six months, and had been quite successful in rustling cattle, but it was, by far, the biggest job they had ever done.

"I make it at least a thousand head, maybe more," a man named Poindexter said.

"Hey, think maybe we could butcher one, have us some fresh beef?" Clayton had not been on the raid with the others. He was a good enough cook the rest of the men didn't mind that he never joined them on any raids.

"What about it, Logan?" Greer asked. "Some fresh beef would be pretty good."

"All right," Logan agreed. "I guess we got enough this time that we ain't goin' to miss one cow."

The Yellow Kerchief Gang was led by Sam Logan. He had started his outlaw career in

New Mexico, riding with two desperadoes, Kid Barton and Coal Oil Johnny. He may have had a last name, but if so, nobody ever learned what it was. The three men terrorized anyone who happened to be on the Santa Fe Trail, whether it be stagecoach, freight wagon, or a single rider on horseback. If they were attacking a stagecoach or freight wagon, all three of them would participate. If it was a single horseman, then only one would approach, slowly, quietly, and without giving any hint of danger. He would ride alongside their mark for a few minutes, carrying on a friendly conversation, then turn to him and suddenly shoot him dead.

Kid Barton and Coal Oil Johnny were the most notorious of the group. They tended to revel in their notoriety, whereas Sam Logan purposely kept a low profile. As rewards were posted, the offers for Kid Barton and Coal Oil Johnny grew, while no reward at all was offered for Sam Logan. Kid Barton and Coal Oil Johnny sometimes took great delight in teasing him for not being worth anything, while the reward on each of them reached one thousand dollars.

Logan, who had not established a name, killed them both as they were waiting beside the road to hold up a stagecoach. When the coach arrived, Logan waved it down, and pointed to the two men, claiming he had overheard them plotting to rob the coach. He not only got the bounty money, a total of two thousand dollars, he also became a hero for stopping a robbery. He used that publicity to get himself hired as city marshal for the town of Salcedo.

Logan's stint as a lawman didn't work out very well for him. When he killed a personal envoy from Governor Lew Wallace, he wound up in his own jail. Tried and convicted for murder, Logan was sentenced to hang. But on the night before the execution was to take place, Logan killed the deputy who was the acting city marshal, a deputy he had personally hired and befriended, and broke jail.

He left New Mexico and went north, all the way to Wyoming, where he organized a group of cutthroats and thieves into the Yellow Kerchief Gang. He resumed his earlier career of robbery, entering a new phase when he started rustling cattle.

CHAPTER THREE

Sussex, Wyoming
Early April 1884

It had snowed that morning, and the cemetery was a field of white, interrupted by grave markers, both crosses and tombstones. The cemetery was crowded with people as Max Coleman and Lonnie Snead were laid to rest. It wasn't just the cowboys from the Powder River Cattle Company, but from nearly all the other ranches in Johnson County. They were all bundled up in mackinaws, parkas, and sheepskin coats, their breath making little vapor clouds in the air, holding their hats in their hands while the parson intoned the last words of committal.

As the mourners began to leave the cemetery, their departure marked by exiting horses, wagons, surreys, buckboards and carriages, William Teasdale trudged through the snow to come over and speak with Frewen. Well dressed, he was a portly man of about fifty. Red-faced and breathing hard, Sir William Teasdale, Lord of Denbigh, like Moreton Frewen, was an Englishman, part of the influx of wealthy Brits who had come to American to invest in and run cattle ranches. Teasdale's ranch, Thistledown, was adjacent to the Powder River Cattle Company.

"When your two men were killed, how many cattle did you lose?" Teasdale asked.

"What? Oh, I don't know, exactly," Frewen said. "But I'm sure it was over a thousand head."

"I've heard that it was at least fifteen hundred head," Teasdale said.

"It may have been. I'm not sure."

"You're not sure?"

"No, not exactly," Frewen said.

"Moreton, you do have investors in your ranch, don't you?" Teasdale asked in an exasperated sigh. "Important men, back in England?"

"Yes, of course."

"Don't you think you owe it to them to be able to render accurate reports as to how just many cattle were rustled?"

"I suppose I do," Frewen said. "But to be honest with you, William, when I learned of the death of two of my cowboys, that sort of pushed everything else out of my mind."

"Yes, well of course it is a shame that they were killed. But you have investors back in England that you must answer to. You can't pass that off by saying you are more concerned with the fact that you lost a couple of mere cowboys. Let's face it, Moreton. The bottom line for both of us is business — cattle business. And the rate of our losses now has just about made our business unsustainable. This cattle rustling is beginning to get out of hand."

"I agree. But I don't have any idea what to do about it."

"William, do come on, won't you? I'm freezing out here."

The summons came from Margaret, Teasdale's wife, who was sitting in the Thistledown carriage wrapped in a buffalo robe. It was a beautiful coach, green with yellow wheels and the Teasdale crest on the door, the letter "T" with two crossbars placed on a shield and surrounded by gold wreathing.

"Yes, dear," Teasdale replied. He started toward the carriage, then turned back toward Frewen. "My offer still stands," he said.

"What offer is that?" Clara Frewen asked when her husband climbed into the backseat of their carriage, a more modest brougham.

"He wants to buy our ranch," Frewen said.

"Has he made a decent offer?"

"Yes, unless you count all the cattle, the house and buildings, and all the horses and equipment. Then his offer is less than one quarter of what the place is worth."

The driver snapped the reins against the team, and the brougham started out of the cemetery, pulling in behind some of the other vehicles.

"Why would he offer you so little? Does he really expect you to take it?"

"He knows that some of my investors are getting worried and he is gambling that I am ready to pull out of the venture altogether."

Northern Colorado

Manny Sullivan lay on top of a flat rock, looking back along the trail over which they had just come. The rider was still following them.

"Is the son of a bitch still there?" Paddy McCoy asked.

"Yeah," Sullivan growled. "We've done ever'thing we could to shake the son of a bitch but he's clung to us like a sandspur. I believe he could track a bird through the air."

"They say Matt Jensen is that good," Mc-

40

Coy said.

"You're sure, now, that it is Matt Jensen?"

"Yeah, I'm sure. Like I told you, I heard that Matt Jensen was askin' questions about us."

"Damn. That's not good. That's not good at all. You think he knows about the robbin' and killin' we done back in Livermore?"

"Of course he knows," McCoy said. "Why else would he be comin' after us?"

"I don't know," Sullivan said. "I'm just wonderin' why he's takin' such a personal interest in us. And I'm also wonderin' how he found out we're the ones that done it."

"How he found out don't matter now," McCoy said. "What does matter is how we are goin' to get shed of the son of a bitch. We're goin' to have to do that, or we ain't never goin' to have any peace."

"How we goin' to get rid of him? We've done ever'thing we could, and we still can't shake him off."

"We ain't goin' to shake him off," McCoy said.

"If we don't shake him off, what are we goin' to do with him?"

"We're goin' to kill him," McCoy said. He pointed to a coulee ahead. "Let's go up through there."

"Ain't you ever been up here before?

41

That's a dead-end canyon," Sullivan said.

"I know it's a dead-end canyon," McCoy said. "One of the reasons I come this way is because I know this canyon real good, and I know it has a cave about halfway up the wall on the left side. And not only that, there is a bunch of rocks around the mouth of the cave so that if a feller don't know it's there, it ain't likely that he will ever even see it. I figure we can hide in the cave till he passes underneath, then we'll shoot the son of a bitch in the back. All we have to do is let him follow us in."

"What if he don't come in?"

"He'll come in, all right. He wants us pretty bad, else he wouldn't be doggin' us so hard."

The two men rode on into the canyon, ground-tied their horses around a bend and out of sight, then climbed up the wall to the cave.

"What did I tell you?" McCoy said. "Get ready. He'll be coming by directly, and when he does, we'll let him have it. He won't even know what hit him."

"We shoulda gone on up to Cheyenne with Plummer," Sullivan said. "If we had, we wouldn't be in this mess now."

"There is a reason why we didn't go into Cheyenne, remember? We killed that deputy up there last year, and there's just too many people that knows us," McCoy said.

"I guess that's right. Still, it don't seem right that Red Plummer has got away scott free and we're the ones bein' hounded. Especially since it was all Plummer's idea in the first place," Sullivan said.

"Yeah, well, it ain't all that bad. Once we get rid of Jensen, we'll get as far away from here as we can," McCoy said. "And don't forget, we got us enough money that we can start over somewhere else. Maybe down in Texas."

Matt had been in this same canyon less than a year earlier, and he knew that it was a dead end. But the two men he was chasing had gone into it, and that left Matt asking the question: did they not know it was a dead end? Or did they know, and were just trying to draw him in to set up an ambush?

It didn't matter. They might think they were setting up an ambush, but as far as Matt was concerned, they had just ridden into a trap.

He rode all the way up to the mouth of the canyon, but instead of riding in, he dismounted and pulled his long gun out of the saddle holster.

"You go on in, Spirit," Matt said. "But

when you hear gunfire, you run like hell, you hear me?"

Spirit started on into the canyon, his hooves making loud clops on the stone floor. Several seconds after his horse entered the canyon a gun roared, and, as Matt had asked him to, Spirit broke into a gallop. The canyon exploded with gunfire as Spirit galloped through, the bullets whizzing harmlessly over the empty saddle, then whining loudly as they ricocheted off the rock wall on the opposite side of the canyon.

When the firing started, Matt tried to locate the men he was trailing, but it was impossible to do so by the sound of the gunfire because it was echoing and reechoing back and forth for the entire length of the canyon. However, he did see a wisp of smoke drifting up from halfway up the wall on the left side, and he smiled because he knew exactly where they were. There was a cave there, a cave that Matt had personally explored.

As he stared toward the area where he knew the cave was, he saw someone rise up to take a look. The acoustics of the canyon were like a giant megaphone, and when one of the two men spoke, Matt could hear him as clearly as if he were standing in front of him.

"What the hell? There wasn't nobody on that horse, was there?" The words *was there, was there, was there,* like the gunshots, were repeated many times down through the length of the canyon.

As Matt studied the area where the two men had positioned themselves, he smiled. He not only knew about the cave, he knew what the men who had taken shelter there might not know. He knew that the cave had another entrance. When he had been up there last year, he had explored the cave just out of curiosity. He had no idea at the time that his curiosity would ever pay off, but now he was about to cash in on that knowledge.

Jacking a round into his rifle, Matt fired toward where he knew the mouth of the cave was, then he repeated it, firing and cocking the lever to jack a new shell in, then firing again.

Matt knew that he didn't have a clean shot from here, but that wasn't why he was shooting. He was shooting to drive them back into the cave, and to let them know that he knew where they were.

"You boys seem to have gotten yourself into a little trap, haven't you?" Matt called up to them. "As long as you are in that cave, all I have to do is wait here until you decide to come out."

"What do you want? . . . What are you chasin' us for?" one of the two men called back down.

"That was my brother and his family that you killed back in Livermore," Matt said.

"You're chasin' the wrong people. We didn't do that. What makes you think we did it?" the other of the two men yelled down at him.

"Jarvis Winslow told us it was you."

"What? That's impossible! The son of a bitch was dead when we left him."

"Sullivan, you dumb shit, you just confessed!" McCoy said.

"Anyhow, I know he didn't tell you."

"He didn't exactly tell us," Matt replied. "But he left us a note in the bank."

"I knew somebody should have went with him."

"Why don't you two come on down with your hands up?" Matt asked. "You know damn well that I've got you trapped there. The only way you can go is to come down, and unless you come down without your weapons, I'll shoot you as soon as you poke your head out."

There was no response from the two men, so Matt waited a few seconds; then he fired again, the one boom sounding like a cannon blast.

"No need for me to be wasting any more ammunition," Matt said. "I'll just wait here until you come out."

"Well you can just wait until hell freezes over, 'cause we ain't about to give up to you."

"Oh, I don't think I'll have to wait until hell freezes over," Matt said. "But I'm willing to wait here as long as it takes."

Now that Matt had them believing that he was going to stay down there, he moved quickly to a part of the mountain that they couldn't see from the cave. It wasn't an easy climb up, but it wasn't impossible, and within half an hour, Matt was on top, standing over the hole that ran, chimney-like, down into the cave.

Matt climbed down the shaft, which was about seventy-five feet long, but at enough of an angle that it was easier to negotiate than had been the climb up. When he dropped down into the cave, he was about two hundred yards behind them. Behind him was all dark, so he could walk almost all the way up to them without being seen. On the other hand, the two men he had been chasing were standing in the mouth of the cave, easily visible because they were backlit by the bright light from outside.

"How about you two boys tossing your guns this way?" Matt ordered.

"What the hell!" Sullivan shouted in shock and fear. It was obvious that neither of the two men had expected Matt to suddenly show up behind them.

McCoy and Sullivan both fired. Although Matt was outnumbered, he had the distinct advantage of being a shadow within the shadows, while they were clearly visible. There were four shots fired, but only two found their mark. Both of the scoring shots were fired by Matt Jensen.

With his gun in hand, Matt approached the two men cautiously. Sullivan had been killed outright, but he saw that McCoy was still breathing.

"I'm dyin', ain't I?" McCoy asked.

"Yeah, you are," Matt replied without emotion.

"I'm dyin' and you're just standin' there watchin'."

"Not much else I can do," Matt said. "But look at it this way. Getting shot beats getting your neck stretched with a rope."

"Yeah," McCoy said. He tried to chuckle, but instead he coughed, and some blood bubbled from his mouth. "Yeah, that's right, ain't it?

"You still lookin' for Plummer? Or have

you already found him?" McCoy asked, his voice strained with pain.

"I'm still looking for him."

"You'll find him in Cheyenne. He's the son of a bitch that got us into this. If I'm goin' down I want him to go down, too."

"I appreciate the information," Matt said.

"Are you just goin' to stand there and watch me die?" McCoy asked. "Aren't you even going to try and patch me up?"

"There's nothing I can do for you," Matt said.

"You son of a bitch! You are enjoyin' it, ain't you? You are enjoyin' watchin' me die!"

Matt remembered the description the sheriff had given him of Jarvis's wife and daughter.

"They had both been raped, Matt. Then their throats was cut and they bled to death. Not only that, we found 'em both naked. The sons of bitches didn't even have the decency to cover 'em up."

"Yeah," Matt replied. "I am."

McCoy drew a few more ragged gasps, then stopped breathing. When Matt knew he was dead, he pushed the two bodies out of the cave opening, letting them fall a hundred feet to the rocky ground below. Then he climbed down after them and, finding their horses, threw the two bodies over the saddles. He had no idea whether he had matched the right body with the right horse or not, but he didn't care.

Looking through the saddlebags, he found a little over six thousand dollars in each bag.

The next day, Matt rode into Livermore with the two bodies draped over their horses. Stopping in front of the sheriff's office, he was met by Sheriff Garrison and a couple of his deputies. In addition, curiosity had drawn at least a dozen townspeople to the sheriff's office.

"Who did you get?" Sheriff Garrison asked.

"Sullivan and McCoy," Matt said. He opened his saddlebag. "And I've recovered twelve thousand dollars that was taken from the bank."

"Twelve thousand?" one of the townspeople replied. "Hell, that's just a little over half the money that was took. Where is the rest of it? Are you keepin' it?"

Matt fixed the questioner with a stare that caused him to gasp, then begin to wilt in fear.

"I didn't mean it like that," he said.

"How did you mean it?" Matt asked.

"I meant, that is, I was just wonderin' where the rest of the money is, is all. I wasn't actually thinkin' you kept it or nothin'."

To the townsman's relief, Matt turned his attention back to the sheriff.

"Before McCoy died, he told me that Plummer had gone to Cheyenne."

"I'll wire the sheriff there," Sheriff Garrison said.

"You can wire him if you want to," Matt replied. "But I am personally going after him. I will send what money I find on him back to the bank here."

"You're a good man, Matt," Sheriff Garrison said.

Matt left the bodies with the sheriff, then remounted Spirit. He looked back toward the man who had asked him about the rest of the money, but the man wouldn't meet his gaze.

Clucking at his horse, Matt rode out of town at a trot. He had a long way to go.

CHAPTER FOUR

*Powder River Cattle Company Ranch, Taney
Creek*
First week of May 1884
Paul Graham, Phil Bates, Emmitt Carol,
and Cooter Miles were in the Taney Creek
line shack. They had come up two weeks
ago to make preparations for the spring
roundup.

"What do you mean? Are you trying to
tell me you've never even *had* a woman?"
Graham asked Emmitt.

Emmitt cleared his throat in embarrassment. "I'm only sixteen. I ain't never really
had the chance to do it. I wouldn't even
know how to go about gettin' a woman
interested in me."

"Hell," Bates said. "There ain't nothin' to
that. All you got to do is go to a whore-
house. If you got the money, whores don't
care how old you are."

"I don't know about that. Mama said she

didn't want me seein' any whores."

"Where is your mama now?" Cooter asked.

"She's down in Denver."

"Then what your mama don't know won't hurt her none, will it?"

"Tell you what, boys," Graham said. "How 'bout the next time we all go into town together, we get this boy broke in. We'll chip in and buy 'im a whore."

"Buy him a whore? Hell, most of the time, I don't have enough money for my own whore, why should I pay for the boy?" Bates asked.

"Because we got to get him broke in good, and I figure the best one to handle that would be Cavalry Mona," Graham said.

"Ha!" Cooter said. "Yeah, Cavalry Mona. Now, I *would* be willin' to help pay for that."

"Why do they call her Cavalry Mona?" Emmitt asked with some trepidation.

"They call her that 'cause near 'bout ever'one in the United States Cavalry has rode her, at least once," Bates said.

"I don't know," Emmitt said. "Is she pretty?"

All three of the other cowboys laughed. "Is she pretty, you ask? Hell, boy, you don't go with whores 'cause they're pretty. You go with 'em because they are there."

"What do you say, Emmitt? You 'bout ready to become a man?"

"I — I think I'd better go down to the creek and get us some water," Emmitt said, taking the bucket and going outside.

Bates laughed a low, knowing laugh. "You know what I think? I think our Emmitt ain't all that fired up 'bout beddin' Cavalry Mona."

"Who knows?" Graham teased. "I'm thinkin' maybe we'll be able to talk him into it," Graham said.

"Whose time is it to cook breakfast?" Bates asked.

"It's your time," Graham and Cooter both replied.

"Well then, I'd better get started."

"I'll give you a hand," Graham offered.

The two men started putting together what they would need for breakfast. Bates got out the flour and lard for biscuits, Graham started carving off pieces of bacon.

"I wonder what the hell is keeping Emmitt with the water," Cooter said. "Maybe I'd better go take a look."

"Hurry back, I ain't got enough water to roll out the biscuits with," Bates said.

Graham got out his book and started writing.

"You're always writin' in that book of

your'n," Bates said. "What is it you're a-writin', anyhow? You writin' a story or somethin'? You goin' to publish a book and become famous? 'Cooking on the Range with Two Gun Pete,' " he teased.

"I'm not writin' a book. I'm just takin' notes is all," Graham said.

Bates walked over to the window and looked outside. "That's funny," he said.

"What?"

"Well, there ain't neither one of 'em come back yet, and I don't even see either one of 'em down to the crick."

Graham walked over to look as well.

"Maybe I'd better go see what's keepin' 'em."

"I'm not sure that's such a good idea," Graham said.

"What do you mean?"

"I don't like the looks of this. I think there might be someone out there keepin' 'em from comin' back in."

Suddenly, a fusillade of shooting erupted and bullets crashed through the window.

Bates moved over to look through the window. "Damn! It's the Yeller Kerchief rustlers!" he shouted.

"Bates, you better get down."

There was another episode of heavy shooting, and Bates cried out.

"I been shot! Graham, I been shot!" Bates said.

Bates went down and Graham went over to check on him. Bates had been hit in the stomach and in the side. He was groaning softly.

"Bates? Bates?"

Bates tried to get up.

"No, I think you'd be better off if you don't move. Wait, I'll see what I can do about stoppin' the bleedin'."

Staying low on the floor, Graham crawled over to the bunk and pulled off a blanket. Returning to Bates, he tore the blanket into a couple of strips and wrapped them around Bates, covering the wounds.

"Thanks," Bates said.

Graham raised up to look outside, and he could see a few people moving around. He took a couple of shots at them, but didn't hit anyone. He took another look at Bates. Bates's eyes were closed and he was breathing in shallow, gasping breaths.

Graham moved over to another part of the cabin and began writing.

Me and Bates was fixin breakfast when the attack come. Emmitt had already went down to the crick after water and when he did not come back Cooter went to see what the matter was and he didn't come back neither. Bates started to go see what was keepin the two of them but I told him I think there might be someone out there that wasn't lettin the other two come back. Then suddenly shootin started and Bates looked out the winder and said, "Damn it's the yeller kerchief rustlers." Then Bates got shot but he didn't get kilt yet.

Over the next two hours, the shooting continued, heavier sometimes than others, but never so light as to give Graham the idea that if he tried to leave he could make it. But he wouldn't leave anyway, not with Bates too badly hurt to leave with him.

"Bates?" Graham called. "Bates, how are you doin'?"

"I ain't doin' all that well," Bates replied, the pain evident in his voice.

"Don't you be dyin' on me now, pard, you hear me? I don't want to be left all alone here."

There were several more shots and the bullets sounded like pebbles rattling off the thick-sided line shack.

"You reckon Emmitt an' Cooter is dead already?" Bates asked.

"I reckon so."

"I'm goin' to die too, ain't I?"

"Pard, I reckon both of us are goin' to die," Graham replied.

"Yeah. Well, at least me 'n you had us a woman. Emmitt never had him one a-tall. Wish we could'a got him to town and done what we was goin' to do."

Bates grew quiet after that, and Graham went back to his writing.

It is now about two hours since the first shot. Bates is still alive, but he is in awful bad shape. They are still shootin and are all around the house. Boy's, there are bullets coming in like hail. Them fellows is all hid behind rocks and such so good that I can't get at them. They are shootin from the crick and from the back of the house.

"Bates, I know you're bad hit, but if you could look out the back and just tell me if they are comin'. It's kind of hard me tryin' to hold 'em off all alone like this. Bates?"

Graham went over and put his ear on Bates's chest to listen for a heartbeat, but he got none.

"You sons of bitches!" Graham shouted through the broken window. He raised up and fired several rounds, but they were fired in frustration only. He knew he didn't hit anything. Nor could he. Then he saw them

58

pull up a wagon and start loading it with brush and weed. That didn't look good to him.

He sat back down and started writing again. He was writing now just out of a sense of need to keep himself from going mad with fear.

Bates is dead. He died at about 9 o:clock. And now I can see them loadin brush and wood and such onto a wagon. They got the tongue drawed up and the wagon is pointed toward the shack. I think maybe they might be fixin to set fire to the wagon and push it down the hill toward the line shack. I don't think they intend to let me get away.

Emmitt and Cooter never did come back. I don't know if they was kilt or not, but I reckon they was. What with them gone and Bates dead, I'm feelin pretty lonesome just now, and I don't mind tellin you I'm pretty dam scairt too. I wish there was someone here with me so we could watch all sides at oncet. They may fool around until I get a good shot before they roll the wagon down at me. I'd love to get at least one of the bastards. I tell you this. I ain't goin to let myself get all burnt up in here. Before they roll that wagon down here, I'm goin to run out of the house, and when I do, I'm goin to come out shootin.

For the time being, the shooting had stopped, except for one or two shots thrown toward the cabin every minute or so just to keep Graham trapped inside. Raising up, he could see them quite clearly now. He thought he recognized one of them.

I see twelve or fifteen men. One looks like Sam Logan, but I don't know if it is or not. If I had me a pair of glasses I might know some of these men.

I've got to look out.

Well, they have just got through shelling the house again like hail. And they got the fire goin good on the wagon and are fixin to push it down on me. Its time for me to go. Goodbye boys, if I don't never see you again.

The wagon came rolling down toward the line shack, hopped up over the low front porch, then crashed into the side. Within moments the line shack was on fire, and though there were no flames inside yet, the smoke was so thick that Graham could scarcely breathe. Coughing and with his eyes watering and burning, Graham picked up Bates's pistol so that he had two guns.

He entertained the hope that because there was so much smoke, it might cover his escape. Holding on to that thought, Graham cocked both pistols, then kicked the door open and dashed outside, firing both pistols.

There was very little smoke outside, most of it being whipped in through the little cabin by the wind. As a result, Graham found himself standing in the open, looking at a ring of men, all wearing yellow kerchiefs. With a shout of rage and fear, Graham continued to blaze away as at least six of the rustlers fired at him. He felt the first two bullets plunge into his body, but the third hit him in the forehead and his world went black.

CHAPTER FIVE

Frewen was in the study of his house reading a letter from London when Clara came into the study.

"Clara, guess what," Frewen said, looking up from the letter. "Your sister Jennie is coming to visit you."

"Oh," Clara said. "What wonderful news that is!"

"I wonder how she will take to the Wild West," Frewen said.

"I'm sure she will get along splendidly," Clara said. "After all, we are Americans, you know."

"Yes, I know, dear," Frewen replied. "But neither you nor Lady Churchill were exactly raised in a log cabin."

Clara laughed. "I may not have been raised in one," she said. "But I am living in one now."

"You call this a log cabin? You have hurt

my feelings," Frewen said, exaggerating a pout.

"This is a wonderful log cabin, and I love it," Clara said. "Does Jennie say in the letter that she will be bringing her child?"

"Yes, the little brat will be with her," Frewen said.

"He is not a little brat," Clara defended. "Winnie is a wonderful child and smart as a whip. Why, with his intelligence, background, and upbringing, I predict that he will do great things some day."

"Ha! Winston Churchill doing great things? That will be the day."

There was a knock at the door to the study and looking toward it, Frewen saw his gentleman's gentleman.

"Yes, Benjamin?"

"M'Lord, Mr. Morrison would have a word with you."

Myron Morrison, foreman of the Powder River Cattle Company, was a big man with gray hair and beard. Enlisting in the Union army as a private, he was a major when the war ended, and with no family and no place to call home, he had come West. After a few "adventures" as Morrison called them (he was never specific about his "adventures" and Frewen had never asked), he began working as a cowboy and now was the foreman of one of the biggest ranches in Wyoming.

"Then by all means, show him in."

Frewen had a smile on his face as he stood to greet his foreman, but when Morrison came in, he had a grim expression on his face.

"Mr. Morrison, what is it?" Frewen asked, his own smile replaced by an expression of concern.

"I have some bad news for you, Mr. Frewen. This morning, Ralph Turner rode out to the Taney Creek line shack to take fresh provisions to the men there. He found the shack burned, and all four of the men dead."

"What? You mean they couldn't escape the fire?"

"No, sir, it isn't that," Morrison said. "There was a burned-out wagon up against the burned-out shack. It looks like it was purposely set afire. There was only one body inside, and it was too badly burned to identify, but we found Graham, Emmett, and Cooter outside, all shot, so we are sure that the body inside was that of Phil Bates, seeing as he was with them."

"Oh," Frewen said. "Oh, those poor men. None of them were married, were they?"

"No, sir."

"Thank God for that, at least."

"Yes, sir. It is bad enough that they all have parents, but it would be doubly worse if they had wives and children. And of course, Emmitt wasn't much more than a child himself. He was only fifteen or sixteen."

"It was the Yellow Kerchief Gang, wasn't it?" Frewen said. "They were the ones who killed Coleman and Snead a couple of weeks ago and they left a yellow flag on a post to brag about it, the bloody bastards. I don't suppose they left a yellow flag this time, did they?"

"No, sir."

"Well, no matter, I'm sure it was them. There's no way of telling for certain, of course, but I've no doubt but that they also did this."

"There was no yellow flag, but we know for a fact that Graham, Emmitt, Cooter, and Bates were killed by the Yellow Kerchief bunch."

"Oh? How do we know?"

"I know you are going to find this hard to believe, Mr. Frewen, but you might recall that the other boys were always teasing Graham about keeping notes on everything that was happening. They all wanted to know if he was writing a book. Well, sir, he had that little tally book with him, and he wrote it all down, everything that happened. They found this lying under him." Morrison handed a small notebook to Frewen. "Read this."

Frewen took the notebook, then pulled his finger back quickly. There was a small spot of blood on his index finger.

"I'm sorry about that," Morrison said. "I thought I got all the blood cleaned away."

"It's all right," Frewen answered. He walked back to the chair and sat down to read.

After Frewen finished reading the journal, he bowed his head and pinched the bridge of his nose. He was quiet for a long moment.

Clara had left the room when Morrison came in, and she returned now. "Mr. Morrison, would you like a cup of coffee?"

"No, ma'am, thank you," Morrison said.

Clara started to ask Frewen if he wanted coffee, but she saw him with his head bowed.

"Moreton? Moreton, what is it? What is wrong?" she asked.

Frewen handed the notebook to her. "Paul Graham, Phil Bates, Emmitt Carol, and Cooter Miles — all killed," he said. "Graham left an account."

"He left an account?"

"Yes, ma'am," Morrison said, nodding toward the book. "You'll find it all written down there in his tally book."

Clara found a chair and settled down to read Graham's account.

"Four at the line shack, and two at on the island in William's Creek," Frewen said. "That makes six good men that we have had killed by the Yellow Kerchief Gang."

After that, Frewen and Morrison remained silent until Clara finished reading Bates's journal. "Oh," she said, sniffing as tears began to run down her cheeks. "Oh, I can hardly stand to read this. How terrible it must have been for him."

"Mr. Frewen, do you have any idea why they might be specifically targeting you?" Morrison asked.

"Targeting me? What do you mean, targeting me? They are hitting all the ranches in the county, aren't they?"

"They are hitting the others, yes, sir; but I've been talking to some of the other foremen, and none of the other ranches have been hit nearly as bad as we have. Like you said, we've lost six good men. There's only been two other cowboys killed in the entire county. And all the other ranchers combined haven't lost as many cattle as we have lost."

"I didn't know that," Frewen said. "I don't know why we should be the ones suffering the most. And I don't have any idea of what to do about it."

"Would you like a suggestion?" Marshal Drew asked Frewen when he went into town to show him the journal. Marshal Drew was not only the city marshal of Sussex, he was also a deputy sheriff, thus giving him some authority beyond the city limits.

"If you have an idea, yes, I would love a suggestion."

"Have you ever heard of a man named Matt Jensen?" Drew asked.

"Matt Jensen? No, I can't say that I have. Who is he?"

"Well, I've never met him either, you understand, but I have read about him, and I've heard a lot about him. He is a lone wolf kind of man who wanders around a lot. And from what I hear, he is the kind of man who puts things right."

"What do you mean by put things right?"

"Well, sir, he's a gunman, Mr. Frewen," Marshal Drew said.

"A gunman? My word, Marshal, are you, a lawman, actually suggesting that I hire a gunman?"

"Yes sir, I am. I think what is happening here now is just the sort of thing where a gunman might be handy to have."

"Do you really think I should resort to something like this?" Frewen asked.

"I'm going to be honest with you, Mr. Frewen. As a deputy, my jurisdiction outside of town is limited, but even so, I wouldn't be able to handle this situation. And there is no way Sheriff Canton can handle it either."

Frewen stroked his mustache. "He certainly hasn't been able to handle it yet, has he?"

"No, sir, he has not."

"All right, let's suppose I did want to hire this gunman of yours, this Matt Jensen. Do you have any idea how I can get in touch with him?" Frewen asked.

"Normally, I wouldn't have the slightest idea of how to locate him, but Mr. Murphy said he saw him at the Cheyenne Club in Cheyenne last week. I don't know if he is still in Cheyenne, but if he is, more than likely we could send a letter to him, care of the Cheyenne Club, and it would get to him."

"Good idea. All right. I will write him a letter," Frewen said.

"You had better make it a good letter so

you can get his attention," Marshal Drew suggested. "A man like Matt Jensen probably gets a dozen or so requests for help a week."

"Don't worry, Marshal. I will find a way to get his attention," Frewen said.

At sea, onboard the White Star Line ship the Baltic

For the first four days of the trans-Atlantic crossing, the seas had been favorable and Jennie had fared well. But this morning, they had run into heavy seas, and for at least twelve hours the ship had been tossed about like a cork. Jennie had become very seasick, though Winnie seemed to be immune to it. The bow was lifted high, and Jennie and Winnie had to hold on because their first-class cabin tilted at about a forty-five-degree angle. It stayed there for a long moment, then the bow plunged back down with such a suddenness that Jennie's stomach seemed to rise to her throat. At the bottom of the wave trough, the ship rolled hard to the starboard, and everything that was loose in the cabin — Jennie's bottles of creams and perfumes, her jewelry box, Winnie's books and journal, shoes, jacket, cap — all slid to the right side of the compartment. Their cabin was on the starboard side, and when it rolled starboard, they could look through the porthole window and actually see the water, not blue as it had been for most of the voyage but a dirty gray, swirling with white caps.

The ship remained in that position for a long, terrifying moment, and Jennie got the impression that they were actually about to capsize.

"Oh, Winnie!" she said, and she put her arms around him, pulling him to her, as much for her own comfort as for his.

Slowly the ship righted itself, then continued on past the upright position, rolling to the port as far as it just had to starboard. Now all the loose objects in the cabin came sliding quickly back to the left, and from the porthole window they could see nothing but sky.

Finally, after another hour of such tossing and pitching about, the seas calmed, and once again the ship was steaming at fifteen knots, stable except for the normal, gentle roll of the waves.

"Are you feeling better, Mama?" young Winston Churchill asked his mother.

"I'll be all right," Jennie answered, although her voice was weak and there was a greenish tint to her skin.

"It is nearly time for dinner," Winnie said.

"I hope that the storm didn't keep the chefs from their work."

"Oh, Winnie, can you actually think of food now?" Jennie asked.

"Yes, ma'am," Winnie said. "We didn't eat lunch, remember? You said you didn't feel like it."

"You go ahead," Jennie said. "I'm afraid I couldn't eat a bite."

"Do you want me to bring you something?"

"No, I . . . wait a minute. Yes, I would love an orange," Jennie said. "I think I could eat an orange."

"I shall try to get one for you."

Normally at this time of day, the first-class dining room was filled with passengers marveling over the fantastic meals provided by the chefs. But this evening the dining room was empty, except for three people who were seated at the captain's table.

Captain Hewitt, seeing Winnie come alone into the dining room, stood and called out to him.

"Here, lad, are you alone?"

"Yes, sir. Mama is ill."

There was a smattering of laughter around the table.

"Yes," Captain Hewitt said. "After the last

twelve hours, several are, I'm afraid. Would you like to join us?"

"Yes, sir," Winnie replied, pleased to have been invited.

The others around the table introduced themselves, and Winnie made a concerted effort to remember the names of each of them so he could call them by name when he left.

"Tell me, young man, what is taking you to America?" Captain Hewitt asked.

"My mother and I are going to visit my aunt and uncle in Wyoming. My uncle owns a cattle ranch, with real cowboys," Winnie said.

"Well, now, I'm sure that will be a wonderful adventure," the captain said.

Captain Hewitt and the others returned to their discussion. They were talking about the Sino-French war.

"The French have taken Vietnam from the Chinese," the American, Congressman Henry Cabot Lodge, said. "But I studied the Vietnamese when I was publishing the *International Review* and you mark my words, the French have done nothing but grab a tiger by the tail. Vietnam is going to come back to haunt them some day."

Winnie listened to the conversation with interest; then, at the end of dinner just before he excused himself, he said good-bye to everyone around the table, addressing each of them by name.

All were impressed with him, and they responded generously.

"Captain, before I return to the cabin, I promised Mama I would try and get an orange for her. Do you think that is possible?"

"It had better be," Captain Hewitt said, and when he raised his hand, a steward appeared instantly.

"Yes, Captain?"

"Get a sack of oranges for young Mr. Churchill, would you please?"

"Yes, sir," the steward said.

The steward disappeared, and within less than a minute returned with a bag of oranges.

"Thank you, sir," Winnie said. "Thank you very much."

When Winnie returned to the room, Jennie was sitting in a chair. Her appearance had improved considerably, though she still looked quite pale.

"Look, Mama, oranges!" Winnie said. "An entire bag of them. Would you like me to peel one for you?"

"Oh, yes," Jennie said. "Winnie, darling, you are a savior."

■ ■ ■ ■

When Winnie's private tutor learned that he was coming to America, she had given him an assignment.

"I want you to write an essay about America," she had said.

"Oh, I know all about America. I have read about it."

"No, not what you get out of books. I want you to record your personal thoughts from your own observations. Don't even think about what is written in all the history and geography books."

"All right," Winnie had said.

Winnie and his mother had taken passage on the *Baltic,* a steam-powered steel ship that could carry one thousand passengers. Two hundred thirty passengers, like Lady Churchill and her son, made the crossing in luxurious accommodations, including a large stateroom with electricity and an attached private bathroom. Winnie began his notebook by writing of their time onboard the *Baltic.*

I like to stand on the promenade and look out to sea and think of the days when

England's ships explored the world. What brave men those sailors must have been to sail this mighty ocean in small wooden ships, propelled only by the wind. When I think of them, I cannot but believe that so very much is owed to so few, by so many Englishmen.

CHAPTER SIX

From the *Cheyenne Leader:*

Justice Dispensed

Word has reached this paper that Manny Sullivan and Paddy McCoy have paid for their heinous crime with their own lives. Readers of this paper may recall reading about these two outlaws in a previous edition. The two outlaws brutally murdered and ravaged the wife and young daughter of Jarvis Winslow, then killed Mr. Winslow as part of their nefarious scheme to rob the bank of Livermore, Colorado.

These contemptible cretins were subsequently located by the dogged determination and excellent tracking of Matt Jensen. Mr. Jensen extended to the outlaws an opportunity to surrender themselves and be brought before the court to answer for their evil deeds. Alas, they did not avail themselves of that generous offer, but chose instead to respond with gunfire. Mr. Jensen answered in kind, and whereas the outlaws missed their mark, the balls energized by Jensen's pistol struck home with devastating effect. Many readers will recognize the name Matt Jensen, as he has achieved no little fame for his many deeds of heroism in serving his fellow man.

Mr. Jensen was not available for an interview, but it is believed that he has continued his quest for justice by going after Red Plummer, the third member of the murdering lot.

The Boar's Head Saloon was on 18th Street just across from the Western Hotel. It was one of the many saloons along Cheyenne's 18th Street that appealed to the lowest-caliber customer. Matt was looking for Red Plummer, and he knew that the Boar's Head was exactly the kind of saloon Red Plummer would frequent.

After Matt reached Cheyenne, he became a semi-regular habitué of the 18th Street saloons, nursing a beer in one, playing cards in another, engaged in conversation in yet another, all the while listening to the conversations of others. Not once did he mention Red Plummer's name, but his quiet observation provided him with all the information that he needed. He learned that, while Plummer was not in town now, he was a frequent visitor. Matt decided to wait for him. He waited for two weeks until, finally, Plummer showed up.

Inside the Boar's Head Saloon, Red Plummer was sitting in the back, drinking whiskey and playing solitaire. Red Plummer was a thin man, with dark, unruly hair, a nose like a hawk's beak, and a large red birthmark on his face. He was also missing the lower lobe of his left ear, having had it bitten off during a fight while he was in prison.

When Matt Jensen came into the saloon, Plummer heard several of the other saloon patrons call out to him.

"Hello, Jensen, you still around?"

"Matt," the bartender called. "We made some fresh cracklins today. They go real good with beer."

Plummer had never seen Jensen up close, but when the others called him by name, he looked over at him. He was a big son of a bitch, with broad shoulders and hard eyes. It was him, all right.

79

For a moment, Plummer panicked. He had already read in the paper what Jensen did to his two pards, and he knew that Jensen was looking for him. It was all he could do to keep from getting up and bolting through the back door. His hands began to shake so badly that he dropped the deck of cards, causing several of them to scatter across the floor.

"Just beer," he heard Matt Jensen say to the bartender. "Hold the cracklins."

"All right, but you're missin' out on a good thing," The bartender said as he drew a beer and handed it to Matt. Matt blew some of the foam off the head, then took a swallow. He wiped his mouth with the back of his hand as he turned his back to the bar to look out over the patrons.

Damn! He's looking right at me! Plummer thought. He grew tense, waiting for Jensen to pull his gun, waiting for the bullet to come slamming into his chest. But nothing happened. Matt Jensen looked right toward Plummer, then passed his eyes around the rest of the room, showing no recognition whatever.

Plummer felt a sense of relief. Jensen hadn't even recognized him.

Matt saw him; he fit Plummer's description

perfectly. But he didn't want to make a scene here in the bar, deciding it would be better to just wait Plummer out until he left the saloon. Then Matt would confront him on the street. The question was, had Plummer recognized him?

Matt had just turned back toward the bar when suddenly a knife flashed by beside him. The blade buried itself about half an inch into the bar.

Drawing his pistol and turning toward the direction from which the knife had come, he saw Plummer getting up from a table with a gun in his hand. Plummer fired, just as Matt, instinctively, moved to his left. The bullet from Plummer's pistol put a hole in the bar exactly where Matt had been but a second before. Matt returned fire, and the impact of the bullet knocked Plummer back into the stove with such impact that that the stove piping was pulled loose. It came tumbling down with a clanging crash as soot and black dust poured forth to mingle with the billowing cloud of gun smoke from the two shots fired.

Matt stood there, holding the smoking pistol in his hand as he looked at Plummer to see if the outlaw represented any further danger.

For a long moment there was absolute

quiet in the saloon, as everyone had been shocked into silence by the sudden and unexpected gunplay. Finally, one brave soul wandered over to look down at Plummer. There was a dark red hole in Plummer's shirt, just over his heart. His right hand was still clutching the grip of his pistol, and his eyes were open and staring sightlessly toward the ceiling.

"Is he dead, Paul?" someone asked.

"Deader than a doornail," Paul replied.

"Sum'bitch, did you see that? He threw a knife and took a shot with his pistol, but still got hisself kilt."

Conversation broke out all over the saloon then, and it was still going on when a police officer came hurrying in.

"Someone want to tell me what happened here?" the policeman asked.

Everyone began talking at the same time, but eventually the policeman got the story. In the meantime, Matt stood against the bar, slowly sipping his beer and watching the policeman work. Finally, realizing that Matt was the one who did the shooting, the policeman came over to talk to Matt.

"I'm not arrestin' you or anything," he said. " 'Cause from what ever'one is tellin' me, this fella started it, first by throwing a knife at your back, then by shooting at you.

Is that true?"

"You heard it right," Matt replied.

"Do you have any idea why he attacked you from behind like that?"

"Because he knew I was going to kill him," Matt replied.

"What?" the policeman responded, surprised by Matt's answer.

"This is Red Plummer," Matt said.

"It is?"

"Damn, Marcus, didn't you even look at him?" one of the other saloon patrons asked. "It was all writ up about Plummer in the paper, how him and two others robbed a bank and kilt the banker and his whole family."

"Yeah, I know about that," the policeman answered. "I guess I just didn't look that close at the body. But if it is Plummer, then as far as I'm concerned, Mr. Jensen, you have done society a service."

"Did anybody see the horse Plummer rode up on?" Matt asked.

"Yeah, I did. It's the dun out there, tied off at the end of the hitchin' rack."

"Officer, would you come with me, please?" Matt said. "I need a witness."

The police officer, and several others from the saloon out of curiosity, followed Matt out to the horse with the black dorsal stripe.

Matt looked through the saddlebags, then pulled out a little sack. Reaching down into the sack he withdrew a thick packet of greenbacks.

"I'll be damned!" someone said.

"If you don't mind, we'll go down to the police station together and count this money out," Matt said. "I'm going to want a receipt, then I'm going to ask you to send the money back to the bank in Livermore."

"I'd be glad to," the policeman said.

Half an hour later, with the money duly counted and secured, and with a receipt in his hand for $9,276, Matt's task was completed, except for the shooting inquiry that the municipal court had scheduled for ten o'clock the next morning. After the inquiry, Matt would have no reason to hang around Cheyenne any longer. It was too late in the day to leave now, so he was going to have to spend at least one more night here. He had been staying at the Western Hotel because of its convenience to all the saloons on 18th Street, and he saw no reason to move out for just one more night. But he did decide that he would like to have a good dinner for this last night, so leaving everything at the Western, he walked down to the Cheyenne Club.

"Mr. Jensen," the manager called out to him, when Matt stepped into the Club. "A letter came for you today."

"A letter for me? And it was delivered here?" Matt replied. "That's strange."

"Yes, sir, I thought so as well. I wasn't sure you were still in town, so I was going to send it back tomorrow. But if you will wait here for just a moment, I'll get it for you."

Matt waited until the manager returned, holding the letter in his hand. "It is from Mr. Moreton Frewen," the club manager said. "Do you know him?"

"No, I don't."

"He's one of the high-toned Brits, you know, a Lord or a Sir or something like that. I never can keep it straight. He's also a member of our club. It could be that he saw you one of the times you were here, and just decided this would be the best place to reach you."

"Could be," Matt agreed, taking the letter. "But I have no idea why he would want to get in touch with me."

Matt walked into the big, spacious parlor room, exchanging greeting nods with some of the other members; then he settled into one of the oversized, leather chairs. Before he opened the envelope, the manager called

85

over to him.

"Would you like a beer? I can get someone to bring it over to you?"

"No, I'm fine, thank you," Matt said. He pulled out the letter, and began to read.

June 18, 1884
My Dear Mr. Jensen:

Your name has been put forth to me by loyal and true friends as someone who can help me deal with a crisis that is striking, not only my ranch, but many ranches here in Johnson County, Wyoming. There is a group of rustlers working the ranges here, stealing cattle with ruthless impunity. Led by a man named Sam Logan, they are organized as well as any military unit and they identify themselves by wearing a yellow kerchief at their throat and a yellow band around their hat. It is this appurtenance to their apparel that provides the sobriquet, the "Yellow Kerchief," by which these scoundrels are known.

Although I am losing cattle at a rate that is unsustainable, it isn't just the loss of cattle that has me concerned. In the last month I have had six of my men murdered by this gang. I, and some of my neighbors, have approached the local constabularies in a plea that something be done, but the problem is clearly bigger than anything the law can handle.

It is my hope that the enclosed draft will be sufficient to hire you to investigate the cause of my cattle loss, and if possible to put a stop to it, and to bring justice to these murderers.

Sincerely,
Moreton Frewen

Matt looked back into the envelope and saw a second piece of paper. When he removed the paper, he saw that it was, indeed, a bank draft, drawn on the Stock Growers' National Bank in Cheyenne. When he looked at the amount the draft was drawn for, he blinked in surprise. It was for five thousand dollars.

"Yes, sir, Mr. Jensen," I.C. Whipple said, as he examined the draft. Whipple was the founder and president of the Stock Growers' National Bank. "We will indeed honor the draft. However . . ."

"However?" Matt asked.

"I have received a telegram from Mr. Frewen. He asks that I have you sign a certificate of acceptance before I release the funds."

"Do you have the certificate?"

"We do. I had it made up as soon as we received the telegram."

"Let me see it," Matt said.

Whipple pulled open the middle drawer on his desk, and took out a document, then he slid it across the desk for Matt to read.

Know all men by these presents, and with my signature here unto affixed, I give oath that I will, to the best of my ability, and within the parameters of law and morality, perform the services requested by Moreton Frewen, and secured by these funds.

"Do you know this man, Moreton Frewen?" Matt asked.

"I do."

"In your opinion, is this document on the up and up?"

"It would be my belief that it is, sir," Whipple said.

Matt nodded, then signed the document. After that, he endorsed the bank draft, and Whipple personally counted out the money.

"That is a great deal of money for one man to be carrying, Mr. Jensen," Whipple said. "If you would like, I would be glad to open an account for you in our bank."

"Thank you," Matt said. "But I'll keep

the money with me."

"As you wish, sir."

"You could give me one more bit of information if you would," Matt said.

"Certainly, if I can."

"Where will I find Moreton Frewen?"

"His ranch is very near the town of Sussex," Whipple said. "That is right in the middle of Johnson County. It is quite some distance from here, two hundred and fifty miles or so. And as there is no railroad that goes in that direction, you will have to go by stagecoach."

"I have a horse," Matt said. "I can make it up in about three days. You wouldn't have a map, would you?"

"There's one in my office," Whipple said. "Come, I'll show you."

Matt followed Whipple into his office, where the banker pointed out the town of Sussex.

"It is a very small town," he said. "But if you follow the stagecoach road north until you reach the Powder River, you can't miss it."

"Thanks," Matt said.

Leaving the bank, Matt walked down to the telegraph office.

MORETON FREWEN — SUSSEX, WYO-
MING
HAVE THIS DAY CASHED THE DRAFT YOU
SENT ME STOP WILL ARRIVE IN SUSSEX
WITHIN THE WEEK TO ASSUME MY DU-
TIES STOP

MATT JENSEN

From the telegraph office, Matt went to
the gun store. There, he bought three boxes
of .44 pistol ammunition and two boxes of
.44-40 shells for his Winchester.

CHAPTER SEVEN

"He is staying in the Western Hotel, in Room 206," Carl Maynard said. Maynard was a teller at the Stock Growers' bank, and he was talking to Pogue Cassidy. There couldn't have been a more unlikely duo than the two men. Maynard was a small man, clean-shaven and nearly bald. He was wearing wire-rim glasses. Cassidy was a big man with red hair and a bushy red beard.

"How do you know what room he's stayin' in?" Cassidy asked. He scratched at his beard.

"He had to fill out a form before Mr. Whipple gave him the money, and that's what he put for his address."

"You say he has the five thousand dollars on him?"

"Yes. Mr. Whipple offered to open an account for him, but he said he wanted the five thousand dollars in cash. That would be two thousand for you, and three thousand for me," Maynard said.

Cassidy chuckled. "Here, now, you bein' a banker and all, how come is it that you don't know how to cipher? What do you mean, three thousand dollars for you?"

"I am the one who brought you this opportunity," Maynard said. "I should be adequately compensated for it."

"Are you plannin' on goin' into this feller's room with me tonight to take the money?"

"What?" Maynard replied with a gasp. "Certainly not! That's not the type of thing I would ever do."

"I see. You don't want to rob anyone with a gun, but you got no problem robbin' with a fountain pen. Is that about it?"

"No, that's not it, at all," Maynard said. "It is just that, in a proposal like this, everyone brings their own contribution to the table. My contribution was in finding the opportunity. Your contribution is in actually doing the deed."

"Yeah, well I'm tellin' you now, I ain't goin' to do it by myself. I'm goin' to have to have someone to help me, and we're goin' to have to pay him at least a thousand dollars. So I make it two thousand for you, two thousand for me, and one thousand for whoever I get to help me."

"All right," Maynard acquiesced. "But I heard him tell Mr. Whipple that he would be leaving tomorrow. So if you are going to do anything, you will have to do it tonight."

There was nobody else with Cassidy. He had told Maynard that just so he could reverse the split and take the three thousand dollars for himself. But as he stood at the bar that night, drinking whiskey to get up his courage to do what had to be done, he asked himself why there needed to be any split at all. He was the one taking the risk.

Then, as he continued to think about it, he realized there was something that Maynard hadn't considered. Once he did the job, Cassidy would have all the money in his hand, and the only way Maynard would ever see a cent of it would be if Cassidy took the money to him.

Cassidy glanced up at the clock. It was five minutes until midnight. If he was going to do this, now was as good a time as any. He tossed down his last drink, wiped his lips with the back of his hand, then started toward the saloon door. He had no intention of splitting the money with Maynard. Once he got the money, he intended to leave town. That would serve Maynard right for trying to cheat him in the first place.

The night clerk at the hotel was reading a book when Cassidy went into the hotel. The clerk put the book down and smiled up at Cassidy. "Yes, sir," he said. "You need a room?"

"I've already got a room," Cassidy said. "A friend of mine said I could stay with him tonight. He's in Room 206."

"Room 206? That would be Mr. Jensen's room. I would not have thought he would be the type to share his room, but if you say. Go on up and knock. I am sure that he is in."

"Yeah, well, I don't want to wake 'im up. Why don't you just give me the key?"

"Give you the key to an occupied room? Oh, no, sir, I'm afraid I can't do that," the clerk said.

Cassidy pulled his pistol and pointed it at the hotel clerk. "I said give me the key to Room 206, you son of a bitch!"

With shaking hands, the clerk took the spare key to 206 from the hook and held it out toward Cassidy. Cassidy took the key, then brought the pistol down hard on the clerk's head. The clerk collapsed on the floor behind the desk.

With the key in one hand and his pistol in the other, Cassidy hurried up the stairs to the second floor. The hallway was well lit by wall-mounted gas lamps that gave off a quiet hissing sound as they burned.

Room 206 was at the far end of the hall. There was also a window there. The window was closed for now, but Cassidy opened it, then stuck his head through to have a look around. Two floors below was the back alley. That was a pretty long jump, but if he crawled out of the window, then hung from the ledge and dropped that way, it wouldn't be so bad. And this would give him a route to get away after he took care of Jensen and stole the money. He left the window up so he wouldn't have to take the time to raise it afterward.

Stepping over to the door that had the numerals 206, he put the key into the keyhole, then turned it as quietly as he could.

It wasn't quiet enough. Even while asleep, Matt heard the lock tumblers click. Quickly and silently, Matt pulled his pistol from the holster that hung from the headboard just above him, then slid out of bed and moved to the opposite side of the room.

The door opened, and in the backlight provided by the hall lamps, Matt saw a man standing there. His right arm was crooked and he was holding a pistol. The man stepped over to the bed, then pointed his pistol before he realized the bed was empty.

"What the hell?" he said in surprise and frustration.

"Are you looking for me?" Matt asked.

Swinging toward the sound of the voice, Cassidy fired, the flame pattern of the muzzle flash lighting up the room. The bullet crashed through the window beside Matt, even as Matt fired back.

The impact of the bullet knocked Cassidy back onto the bed and he lay there with his arms thrown to either side of him, his head back, and his eyes open. His pistol hung by the trigger guard from Cassidy's finger.

"You've been a busy man, today, Mr. Jensen," the police officer said a short while later. Matt was talking to the policeman in the lobby of the hotel, along with several of the other hotel guests who had come down to the lobby out of curiosity. The hotel clerk was there as well, holding a towel to the wound on his head. Two men were carrying Cassidy's body out on a stretcher. "I heard about the incident with Red Plummer."

"Yes, it has been a busier day than I would want," Matt said.

"Did you know Pogue Cassidy?"

"I never saw him before he came into my

room," Matt said.

"Do you have any idea why he broke into your room?"

"Most likely reason, I suppose, is that he wanted to rob me," Matt said.

"I'm sure that's it. I know Cassidy, we have had him in our jail a few times, mostly for fighting and disturbing the peace. But he did serve two years in the penitentiary down in Rawlins for robbery."

"I'd better get a new sheet for your bed," the clerk said. "Like as not Cassidy bled on the one you have."

"Thanks," Matt said. He looked back at the police officer. "Is there going to be an inquiry on this? The reason I ask is because, if there is going to be one, I wonder if we could combine it with the one I have at ten in the morning. I need to get away as soon as I can after that, because I have to be somewhere else."

The policeman chuckled. "Let's see, you have been involved in two shootings in less than twenty-four hours. I'll talk to the chief. I don't see why he couldn't convince the judge to hold both inquiries at the same time."

At ten o'clock that morning, Judge William D. Clanton held a rare double inquiry, one into the death by gunshot wound of Ronald (Red) Plummer, and another into the death by gunshot wound of Pogue Cassidy. Witnesses from the saloon testified first, explaining how Plummer had made the first move. Also introduced into evidence was the account of the bank robbery and murder down in Colorado. Grant Peal, the clerk at the Western Hotel, testified that Pogue Cassidy knew which room Matt was occupying and that when he refused to give him a key to the room that Cassidy hit him over the head and took the key anyway.

When all the testimony was heard, Judge Clanton found no cause for charges to be brought against Matt and he was free to go. Matt thanked the police department and the judge, then he mounted Spirit for the long ride up Sussex.

When Winnie and his mother debarked in New York, they and the other first-class passengers were escorted through customs by courteous and helpful officials. Winnie saw hundreds of passengers from steerage, holding dearly on to all their worldly possessions, poorly dressed and clinging together in apprehension and wonder as they lined up to be processed through Castle Garden. Once they were through customs, Winnie got his first good look at a city that was as big as London, but had a brashness to it that London did not have. He could see the huge sweeping "S" curve of the elevated railroad just off Pier 8. Looking back to the east, he could see the superstructure of the ship he and his mother had just left, as well as the towering masts of the sailing ships that were in port. On the docks, there were many wagons loaded with freight that had been taken from the ships and with freight that would be put on the ships.

Jennie's first act was to hail a cab for them, a hansom cab that allowed Winnie and his mother to ride inside while the driver sat on a seat above and behind them. Having exchanged British pounds for American dollars at the customs office, Jennie passed the fare up through the hole in the roof.

"Disabuse yourself of any idea that I'm a foreigner without knowledge of the city," Jennie said. "I was born here."

"Sure 'n I wouldn't think of such a thing now, m'lady," the cab driver replied in a very thick Irish accent.

Winnie laughed.

"What is so funny?"

"You were afraid he would think you were a foreigner when he is," Winnie said.

Jennie smiled. "I had almost forgotten that about New York," she said.

The cab dropped them off in front of the Jerome Mansion on the corner of Madison Avenue and 26th Street. The five-story edifice, built by Jennie's father Leonard, had a six-hundred-seat theater, a breakfast room that seated seventy people, a ballroom of white and gold with champagne- and cologne-spouting fountains, and a view of Madison Square Park.

Leonard Jerome, who was a major stockholder of the *New York Times,* had defended the newspaper office during the New York draft riots by personally manning a Gatling gun. He was the father of three daughters: Jennie, Clara, and Leonie. The girls were known as the good, the beauty, and the witty. Jennie, who was an exceptionally beautiful woman, was "the beauty." Clara, whose real name was Clarita, was known as "the good," and Leonie was "the witty."

Jerome's wife had given him one more daughter, Camille, who had died at the age of eight. It was also said of him that he had fathered the American operatic singer Minnie Hauk, though the rumor was never substantiated.

"Jennie!" her father said, greeting her with

open arms. "How wonderful of you to visit us!"

Jennie's mother was just as effusive in her greeting, and smothered Winnie with hugs and kisses.

That very evening, Jennie sent a cablegram to London.

LORD RANDOLPH CHURCHILL
WINNIE AND I ARRIVED SAFELY IN NEW YORK. AFTER BRIEF VISIT WITH MOTHER AND FATHER WILL PROCEED BY TRAIN TO WYOMING.

MUCH LOVE JENNIE

For the week they were in New York, Winnie was most struck by the diversity he encountered. Unlike London, where all spoke English and all faces were white, he found New York to be an exciting kaleidoscope.

One can stand on a street corner in New York and hear French, Italian, German, Spanish, Hebrew, and even Chinese spoken. There are white faces, black faces, and yellow faces, for New York appears to be the meeting place for all the people of the world.

On the day they were to leave, Jerome

made his coach and driver available to take them to Grand Central Depot. The coach driver took them ahead of the long line of cabs on 42nd Street and stopped in front, where Red Caps recognizing that the coach represented wealth and tips, hurried over to render their assistance. Jennie went inside the terminal to buy train tickets.

"Sussex?" the ticket clerk repeated after she told him where she wanted to go. "I've never heard of it."

"It's in Wyoming," Jennie said. "My sister and brother-in-law live there."

"Let me look on the map," the clerk said. "Do you know the county it is in?"

"It is in Johnson County," Jennie said.

"Johnson County, all right let me — ah, yes here it is. No, we have no train service there. I'm afraid that the closest we will be able to get you is Medicine Bow."

"Then that is where we shall go," Jennie said. "I am sure that there will be some sort of conveyance available once we reach Medicine Bow. Can you tell me when we will arrive there?"

"When do you plan to leave?"

"The next available train," Jennie said. "And, we will want Pullman accommodations."

"Yes, ma'am, that would be eleven o'clock

this morning. The clerk checked his time schedule. Let's see, this is Tuesday, if you leave on this morning's train, you will arrive in Medicine Bow at five o'clock Friday afternoon."

"Thank you," Jennie said.

Her next stop was the Western Union office in the depot.

THE HON MORETON FREWEN
WINNIE AND I WILL ARRIVE IN MEDI-
CINE BOW AT FIVE PM FRIDAY STOP
                              JENNIE

CHAPTER EIGHT

William Teasdale stood at the bar in his parlor at Thistledown and poured two bottles of Scotch.

"Ah, Moreton, it is good to have a fellow countryman to drink with," he said. "And to have someone who appreciates good whiskey. These Americans and their awful bourbon, except most of the time it isn't even bourbon, it is some indescribable, abominable concoction they call, and rightly so, rotgut."

Frewen chuckled as he accepted the glass of Scotch. "Their drink may be foul," he agreed. "But I have found much about the Americans to admire."

"Well, of course you would say that, wouldn't you? After all, you are married to an American."

"I am indeed, old boy, but that's not the only reason. I find most Americans to be loyal and trustworthy," Frewen said.

Teasdale raised the glass to his lips and held it there for a moment. "Does that include the members of the Yellow Kerchief Gang?" he asked.

"It does not. They have killed six of my men, William. Six. They are fiends of the lowest order."

Teasdale tossed down his drink.

"And how many cattle have you lost?" he asked.

"I told you, I don't know," Frewen answered. "Compared to the loss of human life, why should I be concerned about the loss of a few cows?"

"From what I've heard, Moreton, it is many more than a few cows you have lost," Teasdale suggested.

"I suppose it is," Frewen said.

"I am concerned about every cow I may lose," Teasdale said. "And unlike you, I have no investors back home. That means that I survive or sink on my own, without bringing others down with me. You, on the other hand, have many investors, all of whom will be very concerned about how many cows you have lost."

"It seems to me like we are being singled out for this gang's activity," Frewen said.

"Of course we are going to be targeted," Teasdale said. "We are the two biggest landowners in the county."

"I suppose that is right," Frewen said.

"Look, Moreton, I know that several of your investors are very upset with you because, despite your promise of returning a profit to them, you are losing money, and you have been losing money for over two years."

"I think they know that I am doing my best by them," Frewen said. "Any investment is a risk. At least they aren't holding me personally responsible for the losses."

"Don't you think, though, for the sake of your investors, and especially for your sake, that you should consider cutting your losses before they get any higher?"

"How would I do that?" Frewen asked.

Perceiving a weakness, Teasdale plunged ahead.

"Simple," he said. "You sell your ranch to me, and let me worry about your creditors and investors."

"I thank you for your offer," Frewen said. "But no, I think I'll hang on to my ranch."

"Mark my words, you don't have enough funds to weather this storm," Teasdale said.

"There may not be a storm, if I have my way," Frewen said. He smiled.

"What do you mean, if you have your way?"

"I have hired someone to come to my assistance."

"Who?"

Frewen reached into his jacket pocket and pulled a paperback novel, and held it out toward Teasdale. Teasdale looked at the cover. The cover picture showed a man astride a horse in full gallop. The man had the reins of the horse secured by his teeth and held pistols in both hands. A streak of fire streamed from the barrel of each pistol.

The title was big and bold.

MATT JENSEN
and the
DESERT OUTLAWS

"I have hired this man."

Teasdale looked at the book, then at Frewen, then at the book again. He laughed out loud.

"Matt Jensen? Have you gone daft, Moreton? Matt Jensen isn't even real. He is the hero of a series of penny dreadful novels. What on earth would make you do such a thing?"

"Oh, this story in this book isn't real," Frewen said. "I know that. But Matt Jensen is real."

"What makes you think so?"

"This newspaper article," Frewen said. He showed Teasdale the article he had cut from the *Cheyenne Leader,* telling how Matt Jensen had tracked down and killed two of the outlaws who had robbed the bank in Livermore, Colorado, and killed the banker and his family. "I have already been in contact with him, and I expect he will be here within the week."

"Wait a minute, Moreton. So what you are telling me is that you have hired a gunfighter?"

"He isn't a gunfighter," Frewen replied. "Well, yes, he is. But it isn't like you think. He uses his gun for justice, not for evil."

"I don't know," Teasdale said. "I think you are making a big mistake."

"And I think that I have no other choice," Frewen replied. Frewen took his watch from his pocket and examined it. "I must get back," he said. "Clara will be expecting me."

Shortly after Frewen left Thistledown, Teasdale saddled his horse and rode up to Nine Mile Creek Pass. To anyone who happened to be riding by, this was just another of the many small streams and creeks that were common throughout Johnson County. It was a distance of fifteen miles from Thistledown, and it took Teasdale almost two hours of easy riding to reach it. As he approached the pass, he pulled his rifle from its saddle sheath, tied a piece of yellow cloth to the barrel, then held it up as he continued to ride.

Looking toward the notch at the left side of the pass, he saw the flash of a mirror, signaling that he had been seen, and that he would be allowed to come in. Returning the rifle to its holster, he slapped his legs against the side of his horse, urging it into a trot.

Riding up through the notch, he knew that he was being watched. Although he couldn't see anyone, he could feel several eyes on him. Not until he reached the place where a trail turned hard left did he see anyone. This was the entry guard, and he stood there with his right leg on a stone, the butt of his rifle resting on his leg as he watched Teasdale ride up the trail. At the end of the trail was a small cabin. The cabin had actually once been a line shack on Teasdale's ranch, but was moved from the ranch to this place.

When Teasdale dismounted in front of the cabin, he was met by Sam Logan. Sam Logan was wiry, just under six feet tall, with a pockmarked complexion and a sweeping, very dark handlebar mustache that seemed to hang on to a hooked nose. His dark eyes were set deep in their sockets. His hair was as dark as his mustache.

"Well, now, Mr. Teasdale. Come to pay us a visit, have you?" Logan asked.

Teasdale dismounted, then rubbed his behind. He didn't like riding horses. Normally, he went everywhere by buckboard, carriage, or coach. But a wheeled vehicle was useless here.

"What brings you here?"

"Have you ever heard of a man by the name of Matt Jensen?" Teasdale asked.

"Yeah, sure. Who hasn't heard of him?" Logan asked.

"Then you mean he is real?"

"You damn right he is real."

"You are sure now," Teasdale said. "You aren't talking about some dime-novel cowboy, are you? Because that is the only place I've ever heard of him."

"Well, the books they write about him *are* all full of shit," Logan said, "But Matt Jensen is real. Why are you askin'?"

"Moreton Frewen says that he has hired Matt Jensen to come to his assistance."

"Yeah? Well, if Frewen really has hired him, that ain't goin' to be no good for us. A man like Matt Jensen is nothing but trouble. My advice to you is to get someone to take care of him, and do it quick."

"Get someone to take care of him? What

110

do you mean by get someone? I thought it was your job to take care of the seamier side of our partnership."

Logan shook his head. "Yeah, well, I ain't goin' to go up against Matt Jensen, that's for sure. Not unless I get forced into it. I've got too good a thing goin' here, and I ain't goin' to risk it by gettin' tangled up with Matt Jensen. Leastwise, not unless I have at least half of my men with me. If I was you, I would hire someone to take care of him, and I would do it pronto."

"Do you have any suggestions as to who I might get to take care of him?"

"I don't know, Jensen is . . . wait, yeah, maybe I do have an idea. I know a man who just might be able to do it. He's faster 'n greased lightning, and I know for a fact he has been wanting to face Jensen down. I expect if you paid him enough, he would do it."

"Who is this man, and how do I get in contact with him?"

"His name is Kyle Houston. And he is my cousin. I'll get in touch with him for you."

"You may be good, but I'm pretty damn good myself," Andy Masters said.

"And I'm even better than he is," Andy's brother Aaron added.

"So my advice to you is, clear on out of Trabling now, while you're still breathing," Andy said.

The two brothers owned the Ace High Saloon in the little town of Braggadocio, Wyoming, which was about thirty miles east of Sussex. They had just ordered Kyle Houston out of town.

"I'm not sure you boys want to do that," Houston replied. Houston was a small man, with small, almost delicate hands. In a world without guns, he would be so insignificant as to be overlooked. But there was a reason that the word "equalizer" had been applied to Sam Colt's products. The small man who would be unable to stand up to any challenge in physical match was more than adequate to the task when it came to the use of pistols.

Kyle Houston was not only exceptionally proficient with a pistol, he enjoyed using it and had developed a very thin skin. That was a deadly combination, and had Houston been one to carve notches on the handle of his gun, it would be filled with them.

Earlier this morning, in a dispute in a card game, Houston had run three cowboys out of the saloon, telling them that if they came back, they had better come back armed. The Masters brothers, upon hearing about it,

112

made the same demand of Kyle Houston.

"As far as I'm concerned, you are nothing but a visitor here," Andy said. "And a not very welcome visitor at that. Those boys you ran away are good customers of ours. We can't have someone like you saying who and who cannot come into our saloon. That means you have to leave."

During the entire challenge, Houston had stood still, with a half-smile on his face as he looked at the two brothers. The physical contrast between them was dramatic. Andy and Aaron Masters were both big men, with broad shoulders and powerful arms. Either of them could have brushed Houston aside as one would a fly.

And yet here was Kyle Houston, not only standing up to the two men, but actually relishing the challenge.

"Boys, before we go any futher," Houston said, "I want to hear you say aloud, in front of these witnesses, that I ain't the one that's provoking this fight."

"Why do you need us to say that?" Aaron asked.

"Because I'm going to kill both of you," Houston said, speaking the words as calmly as if he had just ordered a beer. "And I want these witnesses to tell the law that I tried to avoid this fight."

"You don't have to worry about tellin' the law nothin'," Andy said. "Because unless you walk through that door, right now, you are going to be dead."

Houston sighed. "I tried," he said. He held his hands out in front of him, turning his palms up. "I guess it's all up to you, now."

"Draw!" Andy shouted, his hand darting toward his pistol. Aaron started his draw as well.

Although the action seemed instantaneous to those who were watching, and even to Andy and Aaron, Kyle Houston had the unique ability to slow everything down in his mind. He analyzed the situation before him. Andy was the one who had called draw, which meant he had already started his draw when he shouted. Aaron, who didn't start his draw until Andy initiated the sequence of events, was a fraction of a second behind.

That enabled Houston to make his target selection: Andy first, then Aaron. And though Houston fired two times, the shots were so close together that they sounded like one shot.

Andy pulled the trigger on his gun, but by the time he pulled the trigger, he had already been fatally wounded by a bullet to his heart. And though Aaron managed to

114

clear the holster with his pistol, he went down before he was able to get off a shot.

With the two owners of the saloon now lying on the floor, both dead, a stunned silence fell over the saloon patrons. They were awed by the demonstration they had just seen, and spoke, when they did speak, in whispers, lest they say something to anger the little man who was dressed all in black.

Houston looked around the saloon to make certain there were no further challenges, then he put his pistol, which was literally still smoking, back into its holster.

"I think I'll have a whiskey," he said to the bartender.

"I — I don't know," the bartender said.

"What is it you don't know?"

"You just killed the two men who owned this saloon. What happens now?"

"How long have you been working here?" Houston asked.

"Four years, ever since they opened it."

"They got 'ny wives, kids, anything like that?"

"No, neither one of them was married."

"Then it looks to me like you just inherited a saloon."

At first the bartender was surprised by the comment, then its possibility sank in, and a broad smile spread across his face. "Yeah," he said. "Yeah, it does look like that, doesn't it?" He poured the whiskey, slid it in front of Houston, then addressed the others in the saloon, calling out loudly.

"Step up to the bar, boys! Drinks are on the house, compliments of the new owner!"

As everyone was hurrying to the bar they avoided any contact with Houston, not wanting to do anything that might irritate him. However, one man did step up to him.

"Mr. Houston, my name is Clem Daggett. Sam Logan sent me to fetch you."

"Yeah?" Houston said. "What does my cousin want?"

"He wants you to do a job for him."

CHAPTER NINE

Onboard the Western Eagle, on the Union Pacific Line

Ten-year-old Winnie Churchill sat between his mother and the window as the train hurtled across the long, empty spaces.

"Mama, have you ever seen a place so large as America?" Winnie asked.

"Of course I have, dear. I was born here, remember?"

"Does that make me half American?"

"It does, indeed."

"Then if I wanted to be an American cowboy when I grow up, I could be?"

Lady Churchill laughed, and patted her son on the shoulder. "Oh, heavens, darling, I certainly don't think your father would like for you to be running around out here in the American West as a cowboy," she said.

"But Uncle Moreton is a cowboy, is he not? And he isn't even American. I could be an even better cowboy because I am half

American."

"I suppose if you put it that way, you could," Jennie said. "Although I'm not sure that Moreton considers himself a cowboy. I think he considers himself a rancher."

She chuckled. "From what I have heard, though, he is not a particularly good one, but please don't tell him I said so."

"Well, I am definitely going to be a cowboy when I grow up," Winnie said. "I am going to ride a horse and carry a gun and fight wild Indians."

"You are still young. I'm sure that by the time you grow up, some occupation other than being a cowboy will strike your fancy."

While on the train, Winnie continued to write in his journal. He wrote about the Great Lakes and the city of Chicago. But it wasn't until they started across the great western plains that his writing really came alive.

The American plains are a grand and impressive sight, vast, and seemingly life-less but that isn't so, because all manner of creatures reside here from the mighty buffalo to the small prairie dogs. The prairie dogs are most interesting and do not live alone, but construct entire villages as do people. I believe that as the train passes them by they observe us with as much curiosity as we observe them.

When nighttime comes the porter makes up a berth for my mother and me, and provides us with blankets so that we can be snug and warm. It is good to lie in the berth and look through the windows at the darkness which is so well lighted by the moon that one might think it is all a painting done in black and silver.

I would like to see a village of wild Indians, but have not been so fortunate.

At one of the train stops, a man got on who was obviously drunk. He staggered down the aisle, then settled in a seat across the aisle from the seat that Winnie and his mother were occupying. Jennie Churchill was an exceptionally pretty woman, Winnie knew that. He also knew that there were disquieting rumors about her, rumors that, though unsubstantiated, were nonetheless believable because Jennie was not only pretty, she was flirtatious.

But she liked to be in control of her flirting episodes, and always made certain that they were most discreet. She certainly had no interest in interacting with a drunken train passenger. He had no such reservations, however.

"Well now, ain't you a purty thang, though?"

Jennie showed no reaction.

"I'm talkin' to you, sweet thang. You're 'bout the purtiest woman I ever seen."

Jennie continued to stare straight ahead.

"What's the matter, Missy? Do you think you're too good for the likes of Dewey Butrum?"

Winnie got up from his seat and stood in the aisle between his mother and Dewey Butrum.

"Mr. Butrum, to answer your question, my mother is much too good for the likes of you."

"Get out of the way, kid. I'm talkin' to your mama."

"I have no intention of getting out of the way."

"Then I'll just get you out of the way," Butrum said. Standing up, he started toward Winnie, but Winnie kicked him hard in his shin.

Butrum lifted his leg and grabbed his shin, then began hopping around on one leg.

"Ow! You little shit, I'm going to teach you how to respect your elders."

"No, you're not," another man said, and, looking up, Winnie saw that at least three more men had gotten up from their own seats. "If that little fella has the courage to stand up for his mama, we intend to see that nothing happens to him or her. There's an empty seat at the back of the car. You go sit there."

"The hell I will. I like where I'm sittin'," Butrum said.

"Mister, you'll either go back there peacefully, or we will throw you off this train," the man said.

Grumbling, Butrum walked back to the last seat in the car and sat down.

"I thank you gentlemen for coming to our rescue," Winnie said.

The spokesman for the group touched the brim of his hat, and smiled. "I'm not sure we did rescue you, son," he said. "It looked to me like you were doing pretty good on your own."

The three men returned to their seats, and Winnie returned to his.

"You know who those three men were, Mama?" he asked.

"No."

"They were knights."

Winnie's mother reached over, took his hand, then squeezed it. "No," she said. "You are my knight in shining armor."

"Ha! I'm not wearing any armor."

"Oh but you are, dear. You are girded with the armor of courage and righteousness."

Thistledown

William Teasdale was sitting at his desk in the office of his house, examining the figures on the paper before him. So far, he had bought almost two thousand head of cattle from Sam Logan and the Yellow Kerchief Gang, paying them five dollars a head for cattle that would bring him forty dollars a head at the market. For now, all the rustled cattle were being kept away from his main herd in a part of his ranch that was the most remote from what people normally regarded as Thistledown. They would be kept there until the brands could be changed. Once that was accomplished, the stolen cattle would be integrated into his herd.

Teasdale chuckled at how easy it was to convert the capital letter F, for Frewen, to his own brand, which was the letter T with two crossbars. That double-bar T, that stood for Teasdale–Thistledown, was not only branded on the cattle but was painted on the side of his coach, as well as on the sign at the entrance to his ranch.

THISTLEDOWN RANCH
William Teasdale, *Esquire*

Of course there was a double advantage to the rustled cattle: it not only increased his herd and profit, but it also decreased Frewen's herd, and increased his debt. Teasdale was certain that Frewen had not the slightest suspicion that Teasdale himself was behind all his troubles. The only fly in the ointment now was Matt Jensen. But Logan had told Teasdale this morning that Kyle Houston was already in Sussex, just waiting for Jensen to show up.

Sussex was a town with a single road that ran perpendicular to the Powder River. The road, which was appropriately enough called Sussex Road, was flanked on both sides by hitching rails and as many saloons as there were legitimate businesses. There were several horses tied to the hitching rails, most of them within a few feet of one of the eight saloons. The horses nodded and shuddered, swished their tails and stamped their hooves in a vain attempt to get rid of the annoying flies.

Matt Jensen surveyed the town as he rode in. Matt had never settled down in any one place, so in his lifetime there had been hundreds of towns like this, the streets faced by houses of rip-sawed lumber, false-fronted businesses, a few sod buildings, and even a tent or two.

It had rained earlier in the day, and the street was a quagmire. The hooves of the horses had worked the mud and horse droppings into one long, stinking, sucking pool of ooze. When the rain stopped, the sun, high and hot, began the process of evaporation. The result was a foul miasma rising from the street.

It wasn't a matter of finding a saloon, but a matter of choosing which saloon he wanted to patronize. The one he chose was The Lion and The Crown, the biggest and grandest building in the entire town. It was only marginally cooler inside, and the dozen and a half customers who were drinking held bandannas at the ready to wipe away the sweat.

Matt surveyed the place, doing so with such calmness that the average person would think it no more than a glance of idle curiosity. In reality, it was a very thorough appraisal of the room. He was interested to see who was carrying and who wasn't, and how they were armed, what type of weapons they were carrying, and whether or not those who were armed were wearing their guns in such a way as to indicate that they knew how to use them.

There was one man standing at the far

end of the bar who did bear a second look. He was a small man, no taller than five feet, five inches, Matt guessed. He was dressed all in black, including a low-crown hat that was ringed by a silver band. What caused Matt to pay a little more attention to him than anyone else in the room was the fact that, while everyone else in the saloon had given him at least a cursory glance, this man stood at the bar staring pointedly into his drink. It was as if he was purposely avoiding any eye contact.

The heat was making everyone listless and slow-moving. There was nobody at the piano, and even the two bargirls seemed disinterested in working the room. For the moment, they were sitting as far away from the customers as they could, engaged in some private conversation.

The bartender stood behind the bar, wiping the used glasses with his stained apron before he stacked them among the unused glasses. When he saw Matt step up to the bar, he put a glass into place, then moved down toward him.

"What'll it be?" he asked.

"I'll have a beer," Matt said.

The bartender reached for one of the glasses he had just "cleaned" with the stained apron, but Matt pointed to a different glass. It also might have been wiped with the dirty apron, but at least Matt hadn't seen him do it.

"I'll take that glass," he said.

The bartender shrugged his shoulders, but made no comment as he held the new glass under the spigot.

Matt finished his beer, then put the glass down.

"Want another?"

"Not yet," Matt said. "I've got four days of trail stink on me and I need to take a bath somewhere. I didn't see a bathhouse on the way in."

"That's 'cause this town ain't got a bathhouse," the bartender said. "But if you're wantin' a bath, you can take one here. We got a bathing room upstairs. It'll cost you two dollars."

"Two dollars? For a bath? Most of the time it's no more than a quarter," Matt protested.

"Yeah, but since this is the only place in town you can get a bath, that is unless you're planning on bathin' in the Powder River, the boss charges what he can get."

"How many people are willing to pay that?"

"No more'n one or two a week," the bartender admitted.

Matt knew he was being taken advantage of, but he really needed a bath and had been thinking about it for the last twenty-four hours. He put two dollars on the bar.

"The water had better be hot, there had better be soap, and the towel had damn well better be clean," he said.

"Don't worry, it will be," the bartender said as he took the money. "You can't very well take a bath without hot water, soap, and a clean towel, now, can you?"

"I didn't see a hotel, either."

"Not likely you would, seein' as we ain't got one," the bartender said. "We got rooms here, if you want one."

"How much?"

"That'll be two dollars."

"Do you know where I can find a man named Moreton Frewen?" Matt asked.

"You lookin' for him, are you?"

"I am."

"If you're thinkin' you might get hired on out at the Powder River Cattle Company Ranch, I don't think he's hirin' anyone new."

"I'm not looking to be hired. I'm just looking for him."

"Well, if you come in to town from the north, you more'n likely seen his castle."

"His castle?"

127

"That's what folks around here call it. It's made of logs, but it ain't nothin' like any log cabin you've ever seen. Why, I wouldn't be surprised if it wasn't the biggest house in all Wyoming."

"How long will it take to get the bath ready?" Matt asked.

"Not long. Fifteen minutes or so. Are you goin' to be takin' a room here? 'Cause if you are, I'll have the bathtub brought up to your room and filled with hot water."

Matt took out another two dollars. "Yeah," he said. "I'll take a room. But for now, I saw a mercantile across the street. I'm going to go buy a new pair of trousers and a shirt. That is, if the same man that owns this place doesn't own that store. If he does, I probably can't afford it."

"Mr. Oliver don't own it . . . yet," the bartender said. "But he's been tryin' to buy it, and like as not, he will some day."

"Would your name be Matt Jensen?"

The question came from the man at the far end of the bar, the small man dressed in black. Hanging low in a quick-draw holster on the right side of a bullet-studded pistol belt was a silver-plated Colt .44, its grip inlaid with mother-of-pearl. The man's eyes were so pale a blue that they looked like chips of ice.

He had not turned toward Matt yet, but was watching him in the mirror. He tossed the rest of his drink down, then took a towel from one of the bar rings and, very carefully, dabbed at his mouth. That done, he replaced the towel, then turned to look at Matt.

"Hey, you."

Matt did not turn.

"I'm talkin' to you, Mister."

"Are you, now?" Matt said. He knew from the tone of the man's voice, though, that he wasn't being offered a simple greeting.

"You're Matt Jensen, are you?"

Matt didn't answer.

"I seen you once down in Laramie. Matt Jensen. That is you, ain't it?"

"I'm Matt Jensen."

"You're the famous gunfighter, are you?"

"Mister, seems to me like you've got something sticking in your craw. Why don't you let me buy you a drink, then we'll each just go our own way?" Matt said.

"Huh, uh," the man said. "It don't happen like that."

Matt finally turned to face the belligerent little man. "I think I see where you are going with this," he said. "And if you'd take a little friendly advice, I'd say, don't go there."

"Don't go there? Don't go there?" the

little man replied. He turned to address the others. The saloon had grown deathly still now, as the patrons sat quietly, nervously, and yet drawn by morbid curiosity to the drama that was playing out before them. "Is that what you said?"

"That's what I said," Matt said. "Don't go there."

"Is that how you've built your reputation, Mr. Matt Jensen? By frightening people into not drawing against you? Am I supposed to be afraid now, just because I am in the presence of the great Matt Jensen?"

"You're not going to let this go, are you?" Matt asked.

"No, I ain't goin' to let it go," the little man answered. "You see, I make my livin' with my gun, and I've been hired to kill you. Well, sir, I don't want to be hung for murder, so the only way I can justify killin' you is if it is a fair fight. So, that's what I'm wantin' to do now. I want to goad you into drawin' on me."

"What is your name?" Matt asked.

"The name is Houston. Kyle Houston," the man replied. A slow, confident smile spread across his face. "I reckon you've heard of me."

"Yeah, I have," Matt replied.

Houston's smile broadened. "Really? What

have you heard?"

"I've heard that you are a bully and a coward, trying to make a reputation by back-shooting old men and young boys. I heard you've never faced a man down in your life."

Matt hadn't heard any of that, nor had he even heard of Kyle Houston, but he knew that it would make the man blind with rage, and so it did.

Houston's smile quickly turned to an angry snarl. "Draw, Jensen!" he shouted, going for his own gun even before he issued the challenge.

Houston was quick, quicker than anyone else in this town had ever seen. And as he started his draw, a broad, triumphant smile spread across his face. He had caught Matt by surprise, and Matt was going to have to react to the draw.

Then, even before Houston could bring his pistol to bear, he realized that he wasn't quick enough. The arrogant smile left, and one could see in the man's eyes the knowledge, then the acceptance of reality. And the reality was that Kyle Houston was about to be killed.

The two pistols discharged almost simultaneously, but Matt was first and accurate. His bullet plunged into Houston's chest, while the bullet from Houston's gun smashed through the front window of the building.

Looking down at himself, Houston put his hand over his wound, then pulled it away and examined the blood that had pooled in his palm. When he looked back at Matt, there was an almost whimsical smile on his face.

"I'll be damned," he said. "I've been kilt."

"Yeah, you have," Matt replied, still holding the gun.

Houston slid down into a sitting position, his position supported by the bar itself. His right arm stretched out beside him, the pistol free of his hand except for the trigger finger that was curled through the trigger guard. The eye-burning, acrid smoke of two discharges hung in a gray-blue cloud just below the ceiling.

Matt turned back to the bar, then slid his beer toward the bartender.

"I believe I'm going to need something a little stronger than beer," he said.

The bartender drew a whiskey and handed it to him.

"Thanks."

"No problem, Mr. Jensen. If you want anything, just ask," the bartender said.

132

Matt tossed the whiskey down.

"What's your name, barkeep?" he asked.

"It's Moore, Mr. Jensen. Harry Moore."

"Did you know that gentlemen, Mr. Moore?"

"Only by his reputation," Moore said.

"What kind of reputation was that?"

"He was fast with a gun," Moore said. "Folks said he was the fastest."

"That's what folks said, is it?"

"Yes, sir," Moore said.

"And what do you say?"

"I say folks was wrong."

CHAPTER TEN

Behind Matt, the silence was broken as everyone was engaged in spirited and animated discussion about what they had just seen. The gunsmoke had cleared out but the smell of burnt gunpowder still hung in the air as Marshal Drew, the town marshal, arrived.

"What happened here?" the marshal asked. Drew was in his late fifties or early sixties. He was clean-shaven, bald-headed, and with a pronounced paunch. Before the war he had been a Texas Ranger, but when the Texas Rangers were broken up after the war he wandered from town to town, and eventually from state to state, here working as a sheriff's deputy, there as a policeman or city marshal. He had come to Sussex because it was a small town and he hoped to close out his career in a place that offered a minimum amount of stress.

"Houston tried to brace this fella," Moore said.

"Houston started the fight?"

"That's right. Houston drew first."

"You're telling me that Houston drew first, but this man still beat him?"

"That's right, Marshal," one of the saloon patrons said. "Harry is tellin' it like it is."

Marshal Drew stroked his chin as he looked at Houston. Death had made the young would-be gunman's face appear slack-jawed and distorted.

"Mister, if you beat Houston fair and square the way these folks are tellin' it, you must be some kind of a gunfighter," Drew said. "What's your name?"

"Jensen," Matt replied. "Matt Jensen."

"Matt Jensen? Sumbitch! Did Houston know who he was tanglin' with?"

"He called me by name," Matt said.

Marshal Drew looked back toward Houston. "I reckon you run across punks like Houston here more times than you can count, don't you? Tryin' to make a name for himself."

"From time to time," Matt said. "Most men have more sense than he did. And less guts," he added in a begrudging acknowledgment of Houston's misplaced courage. "But I don't think he was trying to make a name for himself. He had another motive."

"What do you mean?"

"He told me he was hired to kill me."

"Hired to kill you? By who?" the marshal asked.

"I'd like to know the answer to that as well."

"Are you here to meet with Mr. Frewen?" Marshal Drew asked.

"Yes, how did you know that?"

"I'm the one who suggested he get in touch with you."

"Do we know each other?" Matt asked.

The marshal shook his head. "We've never met," he said. "But I've sure heard of you. My name is Drew. And if I can be of any assistance while you're, uh, doing whatever it is you are going to do for Mr. Frewen, please, just let me know."

"All right, Marshal Drew," Matt replied. "Thank you, I appreciate that."

Marshal Drew turned to the bartender. "Harry, I'll get Welsh down here to pick up the body and get it cleared away for you," he said.

"No hurry, Marshal," Moore replied with a broad smile. "Havin' Houston shot by a man like Matt Jensen is goin' to bring in the business. Hell, I may get Dysart to come set up his camera. I'll charge people to have their pictures took with Houston's body."

Leaving the saloon, Matt rode down to the end of the street where he had boarded his horse, Spirit, in the livery. Then, trying to stay on the board that crossed the road so as to avoid as much of the mud and liquefied horse apples as he could, he walked back to the mercantile.

There were seven or eight people in the store when he walked in, and from the way they reacted at seeing him, he knew that they had already heard the story of the shooting in the The Lion and The Crown. They moved aside to give him as much room as possible.

The frightened reaction people had to him used to bother Matt. He wanted to yell at them, to ask them if they thought he was going to go berserk and start shooting them all. Now he just turned his mind off to it.

A very overweight man with white muttonchop whiskers came up to talk to him.

"Yes, sir, Mr. Jensen. How may I help you?"

Matt was not surprised that the clerk knew his name. He figured that by now, everyone in town probably knew him. That also meant that Moreton Frewen, the man who had sent for him, knew that he was in town as well.

"I need a pair of trousers and a new shirt," Matt said.

The clerk, evidently believing that he had a gift for fashion, attempted to pick out the trousers and shirt. He chose a pair of fawn-colored trousers and a bright orange shirt.

"Oh, I think you would look very nice in this," the clerk said.

"I would feel better in this," Matt said, picking up a pair of blue denims and a white collarless shirt.

Both Teasdale and Moreton Frewen had telephones in their houses, with direct lines to the switchboard in town. In fact, they were two of only thirty-five private telephones in the entire town; but Teasdale's foreman, Stan Reed, was in town, and shortly after the gunfight occurred, he went directly to the telephone exchange.

The switchboard was in the living room of Gordon Prouty's house. Prouty was the operator. Reed pulled on the bell cord, and Prouty, who was eating a piece of fried chicken, answered the door.

"What do you want?" he asked.

"I want to call Mr. Teasdale."

"It'll cost you a nickel," Prouty said.

Reed gave him a nickel, and Prouty

pointed to a telephone mounted on the wall. "Go over there and pick it up," he said. Prouty connected the line, then turned a crank.

Teasdale was eating his dinner when the telephone rang, and when Margaret started to answer it, Teasdale held up his hand.

"I'll get it," he said. "I'm expecting a call." He hurried over to the phone.

"Hello?"

"Mr. Teasdale, I thought you might like to know that this fella Matt Jensen that ever'one has been talkin' about got into town today."

"How do you know?" Teasdale asked.

"How do I know is because almost the first thing he done after he got here was he got into a gunfight with Kyle Houston."

Teasdale smiled. "Houston kill him, did he? Well, I guess that . . ."

"No sir," Reed said, interrupting him.

"What do you mean, no sir? I thought you said the first thing he did after coming to town was to get into a gunfight with Houston."

"Yes, sir, that's what he done, all right. Only he didn't get killed, he was the one that done the killin'. It's Kyle Houston who is dead."

Teasdale hung up without saying another word.

After he'd made his purchases, Matt returned to The Lion and The Crown Saloon. The bartender waved him over.

"It's Room Four, Mr. Jensen," Moore said, handing Matt a key. "Second room on your left."

Matt climbed the stairs then opened the door to the room. There was a zinc bathtub in the room, filled with water. The little wisps of steam that were rising from the water indicated that the water was warm. Matt slipped down into the tub, where he soaked for nearly an hour. Then, with his skin red from the hot water and soapy scrub, he dried off and walked over to lie down on the bed. Still naked from his bath, he crawled between the stiff, clean sheets, and was asleep within moments.

The room was dark when he woke up. For a moment, he didn't know where he was. Then he remembered that he had taken a room over the saloon. At that same moment, he realized that he was awake because something had awakened him, though he didn't know what it was.

The doorknob rattled quietly, and all confusion and hesitancy were gone. Matt was out of bed, on his feet instantly. Pulling his pistol from the holster that hung on the head of the bed, he moved as quietly as a stalking cat to the wall next to the door. He cocked his pistol, pulling back the hammer as slowly and quietly as he could to silence the engaging sear. With the pistol cocked and loaded, he held it at the ready.

The night breeze pushing through the window cooled his skin, reminding him that he was naked. Damn! He was about to get into a gunfight, and he was naked! How would the paper write that up if he was killed? He could feel the texture of the boards under his feet. He was intensely alert, ready for anything.

He heard whoever was trying to break into his room breathing on the other side of the door. The hall lanterns were lit, and a sliver of light shot in under the door. From the saloon below, he could hear the nighttime revelry, a playing piano, and someone laughing.

Matt waited.

Whoever was coming into his room wasn't breaking into it. They had a key! The doorknob turned again and the door began to swing open, spilling an ever-widening arc of light into the room.

Matt watched the door ease open, away

from him. As it did, the arc of light turned into a bar of light that splashed all the way across to the foot of the bed. A shadow filled the door, gliding in through the opening, backlit by the lantern on the wall in the hall beyond.

"What the hell?" Matt whispered in surprise, letting his breath escape in a rush. The person trying to get into his room was a woman!

Matt grabbed the woman's arm and pulled her inside. He closed the door quickly behind her, the motion pulling her against him. She let out a cry of alarm.

"Who are you?" Matt asked, backing away from her.

"My name is Lily," the woman answered in a frightened voice. "Lily Langtry."

"Lily Langtry? I've heard of you," Matt said, lowering his pistol. "The next question is, what are you doing in my room?"

"I might ask you the same thing," Lily replied. "This is my room. I've been staying here for two weeks."

"What?"

"I'm a friend of Moreton Frewen," Lily said. She chuckled. "However, I am not a friend of his wife, Clara. So when I come to visit, I have to make other arrangements. This room is my other arrangement, and

142

has been for the last two weeks."

"I, uh, don't know what to say," Matt said. "I rented a room, and this is the room the bartender gave me."

"Wait a minute, I think I know what must have happened," Lily said. "I was in Room Three, but I asked to be changed to this room. There is some construction going on down the street, and when they get started in the morning, the hammering and sawing awakens me. I complained about it to Johnny this morning, and he gave me a key to this room. He must not have told Harry. I'll go back across to Room Three. I really didn't expect to see you in here." She paused for a moment, and Matt saw a twinkling of humor in her eyes. "And I especially didn't expect to see so much of you."

Matt felt his cheeks burning, and he was glad that it was too dark for her to see that. He stepped back into the shadow to restore some modesty, if not dignity.

"You don't have to keep looking, you know," he said.

Lily laughed, a low, throaty laugh. "I see your point," she said. "I'll just step back across the hall now. I do apologize for disturbing you. Good night, now."

■ ■ ■ ■

A slight morning breeze filled the muslin curtains and lifted them out over the wide-planked floor. Matt, clean from his bath the night before and wearing his new clothes, moved to the window to look out over the town, which was just beginning to awaken. From the laundry, he could hear the chattering of the Chinese employees as they built the fires to heat the water. Boxes were being stacked behind the grocery store as a team of four big horses pulled a fully loaded freight wagon down the main street.

A stagecoach was sitting at the coach depot, and one man was on top of the coach receiving luggage from another man who was passing it up to him. The door of the coach was open, and passengers were just now getting onboard.

From somewhere in town, Matt could smell bacon frying and his stomach growled, reminding him that he was hungry. He splashed some water in the basin, washed his face and hands, then put on his hat and went downstairs. It was too early for the normal clientele, but there were a couple of people already here and they were sitting at separate tables, staring silently into their breakfast beer. Neither of them paid any attention to Matt as he walked through the saloon. The bartender was not the same one who had been on duty the previous night.

The morning sun was bright, but not yet hot. The sky was clear and the air was crisp. As he walked toward the café he heard sounds of commerce: the ring of a blacksmith's hammer, a carpenter's saw, and the squeak and rattle of the departing stagecoach. He knew that the hammering and sawing must be the construction that Lily Langtry mentioned last night.

Matt smiled as he thought about his encounter with the famous actress. It had been an embarrassing moment, but he had to admit that it was also funny.

Fifteen minutes later, as Matt was enjoying a breakfast of coffee, bacon, eggs, fried potatoes, biscuits and gravy, Lily Langtry came in. Seeing Matt at one of the tables, she smiled and crossed the room to him. Matt stood up.

"Good morning, Mr. Jensen."

"You know my name, Miss Langtry?"

"Of course I do," Lily said. "Would you mind if I joined you?" she asked.

"No, not at all. I would be pleased with the company," he said, pulling out a chair for her.

"My, that's quite a breakfast," Lily said. "How long has it been since you have eaten?"

"It's been quite a while. Not since supper last night," Matt said.

Lily laughed, then, as he held the chair, took her seat. She ordered a cup of hot tea and toast with butter and marmalade.

"You expect something like that to hold you till dinner?" Matt asked.

"No, I'll probably eat a light lunch."

Matt smiled. "I forgot that sophisticated people call supper 'dinner.' "

"Is that what you think I am, Mr. Jensen? Sophisticated?"

"Well, yes, ma'am, being as you are English and famous and all," Matt said.

"Evidently I'm not the only famous one in this conversation," Lily said. "You seemed surprised that I knew your name. But after your — shall we call it deadly encounter? You are the person everyone is talking about this morning."

"I'm sorry about that," Matt said.

"You shouldn't be sorry you killed him. From what everyone is saying, you had no choice. It was either him or you."

"I'm not sorry I killed him, I'm just sorry that it has become the talk of the town."

"I'm also told, however, that the name

Matt Jensen is not just known here in Sussex but quite well known, not only in the West, but throughout the country. You are that Matt Jensen, are you not?"

"Yes, ma'am."

"Oh for heaven's sake, Mr. Jensen, quit calling me ma'am. You make me feel like an old spinster."

"Sorry, Ma'— that is, Miss Langtry. I'm just trying to be polite, is all."

"I think calling me Lily would be very polite."

"All right, Lily it is, then," Matt said.

"Matt, if I may ask, what are you doing in Sussex? This seems like a small and very out-of-the-way town, even for the far West."

"I'm here because I received a letter from Moreton Frewen, asking me to come."

"My," Lily said. "I am impressed that Moreton could crook his finger and bring someone like you to do his bidding."

"He did a bit more than crook his finger," Matt said.

"What did he do?"

"He included a bank draft for five thousand dollars," Matt said.

"Oh, dear. Moreton spends so freely, and the bad thing is, the money he spends isn't his own."

"Not his own money?"

"Well, I suppose it is, in a way. At least, he has control of it. You see, Moreton is very good about getting others to invest in his ideas. He has long had the idea of coming to America and building a huge cattle ranch, an empire, really. The Powder River Cattle Company is the fruition of that idea, and though ostensibly he is the owner, there are so many people invested in the ranch that I fear he is little more than a figurehead. And since his ranch is losing money so badly, I'm not sure how much longer he will be able to hang on."

"I understand that the cattle rustling is very bad here. If you lose too many cows to rustlers, it is hard to turn a profit," Matt said.

"I suppose that is true, but Sir William doesn't seem to be losing money as badly as poor Moreton. In fact, Sir William has offered to buy Moreton's ranch."

"Sir William?"

"That would be William Teasdale," Lily said. "Like Moreton, Sir William is a subject of the Crown. And like Moreton, he has the dream of establishing a cattle empire in the American West. Unlike Moreton, however, Sir William seems to be succeeding."

CHAPTER ELEVEN

Out at Thistledown Ranch, William Teasdale, the subject of Lily Langtry's discussion, was in the ranch office, talking to Reed.

"I thought Kyle Houston was supposed to be the best money could buy," Teasdale said.

"He is damn good," Reed said. "The best I ever saw." Reed scratched at his brown beard, pulled something out, examined it on the end of his finger, then flicked it away.

"You mean he *was* damn good, don't you?" Teasdale asked. "Now he is damn dead."

"Yes, sir, I reckon he is. So, what are we goin' to do about this Jensen fella now?"

Teasdale knew that he wouldn't be able to carry off his cattle rustling — though he preferred to call it his ranch enlargement — scheme unless he had the support of his foreman. He had left it up to Reed to hire the cowboys, men he could trust, men who knew of the arrangement Teasdale had with

Sam Logan and the Yellow Kerchief Gang.

"For the time being, we will just play defensive chess."

"Say what?"

"We will monitor, closely, the moves made by Frewen and Mr. Jensen," Teasdale said.

News of the gunfight between Matt Jensen and Kyle Houston had reached Frewen Castle almost as quickly as it reached Thistledown.

"I am wondering, Mr. Morrison, If I have opened Pandora's box?"

"What do you mean?" Morrison asked.

"This man Matt Jensen," Frewen said. "I haven't said anything to anyone about him, but he is here because I sent for him. And what is the first thing he does when he arrives? He gets into a gunfight."

"Yes, sir, but from what everyone is saying, Houston is the one who provoked the fight. And, from what I understand, he claimed that he had been hired to kill Jensen."

"Heavens, do you suppose Jensen has made so many enemies that there are actually people who will pay to have him killed?"

"That, or . . ." Morrison started, but he let the sentence hang.

"Or what?"

"Or it is somebody local. It could be that someone found out that you hired him and decided to take care of him."

"You mean somebody like Sam Logan?"

"That would be my guess," Morrison said. "He is the head of the Yellow Kerchief Gang. I could see how he might not want someone like Matt Jensen poking around out there."

"But Logan is a desperado himself," Frewen said. "Why would he hire someone else to oppose Mr. Jensen?"

"Because he runs with a gang," Morrison said. "And ultimately, people who run with gangs are cowards."

"That might be so," Frewen said. He looked up at the clock. "Heavens, it is nearly tea time. I had best join Mrs. Frewen. You will excuse me?"

"Yes, sir," Morrison said. "I've got some things to take care of anyway." Morrison hastened his withdrawal. So far he had never been invited to "tea time" and he hoped that he never would.

"I'm sorry I'm late, dear," Frewen said a moment later, when he stepped into the crimson drawing room where Clara Frewen was already waiting. He drew his own tea from a silver tea server, then selected a "biscuit," though the cowboys would have called it a cookie, and took a seat on the opposite side of the table from Clara.

"What is that woman doing here?" Clara asked.

"What woman would that be, dear?" Frewen asked as he took a sip of tea.

"You know very well what woman," Clara replied. "I'm talking about Lily Langtry. She is in town. Though, I'm sure that is not a revelation to you."

"Miss Langtry is a singer, actress, and lecturer of no small renown," Frewen said. "She is performing at theaters all over America."

"There is no theater in Sussex," Clara said pointedly.

"My dear, you know that Miss Langtry and I are old friends of long standing," Frewen said. "It does not seem that unusual to me that she would call upon us if she found herself in the area."

"In the area? And just what area would that be, Moreton?" Clara said. "The closest railroad is in Medicine Bow and that is two hundred miles away. The stagecoach from Medicine Bow only arrives three times per week, and it is a very long and difficult journey."

Clara was a beautiful woman, dainty,

blonde, with her hair worn in the close ringlet fashion of the day. Despite her American heritage, Clara had grown up in Paris, and was often a guest of Napoleon III. Clara and her even more beautiful sister Jennie had been the toast of Paris society. That she would be jealous of Lily Langtry, a much older and not nearly as attractive a woman, seemed ludicrous to all who knew the couple. And indeed, those who knew Clara well knew, also, that she wasn't really jealous, but used this merely as a means of keeping Moreton Frewen wary of any dalliances.

"I only call on her in town because you seem to find her company so objectionable," Frewen said. "And I have no wish to upset you."

"Invite her out for dinner," Clara suggested.

"What? But I thought you didn't like her."

"I don't like her, but that doesn't mean I can't be civil around her. And I would much rather have her come here for a visit than to have you go into town, alone, to visit her. Somehow, that seems so very sordid."

Frewen smiled. "Very well, I shall invite her," he said.

Spirit kicked up sheets of silver spray as he

splashed through the stream. Matt would have paused to give his horse an opportunity to drink if he wanted to, but Spirit gave no indication that he was thirsty.

Once across the stream, Matt turned back around to pay attention to where he was going. For some time now, he had been aware that two men were dogging him, riding parallel with him, and for the most part staying out of sight.

He was pretty sure they were some of Moreton Frewen's men, because he had been on Powder River Cattle Company land for some time now. He had picked them up the moment they started shadowing him.

Matt rode on for a couple more miles, all the while keeping his eye on them until finally he decided to do something about it. He waited until the trail led in between two parallel rows of hills. Once into the defile, he cut off the trail and, using the ridge line to conceal his movement, rode ahead about two hundred yards. He went over to the gully his two tails were using, dismounted, then pulled his rifle from the saddle scabbard and climbed onto a rocky ledge to wait for them. He jacked a round into the chamber.

Matt watched and waited. He saw them come around a bend in the gully and knew that not only had they not seen him, they hadn't even missed him. He waited until they were right on him, then he suddenly stood up.

"Hold it!" he shouted.

"What the hell?" one of the riders yelled. He had to fight to stay on his horse, for the horse had been so startled that it reared. The other rider started for his gun.

"Don't do it!" Matt said, raising his rifle to his shoulder.

"Johnny, keep your hand away from your gun!" the first rider said, just now regaining control of his horse. "There didn't nobody say nothin' 'bout shootin' anybody."

"How did you get here on Powder River Cattle Company land?" Johnny asked.

"You ought to know," Matt replied. "You've been dogging my tail for the last two miles."

"I don't know what you're talking about."

"Don't insult my intelligence, Johnny," Matt said. "That makes me mad."

"What do we do now, Ian?" Johnny asked.

"All right, Mister, we've been dogging you," Ian admitted.

"Why?"

"Because you are on Powder River Cattle Company land, that's why."

"That's good to know, seeing as I intend

to be there," Matt said.

"What are you doing here?"

"I'm just here to pay the ranch a friendly visit, is all," Matt said.

Ian shook his head. "Huh, uh," he said. "We ain't friendly and we don't like visitors."

"Shouldn't you let Mr. Frewen decide that?"

"Our job is to keep people away from him, keep 'em for botherin' him so he don't have to decide whether or not to see saddle bums like you," Johnny said.

"Saddle bum?" Matt held out his arm and examined his newly bought shirt. "Now you are hurting my feelings. And here I thought I had gone and gotten all dressed up to meet Mr. Frewen."

"What do you want to meet him for? He ain't hirin' nobody," Ian said.

"He's already hired me," Matt said.

"Hired you to do what?" Ian asked.

"Well, now, I'm afraid I can't answer that question," Matt said. "He sent me a letter, but he didn't say what he wanted me to do."

"Mr. Frewen sent you a letter?" Ian asked.

"He did."

"You got that letter with you?"

"I do."

"Let me see it," Ian said.

"Now, Ian, that sounds like a demand," Matt said. "And if you stop and think about it, seeing as how I am pointing a gun at you, you really aren't in position to make any demands, are you?"

Ian and Johnny exchanged glances.

"No, sir," Ian said, sheepishly. "Now that you mention it, I don't reckon I am."

"All right, since you've taken that attitude, I'll let you see it," Matt said. He took the letter from his shirt pocket and handed it to Ian.

"But I'm going to take it as a real unfriendly act if something happens to that letter while it's in your hands," Matt said.

"He didn't say nothin' to us about hirin' someone," Ian said, before he started to read the letter.

"Does he tell you all his business?" Matt asked.

"No. But since we're supposed to keep strangers off the property, you would think we would have heard something, don't you?"

"Sounds reasonable to me," Matt said.

"Holy shit!" Ian said looking up from the letter at Matt. "Are you Matt Jensen?"

"I am."

"Let me see it," Johnny said.

Ian handed the letter to Johnny, and

Johnny took a moment to read it.

"Looks like the boss's writin'," Johnny said.

"It is real," Matt said. He held his hand out. "Could I have my letter back, please?"

Johnny returned the letter. "What do you think we ought to do, Ian?" he asked.

"What do you mean, what should we do? Are you crazy? Didn't you read the letter? This is Matt Jensen, for God's sake."

"I'll tell you what to do. Take me to him," Matt said. "I don't want to get jumped by anyone else. They may not be as intelligent as you two are, and I might wind up having to kill them."

"All right, yeah, that's a good idea," Ian said. "We'll take you."

Back at the house, Frewen got up from his chair, crossed the room and planted a kiss on the lips of his beautiful wife.

"My dear," he said. "Don't you know that my life started when I met you? Compared to that lucky day when you agreed to become my wife, nothing from my past — no dalliance, no adventure, no accomplishment of any kind — could ever be of any import."

Clara smiled. "You do have a way of

smoothing my feathers, don't you, Moreton?"

Frewen returned her smile. "Lord, I certainly hope so," he said.

Moreton Frewen's "gentleman's gentleman" stepped into the drawing room.

"Sir Moreton, there is a gentleman by the name of Matt Jensen to see you."

"He's here? Good, good, show him in, would you please, Benjamin?"

"Who is Matt Jensen?" Clara asked as Benjamin left.

"He is someone that I hope I can convince to do some work for me," Frewen replied.

When Matt was led into the drawing room, he saw as handsome a couple as he had ever seen. The woman was blond and beautiful, the man tall and handsome, with a well-groomed mustache. Both were elegantly dressed.

"Mr. Jensen, thank you so much for coming," Frewen said.

"I must confess, Mr. Frewen, that your invitation was quite compelling," Matt said. "In fact, I would say that it provided me with five thousand reasons to come."

Frewen chuckled. "I hoped that would get your attention. I've read a great deal about you, Mr. Jensen. I knew that if I had any hope of getting your attention, I would have to do something dramatic."

"You got my attention," Matt said.

"Good." Frewen turned toward Clara. "Clara, would you excuse us, please, my dear? Mr. Jensen and I are going to talk some business and I fear that some of it might not be suitable for a lady's ears."

"Very well," Clara replied without protesting. She flashed a big smile toward Matt. "If you would excuse me, Mr. Jensen?"

"Yes, ma'am," Matt replied with a slight nod of the head.

Frewen waited until after Clara was gone before he resumed the conversation.

"I hear that there was some unpleasantness last night in the pub."

For a second, Matt had to think about what Frewen was talking about. Then he realized the pub Frewen was talking about was The Lion and The Crown Saloon.

"Yes, I'm afraid there was," Matt said. "The man I shot, Kyle Houston, said that he had been hired to kill me."

"So I heard."

"Do you have any idea who might have hired him?" Matt asked.

"My foreman and I were discussing that same subject," Frewen said. "And we have come up with the idea that it may have been

Sam Logan."

"Sam Logan?"

"Have you ever heard of him?"

"Only that you mentioned him in your letter."

"Yes, well, he is an outlaw, though I have heard that at one time he was a peace officer. I do find that hard to believe, though. I mean, why would a former peace officer become an outlaw?"

"It's really not all that hard to believe," Matt said. "The West is full of outlaws who have gone straight and started wearing a badge, as well as peace officers who have crossed the line to become outlaws."

"Then perhaps the rumors are true. Whatever his background, he is affiliated with a very active gang of cattle rustlers who are operating here in Johnson County with absolute impunity. They call themselves the Yellow Kerchief Gang because they all wear a yellow kerchief, as if it is a point of great personal pride. And, I am sorry to say, they have already killed six of my men, to say nothing of the cattle they have stolen."

"Thank you for the way you put that," Matt said.

"I beg your pardon?"

"When you said that they were causing you trouble, you put the lives of your men above the loss of your cattle. Not all ranchers would do that."

"I assure you, Mr. Jensen, I feel the loss of each life most intensely."

"Did you tell anyone you were contacting me?" Matt asked.

"I did, actually," Frewen replied. "I hoped that just the knowledge that you might be working with me would cause Mr. Logan to have second thoughts about stealing cattle from me."

"How does Logan work?"

"Well, as I said, he is the head of the Yellow Kerchief Gang, and they have gotten very bold, because now they are quite large. They succeed by overwhelming numbers. And Logan seems to understand military tactics. He knows where he will be able to enjoy numerical superiority, and he will ride in, bold as you please, with a group of ten or twelve men against two or three, four at the most, and proceed to cut out cattle. On one such raid, he took over fifteen hundred cattle."

"So, what, exactly, do you want from me, Mr. Frewen?"

"I want you to protect me and mine," Frewen replied.

"For how long?"

"At least until we are able to take our

162

cattle to market."

"All right," Matt agreed.

"Oh, and there is one more thing," Frewen said."

"What would that be?"

"My sister-in-law and her young son Winnie are coming to America for an extended visit. They will arrive by train in Medicine Bow on Friday. From there, they will have to travel by stagecoach until they reach Sussex. If you would, I would like for you to be there to meet them, then ride in the coach with them back here to the ranch. I know that may sound a bit odd to you, but I'm more than just a little concerned about their safety."

"All right, I'll do that," Matt agreed. "But tell me, do you have any specific reason to be worried? Is there something I should know?"

"I have no specific reason to be worried," Frewen admitted. "It is just a feeling I have. I'm sure it's foolish."

"Not foolish at all," Matt said. "I stay alive by paying attention to such feelings."

CHAPTER TWELVE

Two days later, Teasdale left Thistledown and rode out to Nine Mile Creek, again going through the ritual of displaying a yellow flag tied to the barrel of his rifle. There were half a dozen horses tied up out front, and when Teasdale dismounted and tied his own horse off, Sam Logan stepped out onto the front porch.

Logan was holding a cup of coffee, and he had a yellow kerchief at his neck.

"Hello, Bill," Logan said.

Teasdale winced. "You don't have to call me Sir William, as I know that there is no regard for titles in this country. But I would prefer it if you would call me Mr. Teasdale."

"All right, if that's what you want. I just thought that, what with us bein' friends and all, that we would be callin' each other by our Christian names."

"We are not friends, and there is certainly nothing Christian about our relationship,"

Teasdale said. "We have a mutually beneficial working partnership, and that is all."

"Well, Mr. Teasdale, if you ain't too good to drink coffee with us, come on in and have a cup," Logan invited.

"I'll do that," Teasdale replied.

There were five others inside the shack who, like Logan, were all wearing yellow kerchiefs.

"I am sure you have heard by now what happened to Kyle Houston," Teasdale said.

"I've heard."

"I thought you said he would be able to take care of this man, Jensen," Teasdale challenged.

"I thought he would," Logan said. "You don't think I would send my own cousin out to be killed, do you?"

"Well, he was killed, and this puts us back to where we started."

"Not quite where we started," Logan replied with a big smile. "I've got another hundred and fifty cows for you," Logan said. "That will be another seven hundred fifty dollars."

"Where did you get them?" Teasdale asked.

"Does it matter?"

"Yes, it matters. You know damn well it matters. I told you, I will support you and

165

your people only so long as you continue to conduct all of your operations against the Powder River Cattle Company, Limited."

"Well, if it makes you feel better, I'll tell you that we did take these cows from the Englishman," Logan said. "And I've already got my men changing the brands."

"Good," Teasdale said. "But that doesn't solve the problem of Matt Jensen, does it?"

"You don't have to worry about Matt Jensen. I'll find a way to take care of him."

"You are going to take care of him?"

"Yes."

"I thought you said you didn't want to deal with him."

"I don't want to deal with him alone, and I won't. But that doesn't mean he can't be dealt with."

Teasdale smiled. "That's what I like to hear," he said. "And you'll have a few days to decide how to do it, since he's going to be gone from now until Friday."

"Gone? Gone where?"

"He is taking a stagecoach down to Medicine Bow to meet Frewen's sister-in-law and nephew. He is going to ride back in the stagecoach with them."

"Is he now?" Logan said. "Hmm, that is interesting."

"What do you mean?"

"I mean being in a box like that, riding in the coach and all, Jensen is going be sort of hog-tied. That will make it easier to get to them."

Because Matt would be riding from Medicine Bow to Sussex on the stagecoach with Mrs. Churchill and her son, he decided to leave Spirit back at Frewen's ranch and make the trip to Medicine Bow on the coach. That gave him the opportunity to scout the terrain on the way down, to pick out areas where he would need to be particularly alert.

In Medicine Bow, the railroad kept a roundhouse of five stalls in which locomotive engines were kept. Before proceeding on west, depending on the size of the train, one or more engines would be added in order to assist the train up the steep grade to Carbon, the next stop. The army maintained a supply depot there as well, and, because this was the shortest way to the Black Hills, it was a stop that was far busier than its population would suggest. There were a few stores in town, mostly to cater to travelers, three saloons, the Railroad Hotel and Restaurant, a Freight Company, the stagecoach depot, and a handful of houses.

Matt was standing on the brick platform

as the engine came thundering in, steam gushing from the driver wheels, smoke streaming from the stack and glowing embers falling from the firebox to leave a shimmering trail of gold between the tracks. There was a squeak of steel on steel as the train shuddered to a stop; then, even though the train was still, it wasn't quiet. The relief valve vented steam in loud sighs, the bearings and journals popped and snapped, and the bell rang. The engineer, with his pipe in his mouth, looked down from his lofty perch as he wiped the sweat from his face with an oversized red kerchief. Enjoying a few minutes of respite, he leaned on the windowsill to observe the activity on the platform.

The conductor stepped down first, followed by a porter who put a boarding step in position for the detraining passengers to use. Matt leaned against one of the posts that supported the platform awning and crossed his arms across his chest, observing each of the passengers as they disembarked.

He saw one rather plump young woman with a boy of about ten, and he straightened up from the post and started toward them. But before he got close enough to speak to them, he heard the boy call out.

"Papa!"

A bearded man wearing a brown suit embraced the woman and the boy, and Matt returned to his post.

A man and woman got off the train. Three women stepped down, followed by a family of four, then a couple of men left the train, and Matt knew without having to ask that they were drummers.

Because there was a long pause after the drummers disembarked, Matt was beginning to think that perhaps Mrs. Churchill and her son had missed the train. He was about to go back into the depot when a young boy stepped down. He stood on the depot platform with his hands on his hips, looking around in what was obviously great curiosity. There was something about the boy that caught Matt's attention. He did not look like most of the young boys Matt had seen. He was much better dressed, wearing dark blue trousers held up with buttons rather than straps or suspenders, a white shirt with blue cuffs, and a dark blue neckerchief.

A moment after the boy stepped down, he was followed by an exceptionally pretty woman, with dark, upswept hair and amber eyes. She reached down to touch the boy on the shoulder and then glanced around the depot platform as if looking for someone.

Frewen had described her to Matt.

"She will, no doubt, be the most handsome woman you will see on the train, so I don't think you can miss her."

If this was Lady Churchill, Frewen's description of her had been very accurate. If she wasn't the prettiest woman he had ever seen, she was certainly the "most handsome" he had seen detrain. He walked up to her.

"Excuse me, Ma'am, but would you be Missus, uh, that is Lady Churchill?"

"I am," she said. "And you are?"

"My name is Matt Jensen, ma'am," Matt said. "I've been sent by Mr. Frewen to ride in the coach with you and the boy from here to Sussex."

"Do you have some proof of that?"

Matt smiled. "Your sister said you would ask for some proof that I am who I say I am. She wrote a letter and asked me to give it to you." He pulled the letter from his shirt pocket.

Dear Jennie,

How wonderful it is to have you and young Winnie pay us a visit. The tall, handsome gentleman who should be standing before you right now is Matt Jensen. He has a widespread reputation

170

of being someone who is proficient with a gun, and has been tested many times.

You may wonder why I tout his proficiency with a firearm. That is because there are evil men about right now, and I persuaded Moreton to call upon Mr. Jensen to escort you from Medicine Bow. You will be safe with him. But knowing you as I do, I can't help but wonder if he will be safe with you.

Please forgive the joke.

Your loving sister,
Clara

Jennie smiled as she finished reading, then folded the letter and returned it to the envelope. "Apparently my sister and my brother-in-law have put me in your hands," she said. She flashed a huge smile. "And they appear to be such strong hands, too. I shall try not to be any trouble."

"Lady Churchill, I'm sure you will be no trouble at all."

"Lady Churchill is so cumbersome, and so bloody British. I'm back in America now. And since we are going to spend some time together, I would really appreciate it if you would call me Jennie."

"Oh, I don't know," Matt said. "I think that would be awfully forward of me if I

171

called you by your first name."

"And rude if you refused my specific request that you do so, Matt," Jennie said.

Matt smiled back at her and remembered that Lily Langtry had also asked him to call her by her first name.

"Well, now, I wouldn't want it to get back to Mr. Frewen that I was rude to his sister-in-law. If you really want to be called Jennie, I will oblige you."

"I do," Jennie said. "Will we be taking the coach tonight?" she asked.

"No, ma'am, the first coach for Sussex doesn't leave until eight o'clock tomorrow morning. I've got rooms for us here at the hotel."

"I'm afraid I have a rather large traveling trunk," Jennie Churchill said.

"Don't worry about it. I'll have it sent to the hotel," Matt said.

For the entire conversation between Matt and his mother, Winnie had kept his eyes glued on the pistol at Matt's side.

"Are you a real cowboy?" Winnie asked.

"I suppose that in a manner of speaking, you could say that I was a cowboy, in that I have punched a few cows in my day. But I don't do that very much anymore, so you couldn't rightly call me one. I tend to move around quite a bit."

"Punched cows?" Winnie asked. He laughed; then, as if boxing, threw a punch. "You have punched cows?" he asked again.

Matt laughed with him. "I reckon that is a strange way of saying it, but when cowboys ride herd on cows, they use the term 'punching cows.' "

"Uncle Moreton has cows, doesn't he?"

"Yes."

"Then while I am here, I shall want to 'punch' a cow."

"I'm sure you will get the opportunity," Matt said.

"Would there be a restaurant in the hotel, Matt?" Jennie asked. "We haven't eaten since lunch, and I'm sure Winnie is hungry. I know that I am."

"The hotel has a very good dining room," Matt said.

"Would you take dinner with us?" Jennie asked.

"I would be honored to."

"Will I get to see any wild Indians while I am here?" Winnie asked.

"I'm sure that while you are here, you will see some Indians."

"Are they wild?"

"There is no such thing as a 'wild' Indian," Matt said. "The Indians were living here with their own culture for thousands of years before the white man ever came."

"I meant no disrespect, sir," Winnie apologized.

Matt laughed at the boy's excellent vocabulary. "Young man, I don't think it would be in your nature to show disrespect to anyone."

When they reached the hotel, Matt made arrangements for the trunk, then led Jennie and Winnie into the dining room.

CHAPTER THIRTEEN

"You're sure he'll be on the stagecoach coming from Medicine Bow?" Logan asked.

"I'm quite sure," Teasdale said. "Mrs. Frewen told my wife that she was expecting her sister and nephew, so she convinced Frewen to send Jensen to Medicine Bow to meet them and take the coach back to Sussex with them."

Logan nodded. "Good. We can not only get rid of him, we can make it look just like the coach was held up. Which it will be."

"Remember, no harm is to come to Lady Churchill or her son," Teasdale said.

"Why not? If they get kilt too, it would just make it seem even more like it wasn't nothin' but a stagecoach holdup."

"No!" Teasdale said. "Nothing is to happen to the woman or her child. I must insist on that."

"All right, nothing will happen to them. They'll just have a little excitement they can talk about when they get back to England."

"And, while I don't want to tell you how to run your business, I would suggest that you don't wear your yellow scarves for this."

"Oh, don't worry none about that," Logan said. "We won't be the ones doin' it. I've got some friends that sort of specialize in holdin' up stagecoaches."

Back in Medicine Bow, Matt, Jennie and Winnie were taking their dinner at the dining room of the Railroad Hotel. "I'm quite sure I have never eaten buffalo," Jennie said after they ordered their dinner. "What does it taste like?"

"It has a somewhat lighter and sweeter taste than beef," Matt explained. "And it's not as fat."

"Have you ever shot your gun?" Winnie asked.

"I've shot it, yes."

"Have you ever shot anyone with it?"

"Winnie!" Jennie scolded. "What an awful question to ask!"

"It's all right," Matt said. "I know that boys his age are interested in such things."

"Well, have you?" Winnie asked.

"Yes," Matt answered without elaborating.

"I have read of cowboys, and how they can draw their guns very quickly and shoot very accurately," Winnie said. "Are you very fast, and can you shoot very accurately?"

"There is something much more important than being fast and accurate," Matt said.

"What could possibly be more important than that?"

"The most important thing in any fight is who is right and who is wrong. You must always be on the side of right, and by that I don't just mean what is legal, I mean what is morally and ethically right."

"I will remember that, Mr. Jensen," Winnie said.

Although there was a stagecoach depot, the Railroad Hotel had an arrangement with the stagecoach company to stop at the hotel to deliver or pick up passengers. Matt, Jennie and Winnie barely had time to finish their breakfast the next morning before the coach arrived out front to pick them up.

Winnie was most intrigued by the great Concord Coach. Considered the finest passenger vehicle of the time, the stagecoach could seat as many as nine people on the three inside benches. It was big, with the driver and another man sitting up over the front wheels. The team consisted of six horses, more horses than Winnie had ever seen in one team.

For this trip, there were only six passengers and Matt was glad, because the fewer passengers there were, the more comfortable was the coach.

Matt secured the backseat for them because he thought it would be more comfortable if they were looking forward. Also, the mounting of the coach on the leather through braces, plus the heavy load in the boot, meant that anyone sitting in the front seat would be leaning forward slightly, whereas those on the rear seat would have some support for their backs.

They started out with Winnie riding between them, but as the trip grew longer, he asked to be by the window so he could see outside. That rearrangement put Jennie in the middle of the seat, pressed up against Matt. Matt thought the closeness would make Jennie uncomfortable, but she didn't seem to mind.

"How long before we get to Uncle Moreton's ranch?" Winnie asked.

"We'll be there by this time tomorrow," Matt replied.

The coach averaged between five and seven miles per hour while underway, but every twelve miles the driver would blow his trumpet as a signal to the operators of the way stops. The stops were very brief, just long enough for the passengers to attend to whatever personal needs may be necessary, and to attach a new and fresh team which, because the hostler had been notified by the bleat of the trumpet, was already in harness waiting to be attached to the coach.

At their noon stop they had a meal of stewed dried apples, fried ham, biscuits, and coffee. For supper that evening they had eggs, potatoes, beans, steak, honey, and baked bread. Matt had taken many stage-coach trips and he knew that this was much better food than the normal fare. He was sure that the meals weren't up to the standard that Jennie was used to, but he was pleased that she didn't complain.

By late afternoon, the other three passengers had left the coach so that only Matt, Jennie and Winnie remained. Then it got dark, but the coach continued.

"I would have thought we would be stopped for the night by now," Jennie said. "Where will we stop?" Jennie asked.

"We won't."

"You mean we will be riding in this thing all night long?"

"Yes, but it won't be so bad," Matt said. "There are only three of us, so it shouldn't be that hard for us to get some sleep."

"Get some sleep where? How?"

"Here," Matt said. "Let me show you."

Reaching up to the middle and the front seat, Matt folded them down. The result was a flattened cushioned area that could be used as a bed.

"We've also got blankets," Matt said, producing them from a compartment under the middle seat. "And believe me, the nights up here are cold, even at this time of year."

Spreading one blanket out over the folded-down seats, Matt invited Jennie and her son to lay down. Then he lay down beside them and pulled the other blanket over them.

Jennie chuckled.

"What is it?" Matt asked.

"I had almost forgotten how quaint America could be," Jennie said with a chuckle. "I've known you only two days and already we are going to bed together."

Matt cleared his throat in embarrassment. "If you would prefer, I can ride on top of the coach tonight."

"Nonsense. Please forgive my joking. I meant nothing by it."

The coach was well sprung and the road was smooth, and that, plus the normal exhaustion of travel, enabled all three to get to sleep rather quickly that night. When they went to sleep, Winnie was lying between Matt and Jennie. But when Matt woke up at one of the middle-of-the-night stops, Jennie had changed places with Winnie and was now lying with her head on Matt's shoulder.

"Uhmm," she said, sleepily. "Why have we stopped?" She kissed Matt just under his ear, and he sat up quickly.

"To change teams," he said.

"Oh!" Jennie gasped. She put her hand over her mouth. "Oh, my goodness what did I . . . oh, please forgive me. I must have been dreaming!"

"It's all right, no harm done," Matt said. "I'll, uh, step outside and see what is going on."

They were at the Soda Lake way station, and here the driver and guard that had brought the stage from Medicine Bow were being relieved by a new driver and guard. Matt was standing outside the coach as the switch was made and he recognized Ed Mercier, the new driver, and Gary Conners, the new shotgun guard. Their regular route was between Sussex and the Soda Lake station, and Matt had met them on the way down. The driver and guard were both small men, the company believing that the smaller the drivers and shotgun guards were, the less they would weigh and the easier it would be on the horses.

"Hello, Mr. Jensen," Ed said as he approached the coach. "Did you meet the passengers you went for?"

"Yes, they are asleep in the coach," Matt said.

"Ah, then I'll shut up so as not to wake them," Ed said. He took a chew of tobacco, then walked forward to check on the horses. In the meantime, the driver who had brought them this far stretched and yawned, then headed for the way station and some much-needed sleep.

Ed came back from checking the team, spit out a wad of tobacco, then signaled to his shotgun guard. "Climb up there, Gary, and let's get this thing on the road."

By mid-morning the next day, they had picked up three more passengers: a grandmother, mother, and daughter. The young girl was about nine years old and she quickly developed an interest in Winnie.

"I've never heard anyone talk like you do," the little girl said. "Where do you live?"

"Blenheim Palace near Oxford," Churchill said.

The girl's eyes grew big. "You live in a palace?" she asked. "Are you a prince?"

Winnie laughed. "No," he said. "Your papa has to be a king or your mama a queen for you to be a prince. Papa isn't a king. He is a lord, but it is an honorary title only, because he is the third son of the Duke of Marlborough."

Matt was listening to the conversation with amusement as he was looking through the window. That was when saw the riders on the crest of a hill looking down toward the coach. They watched the coach with what seemed to Matt to be an intense degree of interest for a long moment, then all three disappeared on the other side of the hill.

It may have been nothing, but Matt got the feeling that they were up to no good. Without saying anything to anyone inside the coach, he opened the door then climbed up on top.

"My word!" one of the other women said. "Where is he going?"

When Matt got on top of the coach, he moved forward, then tapped the driver on the shoulder.

"Ed, I just saw three riders up on top of the ridge. Maybe it was nothing, but seemed to me like they were checking us over pretty close."

"It's good that you spotted them," Ed

said. "We'll be doing a hairpin turn around the pinnacle up there. There's a perfect spot for an ambush just around on the other side."

"How hard would it be for me to go over the hill here, and get behind them?" Matt asked.

"Not all that hard, I don't reckon. Don't know if you could get there before I do, though."

"I can if you slow the team down to a walk," Matt said.

"All right," Ed said. He pointed ahead. "Your best bet would probably be to just step off the top of the coach right there just this side of that big rock. That's about as easy a way across as any."

"Ha," the shotgun guard said. "Like you've clumb over it before."

"I didn't say I'd ever clumb over it," Ed said. "But I've been driving this route for three years, and I know it pretty well."

"Have you been held up here before?" Matt asked.

"Four times," Ed answered.

"There won't be a fifth," Matt said. "At least not today."

As the coach approached the rock Ed had pointed out, Matt jumped easily from the top of the coach onto the side of the hill.

"Remember, drive slow enough to give me a chance to get over."

"You got it, Matt," Ed called as he pulled back on the reins, slowing the team to a walk.

From inside the coach, Winnie saw Matt.

"Mama, Mr. Jensen is climbing over that hill and he has his gun in his hand."

"Maybe he just doesn't want the gun to fall out of his holster," Jennie suggested.

"But why is he climbing that hill?"

When Matt reached the top of the hill, he saw three men waiting behind a row of sagebrush, guns in hand, looking toward the end of the butte where the road would make its turn. He also saw three horses, ground-tethered. Untying the horses, he slapped them on their rumps and sent them running. Then he squatted behind a big rock.

"What the hell! Our horses is gettin' away!" one of the men said. The three came running back toward their horses.

"You boys just stop right there," Matt said, raising up from behind them.

When the three men whirled around, they saw Matt holding his pistol leveled on them.

"Nice day, isn't it?" Matt asked.

"Who are you? What are you doing here?" The man who asked was bald-headed, and had a full mustache.

"Funny you would ask that question, because I was about to ask you the same thing."

"We wasn't doing nothing," the bald-headed man said.

"Really? Because it looked to me like you were waiting for the stagecoach to come around so you could rob it."

"We wasn't doin' no such thing."

"I don't believe you. I'm a passenger on that stagecoach, and I wouldn't want to get held up or anything, so here is what we are going to do. You," he said, pointing to the only one of the three who was wearing a hat. "I want you to use your hat as a bag, and I want you to put your gun in there, then collect the guns from the other two, and bring all of them over here to me."

"Why would we want to do that?"

"Because I'll kill you if you don't," Matt said, easily.

"Do it, Carter," the bald man said.

Carter put his own pistol in the hat, collected the other two pistols, then walked over to put them down where Matt told them to.

"There they are," Carter said.

"Good man. Now the three of you just walk over there and have a seat for a while,"

Matt said.

When the three responded, Matt picked up the hat with the pistols, then walked out into the road just as the coach came around the turn. He waved at the driver, and Ed started pulling back on the reins, bringing the stage to a halt.

"I'll be damned," Ed said, looking toward the three men who were sitting on the side of the road. "Hello there, Carter, Hodge, Decker. How are you boys doing?" He laughed.

"You know these men, Ed?" Matt asked.

"Oh, I should say that I do," Ed replied. "They've done held me up twice. I guess it would have been three times if you hadn't stopped them."

"Hey, where you goin' with our guns?" the baldheaded one asked. "Them guns cost money and you're stealin' 'em."

"I'm not stealing them," Matt said. "I tell you what. I'll leave them with the marshal in Sussex."

"There ain't nothin' right about you doin' somethin' like that," one of the would-be robbers said.

"Ha," Ed said. "Since when did you boys worry 'bout what's right?"

"I hope you can find your horses," Matt

said as he stepped back into the coach. "If not, you are going to have a very long walk."

CHAPTER FOURTEEN

When the carriage carrying Moreton and Clara Frewen came into town to meet the stagecoach from Medicine Bow, they saw Teasdale's coach there as well. Teasdale was standing alongside his coach with his arms folded across his chest.

"I wonder what William is doing here," Frewen said as their driver pulled to a stop.

"Is Margaret with him?" Clara asked. "Maybe they have come to meet Jennie."

"I don't know," Frewen said. "I'll walk over there and see. If he is, I'll lift my hat. If I don't lift my hat, she isn't there."

"All right," Clara said, remaining in the carriage as Frewen stepped down.

"Hello, William," Frewen said.

"Moreton," Teasdale replied.

"Are you meeting someone on the stage?"

"No. I just thought as long as I was in town, I would meet it and see if there is any mail for me."

"Margaret didn't come with you, did she? Clara is over in the carriage and wanted to know."

"No, she's at home."

Frewen turned toward Clara and shook his head.

"What brings you here?" Teasdale asked.

"Don't you remember? We told you that Clara's sister Jennie and her son are coming to visit us."

"Oh, yes, I do remember. Well, I hope they have a very pleasant visit."

"I intend to make certain their visit is pleasant. They should be on this coach. And I'm sure they are, or I would have gotten a telegram from Mr. Jensen informing me that they aren't."

"Jensen? Isn't that the gunfighter you hired? You mean you sent the gunfighter to escort your sister-in-law and your nephew?"

"Who better to send for protection than someone who knows his way around firearms?"

"But he killed a man the first night he was in town, didn't he? That's the kind of man you want escorting your kin?"

"If you have heard that he killed a man, you have also heard that the man he killed provoked the fight," Frewen said.

"Kyle Houston. He was supposed to be

very good with a gun, I've heard," Teasdale said.

"Evidently he wasn't good enough," Frewen replied with a chuckle.

"You laugh about this," Teasdale said. "But just how safe do you think someone like Matt Jensen is? He obviously draws men like Kyle Houston to him, men who want to make a reputation for themselves. I mean, do you really want someone like that around?"

"That is exactly the kind of man I want around," Frewen said.

"I hope you haven't made a mistake," Teasdale said.

"I'm sure I haven't, but I do appreciate your concern. I'd better get back over to Clara. She doesn't like to sit alone for too long."

As Frewen returned to his carriage, Teasdale controlled a smile. If things went the way he hoped, the only way Matt Jensen would be on that stagecoach would be if his body was sprawled out on top. If someone like Kyle Houston hadn't been able to take care of him, then it was obvious that one man couldn't do it. But Logan had told him this would be three men, three professionals who knew guns, and who had experience holding up stagecoaches.

"Coach is comin' in!" someone shouted.

"Coach is comin'," another repeated, and those people who were in the part of town near the stagecoach depot paused long enough to watch the arrival.

Ed liked to depart and arrive with a bit of a show, so, though he didn't whip the horses into a gallop, they were at a rapid trot as the coach came moving quickly down Sussex Road. He pulled the team to a stop in front of the stage depot, then set the brake.

"Hello, Ed!" the depot manager called. "Any trouble?"

"Ha!" Ed replied. "No trouble for us, thanks to Mr. Jensen."

Hearing that, Teasdale looked toward the coach. He saw a man step down, then help three ladies in the coach exit, including Jennie Churchill, whom he recognized. Teasdale had never met Matt Jensen, but he knew without having to be told that this was him.

"Jennie!" Clara Frewen called and she and Jennie ran toward each other with arms extended, meeting in the middle with a big embrace. Winnie stood quietly alongside his mother until Clara bent down to greet him as well.

"My, how you have grown!" Clara said. "I

certainly hope you don't consider yourself too big now to give your aunt Clara a hug."

Winnie smiled and complied with Clara's request. When Frewen extended his hand, Winnie took it and they shook hands.

"Oh, you must be exhausted, poor thing," Clara said.

"Perhaps more exhilarated than exhausted," Jennie replied. She extended her hand toward Frewen. "It was so wonderful of you to agree to receive us as guests," she said.

"You are always welcome in our home, Jennie," Moreton said. "I see you met Mr. Jensen."

"Indeed we did," Jennie said. "It was very thoughtful of you to send him for us. He was not only the perfect gentleman and a pleasant traveling companion, he also saved us from what could have been an unpleasantness."

"Our stagecoach was almost robbed!" Winnie said excitedly. "But Mr. Jensen prevented it."

"Oh, how frightening that must have been!" Clara said.

"Frightening? No," Jennie said. "It was exciting! Wasn't it, Winnie?"

"Yes, very," Winnie replied.

Marshal Drew was one of those who had

come to meet the stage, and upon overhearing the conversation, he walked over to the driver who was talking to the depot manager.

"Mr. Frewen's guests are talking about a holdup," Marshal Drew said.

"That's right, there was a holdup," Ed replied. "Well, no, there weren't really no holdup."

"Was there, or wasn't there?"

"There wasn't, but it ain't cause the robbers didn't try." Ed laughed. "They was waitin' for us like they done before, only Matt here, he seen 'em from the coach. It was back at Crowley Ridge it was, you know where the road makes a real hairpin turn around the end of it? It's real near Teapot Dome. Anyhow, Matt clumb up over the ridge and then come down behind 'em. And when me 'n Gary got there, we seen Carter, Hodge, and Decker sittin' just as purty as you please on the side of the road. And there was Jensen standin' in the road waitin' for us, holdin' on to all their guns."

"You weren't carrying any money this time, were you, Ed?"

"Nope, nary one red cent," Ed replied.

"Then I don't understand why they tried to hold you up. Ever' time they've done it before, you've had something to rob."

"Yeah," Ed said. "Well, truth is, I don't know why they tried it, either. All I know is they did try it, and, thanks to Matt Jensen, they didn't get away with it."

Matt walked up to the marshal, carrying Pete's hat with three pistols.

"Here you go, Marshal," he said. "I told the men I took these guns from that they could get them back from you."

"Ha!" Marshal Drew said. "There's a fat chance of that happening."

Frustrated at seeing Matt Jensen still alive, Teasdale turned back to his coach. "Take me home, Mr. Reeves," he said to his driver.

Matt accepted an invitation to eat dinner with Frewen and his family that evening, but when Frewen offered him a bed in his guest room, Matt declined.

"If you have a spare bed in the bunkhouse, I'd rather stay there," Matt said. "I think it would give me more freedom to ride around, and if I'm going to find and stop the rustlers, that's what I'm going to have to do."

"All right," Frewen agreed. "I also have several line shacks, one less than I did have, since Logan burned one of them, but if you find yourself near one of them, feel free to spend the night there. They are all occupied,

195

but I would be glad to give you a letter that would identify you so that — no, wait, that won't do any good. There are several of them who can't read."

"You could give him a paybook," Clara suggested.

Frewen smiled. "Yes, that's a good idea. They would all recognize that."

"A paybook?"

"Shortly after I started ranching, I learned that there is a rather quaint custom among some of the cowboys to show up at payday on the larger ranches, and stand in line to draw their pay — whether they work there or not. Apparently I was an easy mark, because my bookkeeper pointed out to me some months I was paying from one to two more cowboys than actually work for me."

"So now any cowboy who shows up for pay must present his paybook," Clara said.

"It was her idea," Frewen said. "If you are challenged by anyone, all you would have to do is show them your paybook."

"All right," Matt said. "Give me a paybook and I'll carry it."

After dinner, Matt walked out onto the front porch and stood there for a moment, enjoying the quiet. He sensed someone coming up behind him, and recognized her perfume.

"Hello, Jennie," he said without turning around.

"Oh, my, I have heard that you are one of the most noted men of the West," Jennie said. "But I didn't know you had eyes in the back of your head."

"I don't," Matt said. "It's just that you are wearing perfume and that makes it hard to sneak up on a person."

Jennie laughed, a low, throaty laugh. "Of course," she said. "I should have thought of that. Do you like it? It is *Fougère Royale* from the House of Houbigant in Paris. I was assured by Paul Parquet, my *parfumerier,* that this scent would madden men. Does it have that effect on you?"

"It smells good," Matt said.

Jennie threw her head back and laughed. "It smells good," she repeated. "Matt, you are just too precious. I shall have to tell Monsieur Parquet the next time I see him that you said his perfume 'smells good.' "

Jennie came up to stand close to him, much closer than she needed to stand.

"Oh, my," she said. "The stars are even more beautiful here than they are at sea. They are so close it is almost as if you could reach up and touch them."

"It's the clear mountain air," Matt said. It was the reason he had heard given, but in truth he had seen stars like this for most of his life, so he couldn't always relate to what people were talking about.

"Moreton said that you turned down his offer to stay in a guest bedroom," Jennie said.

"Yes."

"But that is silly. Where will you sleep?"

"I will sleep in the bunkhouse, or wherever I happen to be when I get sleepy," Matt replied.

"Like last night, when we slept together in the bed?" There was a throaty, flirtatious tone in her voice.

"Yes."

"I seem to have a memory of something — something that I'm sure would be most embarrassing to me if I could remember it clearly."

"No need to be embarrassed," Matt said.

"Then, something did happen, didn't it?"

"Not really."

"Oh, wait," Jennie said. "I remember now. I believe that at some time in the middle of the night I kissed you. Is that right?"

"Yes."

"I am so sorry," she said. Jennie put her hand on his cheek and moved her fingers softly over the stubble. "And if memory serves me, it was right here."

Matt took her hand in his and gently, but firmly, pushed it back down. "As I said, Mrs. Churchill, you have nothing to apologize for, or to be embarrassed about."

"I am glad you are so forgiving," Jennie said. "When will you be leaving on this sojourn of yours, this quest to find the rustlers Moreton was talking about over the dinner table?"

"First thing tomorrow," Matt replied.

"And you will be sleeping in the — I believe you called it a bunkhouse — tonight?"

"Yes."

"Then, before you go, perhaps you would like to come back inside for a drink."

"I wouldn't want to be a bother to anyone," Matt said.

"Oh, you wouldn't be a bother to anyone. That is, if you came to my room to have the drink. There would only be the two of us. And I assure you, we would be — quite alone," she added, her voice now almost a purr.

Matt had been trying to tell himself that Jennie was just being flirtatious, but she was taking it into an area where he wasn't comfortable. He needed to stop it now, before she got the notion that he was open to the idea.

"Mrs. Churchill, I do thank you for the kind invitation, but it wouldn't be right. You are a married woman and —"

"Lord Randolph and I have an understanding," Jennie said.

"Yes, ma'am, maybe you do, but I don't. Like I said, you are a beautiful woman, Mrs. Churchill. In fact, you may be one of the — if not the — most beautiful women I have ever seen. If I let myself take advantage of you, a simple understanding between you and your husband wouldn't be enough. Because then I would want you exclusively, you see, and if someone got in my way, I couldn't promise you that I wouldn't kill him. And that would include your husband."

Matt had gone over the top with his declaration, but when he heard Jennie gasp, and saw the look of shock, and even a little fear, in her eyes, he knew that it had exactly the effect he wanted. She stepped back, opening a little distance.

"Mr. Jensen," she said. "I wouldn't want you to get the wrong idea. I was just being a bit flirtatious. It is a naughty pastime of mine. But you must know that I love my husband most dearly, and would never do anything to hurt him."

"I'm sure of that," Matt said. "That is why I wasn't questioning you. I want to make it clear that I was referring to myself. I am not beyond letting a beautiful woman make me do things that I have no business doing."

"Well in that case, perhaps I had better be somewhat more reserved around you," Jennie said. "I, uh, am sorry if my conversation discomfited you in any measure. I'll just bid you good night and be on my way."

"Good night, Mrs. Churchill," Matt said as she stepped back inside.

Matt waited until he heard the door shut behind him, then he looked out into the night and smiled.

Clara had seen her sister go out onto the porch, so she moved without fanfare to the front window so she could look outside. She knew that Jennie was an outrageous flirt, and had been even from the time when they were girls together in Paris. Among the sophisticates of Europe, Jennie could play these dangerous games, skate to the edge to entice, even madden men, then jump back from the abyss with no further damage done.

But this was America. And not only America, it was the West, and Clara knew that Jennie had never encountered men like Matt Jensen, strong and principled men with codes of honor, men who could not be trifled with. She breathed a sigh of relief when she saw her sister step away from him, then start back inside. She turned away quickly so she would not be discovered spying.

Chapter Fifteen

For the next week, Matt rode over the land that made up the Powder River Cattle Company. He covered not only the land that Frewen held deed to, but also the land that was considered open range where Frewen's cattle sometimes roamed in search of fresh graze. A couple of times, he was challenged by some of Frewen's cowboys. These were the ones who were staying in line shacks rather than the bunkhouse, so they had not met him. When he showed them the pay-book Frewen had given him, they accepted him as one of them, so he was able to enjoy free roam of the range.

He came across the line shack that had been burned out, and paused for a moment to have a look around. He had read the account of those last hours as kept by Paul Graham, one of those killed. It was easy to see what happened here because the charred remains of the front part of the wagon were pushed into the burned-out house. The back part of the wagon, including the rear wheels, was still intact. He thought about the young cowboy, forced out of the line shack by the fire, only to be ruthlessly gunned down by the outlaws.

Later that same day, Matt happened upon two of Frewen's cowboys. One was lying on the ground and the other was sitting beside him. The one on the ground had blood all over the front of his shirt.

"What happened here?" Matt asked, dismounting and hurrying to the side of the wounded cowboy.

"It was the Yellow Kerchief Gang," the uninjured cowboy said. He was about sixteen, and the cowboy on the ground didn't look any older. "They shot Burt, and took the cows we was watchin'. Burt's hurt real bad."

The young cowboy wiped tears from his eyes.

It only took one glance for Matt to see that Burt was more than badly hurt. Burt was dead. He confirmed it when he was unable to find a pulse.

Matt had seen both cowboys before, but he hadn't learned everyone's name yet. "I saw you back at the ranch, but I don't know your name," Matt said.

"My name's Jeff. Jeffery R. Singleton. This here is Burt Rawlings," he added, pointing to the cowboy on the ground.

"Well, Jeff, I'm sorry," Matt said. "But your friend Burt is gone."

Jeff was small, barely over five feet tall, and couldn't have weighed over 120 pounds. He was young, but Matt was reasonably sure the boy wouldn't be much bigger when he was full grown.

Jeff wiped away another tear. "Yes, sir, I was sort of afraid of that. I was hopin' I was wrong, though. Me 'n Burt, we was goin' to go into town this Friday on our day off. We was goin' to buy me a French harp and Burt was goin' to teach me to play it. You should hear him. Burt is just real good at playin' the French harp. He can play most . . ." Jeff stopped, and choked back a sob. "That is, he *was* just real good at playin' the French harp. He could play most any song you ever heard tell of."

"The men who did this," Matt said. "How many were there, and which way did they go?"

"They was only two of 'em. They was waitin' over there behind them rocks. When we come up, they shot Burt off his horse afore either one of us even seen 'em. Then they both come out from behind the rocks and they throw'd down on me. I prob'ly should'a fought back, but they had the drop on me. They took mine and Burt's guns with 'em when they rode off with the cows."

"They took the cows, you say?"

"Yes, sir. Fifty of 'em, I'd say."

"Which way did they go?"

"That way," Jeff said, pointing west. "Of course, that's about the only way they could go with them. Couldn't go south 'cause that way is the Injun reservation. They couldn't go north, 'cause there ain't no water that way, an' them cows was already a-gettin' plenty thirsty when me 'n Burt was herdin' 'em. And they couldn't go back east, 'cause that's back toward the main part of the ranch."

"I'm going to help you put Burt's body on his horse. You take him back to Mr. Frewen. Tell him I'm going after his cattle and the two men who took them."

"Yes, sir," Jeff said. "You be careful 'round them two, Mr. Jensen. I mean, I know you are a gunfighter an' all, but them two don't fight fair. Like I said, they just rose up an' shot Burt without so much as a fare-thee-well."

Matt didn't like the use of the term "gunfighter" but he didn't challenge Jeff. "I'll be careful," is all he said.

It took a few minutes to drape Burt's body over the back of his horse and to use Burt's lariat to tie him onto the saddle so he wouldn't slide off on the ride back to the big house. Matt made certain that the body was very securely tied, because he knew that if it fell off, Jeff probably would not be able to get him back onto the horse.

Then, when Burt was secure, Jeff swung into his saddle and started back.

"Jeff, I'll find the ones who did this," Matt promised.

"Yes, sir, I'm sure you will, and I'll appreciate that," Jeff said. "Only, it ain't goin' to bring Burt back."

Matt watched Jeff for a moment, then he mounted Spirit and started off in the opposite direction. It wasn't hard to track the rustlers. The fifty head of cattle left a trail of footprints and cow plops that was even better than a series of painted arrow signs.

Matt caught up with the cattle thieves in less than an hour. There were two of them, both wearing yellow kerchiefs, and both wearing hats that had yellow hatbands. Because they were concentrating on the cows they were herding, neither of them saw Matt. About half a mile ahead was a good, wide, clear stream of water. Matt recalled that Jeff had mentioned that the cattle were already thirsty, so he knew that was where they were going. Detouring around the herd, he rode hard and reached the stream before the two rustlers and their cattle arrived.

He was waiting just out of sight as they rode up.

"Get all of 'em up here, Zeke. Let's get 'em watered, then get on. The quicker we are out of here, the better I'll feel," one of the two men said. The man who called out was average size in height and weight, distinguished by a terrible red scar that streaked down the left side of his face, starting on the forehead, coming through the eyelid which also bore the scar, then down across his cheek before turning back up, like a fishhook at the corner of his mouth.

"You don't have to worry none about gettin' 'em up here," Zeke said. Zeke had a full, very dark beard. "They've done got a whiff of the water. They ain't no way we could stop 'em, even if we wanted to."

"Ha! You got that right."

The two rustlers rode up to the stream together, let their horses water, then moved to one side to watch as the fifty cows hurried up, then spread out along the bank to begin drinking.

"Woowee! Look at them bastards drink,

Clem. Now I would say that is one thirsty bunch of cows," Zeke said.

"Have you got a count? How many is there?" Clem asked.

"They's fifty-three of 'em."

"Ha! And seein' as we get a dollar a cow, that's fifty-three dollars we can split," Clem said.

"Yeah, and don't forget the guns we took off them two cowboys. They ought to bring five or ten dollars apiece, anyway."

"Next time we go into town, I'm goin' to get me a bottle of whiskey and the best lookin' whore I can find," Clem said. "What are you going to do next time you go to town?"

"I'll tell you what he is going to do next time he goes to town," Matt said, suddenly appearing from behind a large outgrowth of sagebrush. "He is going to hang. Both of you are."

"What? Who the hell are you?" Zeke shouted. He started for his gun.

"No, don't do it!" Matt called, but Zeke continued with his draw.

Matt waited until the last moment, hoping Zeke would come to his senses, but he didn't. Matt had no choice but to shoot, and his bullet hit Zeke in the forehead. Zeke pitched from the saddle, dead before he hit the ground.

Clem may have had a notion to draw as well, but seeing what happened to Zeke, he threw his hands up.

"No!" he said. "No, don't shoot! I ain't drawin' on you!"

Matt rode toward Clem until he was just a few feet away. He could see the hate and anger in Clem's eyes.

"Throw his carcass across the back of his horse," Matt said.

"You're the one that kilt him. You do it," Clem said.

"All right, I'll do it. But if I do, then I may as well take both of you back that way," Matt said, and he pulled the hammer back on his pistol and aimed it directly at Clem's head.

"No!" Clem shouted, holding his hands out. "I'll do it, I'll do it."

"Good thinking," Matt said.

A few minutes later Zeke was belly-down on his horse, and Clem was mounted, with his hands tied to the saddlehorn. Matt looped his rope around Clem's neck.

"What? Look here! What are you a-doin'? You ain't a-fixin' to hang me, are you?"

"Not here. At least, not as long as you do things my way," Matt said as, holding on to the other end of the rope, he mounted

Spirit. "Let's go."

"Where are we a-goin'?"

"We are going to meet the man whose cows you were stealing, and some of the men who were friends of the one you killed," Matt said.

"You don't plan for me to ride like this, do you? With a rope around my neck? Don't you understand? Anythin' could happen. My horse could step into a gopher hole, I could fall off, my horse might even decide to take off runnin'. If anythin' like that was to happen, why, my neck would get broke."

"Yeah, it would, wouldn't it?" Matt replied.

"This ain't right!" Clem called as Matt gave Clem's horse a slap on the rear to send him on.

"If I were you, I'd do less talking and pay more attention to your riding," Matt said easily. "You don't want to fall off, do you?"

"No!" Clem said, his answer reflecting his concern.

It took Matt and Clem better than an hour to ride back to Frewen Castle. For the entire time back to the ranch, Clem kept clucking soothingly to his horse.

When Matt returned with one man belly-down across a horse and another with his hands tied to the saddlehorn and a rope around his neck, the arrival generated a lot of attention among the Frewen cowboys. They were especially interested in the fact that the dead man and Matt's prisoner were both wearing yellow kerchiefs.

"I'll be damn if Jensen ain't caught hisself a couple of Yellow Kerchiefs," one of the cowboys said.

"That's them!" young Jeff said, pointing to the two men. "That's the two men that jumped us, and kilt Burt!"

"What the hell did Jensen bring one of 'em back alive for?" one of the other cowboys said. "Hell, let's just shoot the son of a bitch now!"

"Shootin' is too good for him. Let's string 'im up. Hell, it won't be hard to do. He's done got the rope around his neck."

Several gathered around then as Matt rode straight to the barn. Once there, he threw his end of the rope over a beam that extended out over the top of the barn door, then pulled it just tight enough to put pressure on Clem's neck. After that, he tied his end of the rope off then started toward the big house.

"What? What are you going to do? You can't leave me like this! I could hang!" Clem called out in fear.

Clem was sitting on his horse right in

front of the barn door. The rope around his neck went up and over the protruding beam, then was tied off at the other end, so that it formed an inverted "V."

"You won't hang, as long as you can keep your horse still," Matt called back over his shoulder.

"You can't do this! You can't leave me here like this!" Clem called out to him. "It ain't right!"

"Mister, I would quit yelling if I was you," one of the cowboys said. "You're liable to spook your horse. Besides which, if you don't shut up your caterwaulin' I'll slap your horse on his ass myself."

The other cowboys laughed.

"Ahh," Clem said, realizing then that what the cowboys said was true. "Stay here, horse," he said as calmly as he could. "Don't you be tryin' to go nowhere."

When Matt came back out a few minutes later, Moreton Frewen and his wife Clara, as well as Jennie Churchill and her son Winnie, followed him out of the house and across the yard toward the barn. There, they saw one horse with a body draped across it and another horse, in the saddle of which sat a man with a rope not only around his neck, but looped over a protruding brace, as if he were about to be hanged.

"What do you want to do with him?" Matt asked.

"This is the feller that kilt Burt! I say hang the son of a bitch!" one of the cowboys shouted, then seeing the reaction of the two ladies, he took off his hat. "Sorry ladies," he said. "I didn't mean to go cussin' in front of you."

"I think we should take him into town, give him a trial, and then hang him," Frewen said.

"Do we have a judge in this town?" Matt asked.

"I'm a judge," Frewen offered.

"All right," Matt said. "I'll take him into town and turn him over to Marshal Drew."

As Jennie watched Matt ride off, she felt a strange mix of emotions. She had never met anyone quite like Matt Jensen. He was the perfect gentleman, kind and sensitive, gentle and patient with her son. But he was also, without doubt, the most dangerous man she had ever met. Despite that, or maybe even because of it, she still found him handsome and exciting and would have enjoyed an innocent dalliance with him. Except that she knew, instinctively, that a dalliance with

Matt Jensen would be anything but innocent.

When Matt took his macabre procession into town it generated as much attention as it had when he had arrived back at Frewen Castle. Men and women came out of houses, stores, and saloons to stand on the side of the street and watch as he passed by.

"Them's Yellow Kerchiefs," someone said.

"Who's that leadin' 'em?"

"Don't you know? That's Matt Jensen. He's the one that kilt Kyle Houston."

Not content to just watch Matt ride by, most of the town moved out into the street then began walking along behind him, following him to Sikes' Hardware Store, which was also the location of the Welsh Undertaking Parlor. By the time he got there, Sikes and Welsh were both outside, drawn by curiosity as to what had caught the attention of the whole town.

"Get this one buried," Matt said, nodding toward Zeke's body.

"What's his name?"

Matt looked toward Clem. "I heard you call him Zeke. What's his last name?"

"I don't know," Clem said. "He never told me."

"It's Holloway," a woman's voice said.

215

The woman who spoke was wearing the revealing attire of a bargirl. Several looked at her, the expressions on their faces reflecting their curiosity.

"Tell me, Lucy, how come it is you know his last name?" Welsh asked.

"He told me once that his last name was Holloway."

"You're doin' business with one of the Yellow Kerchief men?" someone said accusingly.

"How was I supposed to know he was a Yellow Scarfer?" Lucy replied. "He didn't have his yellow kerchief on when I seen him. Fact is, he didn't have nothin' on a-tall, last time I seen him."

The entire town laughed.

CHAPTER SIXTEEN

The next morning in Sussex, a crowd had gathered around Sikes' Hardware Store to stare at a gruesome display. The object of their attention was Zeke Holloway's body. He was tied to a board with his arms folded across his chest and a gun in his right hand. His yellow scarf was still in place around his neck, but he wasn't wearing a hat. His eyes were open and sightless. His face was bluish white, all the blood having drained down from his head; and because of the paleness of his skin, the contrast between the black of his beard, and the white of his face was even more striking. The bullethole between his eyes was black and bloodless. Above the door was a sign.

Zeke Holloway
Yellow Kerchief Rustler
Killed by Matt Jensen

For the moment, Welsh was busily constructing two coffins, one for Zeke and one for Clem, who was about to stand trial. A few pointed out to Welsh that Clem had not been found guilty yet, but Welsh said he was confident that he would be.

"And even if they don't find him guilty, it ain't like the coffin is goin' to go to waste. There is bound to be someone that's goin' to be needin' one sooner or later."

Zeke Holloway would be buried just as he was now, without embalming, his skin pale and the blood still on his shirt. But it was different for Burt Rawlings, who had already been brought to Welsh to be prepared for burial. He had been embalmed, and cosmetics applied to his face and hands in order to restore some color to the body. He was also dressed in a suit and tie, though no one who knew him had ever actually seen Burt in a suit.

Burt didn't need one of the wooden coffins Welsh was making, because Moreton Frewen had bought one of the manufactured coffins Welsh kept on hand for the more affluent of his customers. It was called the "Eternal Cloud" and it was a beautiful casket, painted with a shining, black satin finish, and adorned with silver. The ad for the coffin boldly announced:

This Coffin is **guaranteed** to last for ONE THOUSAND YEARS!

Nobody ever thought to ask how a disappointed customer would be able to collect on the guarantee.

Rawlings was laid to rest later that morning, borne to the cemetery in a glass-sided hearse. His funeral was attended by half the people from the town and a significant number of people from the county.

From the window of his cell, Clem was able to watch the funeral cortege as it passed by the jail.

"Why have so many turned out for one cowboy's funeral?" Clem asked the deputy marshal.

"They are all turnin' out 'cause he was just a boy, only seventeen years old, and ever'body thinks it is a dirty shame that someone who's never done no evil to anyone gets murdered in cold blood," the deputy replied. "And seein' as you're the one that done it, well, I reckon there'll be about that many turn out to watch you hang."

Clem, who was standing on his bed so he could see out the window, stepped down, then sat on his bunk with his elbows on his knees, and his head in his hands.

He thought of a fishing hole that was near

the house where he had grown up back in Missouri, and he wished with all his heart that he could be there now.

"Clem, get on back here and feed the chickens now!"

"I done fed 'em, Ma," Clem lied. "I just need to catch me a couple more fish here."

"You haven't fed them. I know you haven't."

"Leave me alone. If you want your goddamn chickens fed, feed 'em yourself."

"Clem, how can you talk to me that way? I am the one who gave birth to you!"

"Yeah, well I didn't ask to be born. Now just feed your chickens and leave me be."

Clem couldn't wait to get out of Missouri. He intended to go West and strike gold. He knew there was gold out here, he had read about it. All you had to do was find a stream then start sifting through that stream with a pie pan, and you could find as much gold as you wanted.

Or so he had thought.

The reality was much different. The reality was that he didn't find any gold, and in order to eat, he had turned to stealing. After that it was an easy step to fall in with murderers and thieves, and now he was about to pay the price.

When Moreton Frewen told Matt that he

was a judge, he wasn't exactly lying, but he was stretching the truth. He was a member of the Magistrate's Court in the Judiciary of England and Wales. In this appointed but unpaid position, his authority was limited, even in England. He had no authority whatever in America, except for an honorary recognition of his status, but he believed in the principle of *fiat justitia ruat caelum,* "let justice be done," regardless of the circumstances, so when the occasion called for it, he merely assumed the authority.

Because The Lion and The Crown Saloon was the largest building in Sussex, arrangements were made to hold the trial there. Nearly everyone who had attended Burt Rawlings's funeral that morning were now present at the saloon turned courtroom. The tables had all been moved to one side, except for three: one to be used by Frewen as the judge's bench, the second to be used by the defense counsel and the defendant, and the third to be used by the prosecutor. The chairs were then put out in rows, theater-style, but there were far too many people for the chairs, so the rest of the attendees were lined up along the bar and the walls. Two of the bargirls who worked The Lion and The Crown, Lucy and Rose, were sitting up on top of the upright piano. Their crossed bare legs were the object of attention of many of the cowboys who had come into town for the trial.

There were only two lawyers in town, so Frewen appointed one to act as the prosecutor, and the other to act as defense counsel. Orin Dempster, the court-appointed lawyer for the defense, registered a protest before the trial even got underway.

"Mr. Frewen, I submit, sir, that you do not have the authority to preside over this trial," Orin Dempster said. "This is clearly a case of *coram non judice,* a legal proceeding without a judge, with improper venue, without jurisdiction."

"I am a duly appointed Magistrate," Frewen said.

"In England, sir, not in America, and certainly not in Wyoming. We could quite easily send to Buffalo for a judge," Dempster insisted.

"No need to waste the judge's time," Frewen said. "I am quite capable of presiding over the trial."

Clem was sitting at the table with Dempster and with Marshal Drew.

"You got no right to try me," Clem called out.

Frewen looked over at Clem. "You are not to speak until you are asked to speak."

"But this here feller is right," Clem said. "You can't try me."

"If you speak again, I will have you gagged," Frewen said.

Clem opened his mouth as if to speak again, but closed it before he uttered a sound.

"Your Honor, I want my protest to go on record," Dempster said.

"Duly noted," Frewen said. "Marshal Drew, would you bring the prisoner before me, please?"

Marshal Drew prodded Clem before the table that Frewen was using as his bench.

"Would the prisoner state his name, please?" Frewen said.

"Clem."

"And what is your surname?"

"My what?"

"Your last name. I shall require your last name."

Clem smiled. "You do, huh? Well, you ain't goin' to get it. I reckon that means you can't try me, don't it?"

"It will not prevent the trial from taking place," Frewen said.

Clem turned toward Dempster. "Can he do that? Can he still have the trial even if he don't know my last name?"

"Your Honor, I am filing a second protest," Dempster said.

"Your protest is noted," Frewen said.

"What's that mean?" Clem asked Dempster. "These protests you are filing."

"That means that whatever the verdict is as a result of this trial, there is a possibility that it might be overturned," Dempster said.

Clem grinned broadly. "Is that a fact?"

"It could take as long as a month," Dempster said.

"That's all right, I've got a month."

"Wrong, sir. You have all eternity," Frewen said.

"What? What do you mean? What do you mean I have all eternity?"

"I mean, sir, that if this jury finds you guilty I will sentence you to hang tomorrow," Frewen said. "That being the case, if the verdict is overturned next month, it will be of no consequence to you, because your carcass will be a worm feast."

"No, that ain't right!" Clem said.

"Killing Burt Rawlings wasn't right, either," Frewen said. "Mr. Gilmore, you are the prosecutor. Make your case, please."

"The court calls Jeffery Singleton to the stand," Gilmore said.

Jeff, all cleaned up now and wearing his best denims and shirt, took the stand and was sworn in.

"Mr. Singleton, did you see who killed Burt Rawlings?"

"Yes, sir, I did."

"Is he in this courtroom now?"

"One of 'em is," Jeff replied. "The other 'n is tied up to a board that is standin' up in front of Sikes' Hardware Store."

There was a smattering of laughter throughout the court.

"Would you point to the murderer please?"

"It was him," Jeff said, pointing to Clem.

"Let the record show that Mr. Singleton pointed to the defendant."

Gilmore walked over to the bar where there lay two pistols. He picked both of them up and brought them over to show to Jeff.

"Do you recognize these pistols?"

"Yes, sir. That there'n is mine," Jeff said, pointing to one of them. "The other'n belongs — uh, belonged to Burt."

"Thank you. Let the record show that the witness identified the two pistols, one as belonging to him and the other belonging to the decedent, Burt Rawlings." Gilmore turned to Dempster. "Your witness."

Dempster did not get up from his chair. "Was it daylight or dark when you saw the men who shot your friend?"

"It was daylight," Jeff said.

"And you are sure that the defendant was one of the two men you saw?"

"Yes."

"Could it be that perhaps the sun was shining in your eyes so that your vision was restricted?"

"No."

"You say that with such resoluteness. How can you be so sure?"

"Because it was mid-mornin', and this Clem feller, and the other'n, the one that's tied to the door down to Sikes' Hardware, the first time I seen 'em, they was standin' west of me. Burt, he never seen 'em at all, 'cause they was still hidin' behind the rocks when they shot him."

"No further questions," Dempster said, realizing that every question he asked was just making the case worse for his client.

"Witness is excused," Gilmore said. "Prosecution calls Matt Jensen."

Like Clem before him, Matt was sworn in, then he took his seat.

"Mr. Jensen, you are the one who brought in Zeke Holloway's body, are you not?"

"I am."

"And you killed him?"

"I did."

"You also brought in Clem and these two

pistols. Where did you get the pistols?"

"Clem and Zeke had them on their persons."

"What were Clem and Zeke doing when you encountered them?"

"They were herding stolen cattle."

"How do you know the cattle were stolen?"

"They had the Frewen brand," Matt said.

"Objection, Your Honor!" Dempster said.

"What is the objection?" Frewen asked.

"I object to the fact that the stolen cattle had the Frewen brand."

"I don't understand the objection. Are you saying they did not have the Frewen brand?"

"No, sir, I'm sure they did have the Frewen brand."

"Then what is the objection?"

"The objection, Your Honor, is that if the stolen cattle had your brand that means they belonged to you."

"Now that, Mr. Dempster, is a brilliant deduction," Frewen said sarcastically. "Yes, the cattle with my brand do belong to me."

"And that is exactly my point, Your Honor. I suggest that since you have a vested interest in the outcome of this trial that you might be incapable of rendering a fair and honest verdict, and I ask that you recuse yourself."

"Are you challenging my honesty, sir?"

"No, I wouldn't say that. It's just that . . ."

"Just what?"

"Just that . . . well, sir, I will be filing a protest on that as well," Dempster said, knowing that he was losing the battle.

"Please feel free to do so," Frewen said. "Do you have any questions of this witness?"

"Yes," Dempster said. "Mr. Jensen, you openly admit here, in this court, that you shot and killed Zeke Holloway?"

"Yes."

"Why did you shoot him?"

"Because he tried to shoot me."

"And why is it that while you shot Mr. Holloway, you did not shoot the defendant?"

"Because he didn't try to shoot me," Matt answered, easily.

"Thank you, no further questions. Defense calls the defendant to the stand."

Sullenly, Clem took the stand.

"Did you kill Burt Rawlings?"

"No, it wasn't me, it was Zeke that done the shootin'."

"No further questions," Dempster said.

"Redirect?" Frewen asked.

Gilmore didn't approach, but asked from his chair. "How do you know it was Zeke

Holloway who killed Burt Rawlings?"

"Because I seen him do it."

"Were you also shooting?"

"Yeah, but it was Zeke who done the actual killing."

"No further questions."

"Closing argument, Mr. Dempster?" Frewen offered.

"I continue to protest your authority to conduct this trial. And I especially protest your authority to order capital punishment," Dempster said.

"Noted," Frewen said without further discussion.

"And, you heard my client. He says he didn't do it. He says that the actual killing was done by Zeke Holloway. I submit that since both were firing, it is impossible, even for an eyewitness, to testify as to which gun the bullet came from that killed Burt Rawlings. And, since our system of law requires guilt be established beyond any reasonable doubt, then the jury will have no recourse but to acquit."

Dempster sat down and Clem looked at him.

"That's the best you can do?" he asked.

"Under the circumstances, yes. That is the best I can do," Dempster said.

"Summation, Mr. Prosecutor?" Frewen asked.

"My summation is simple enough, Your Honor. Mr. Singleton saw the defendant kill Burt Rawlings. Mr. Jensen recovered the pistols and the cows the defendant and Zeke Holloway stole, which establishes motive and means. And Mr. Clem No Last Name claims that he was present during the shooting, indeed that he was shooting as well, though he says that it was a bullet from Holloway's gun, and not his, that killed Mr. Rawlings. His own testimony is *prima facie par delictum actus reus,* unimpeachable evidence that the crime was committed and that he was there. That means, Your Honor, that he bears equal responsibility. Under the law, if he is participating in the shooting, he is guilty of murder whether any of his bullets struck the victim or not."

"Thank you. The jury may now retire to consider the verdict," Frewen said.

"Mr. Frewen," the jury foreman said. "There's no need for us to retire to consider the verdict. We can talk it over right here, amongst ourselves. Won't take more'n a minute or two."

"Very well. Make your decision."

The twelve men gathered together for a moment to discuss it. Though they spoke too quietly for anyone else to hear, it was obvious that there was little or no disagreement among them. Then they retook their seats.

"We got the verdict now," the foreman said.

"What is the verdict?"

"We find the son of a bitch guiltier than hell."

There was laughter and applause from the gallery.

"Marshal Drew, bring the defendant before me again, please."

Again, Marshal Drew prodded Clem up to stand before Frewen.

In keeping with his English heritage, Moreton Frewen put a black cloth called a "sentence cap" over his head. This was the custom in the English courts and worn only when a death sentence is about to be passed.

"Clem, No Last Name, this court sentences you to hang tomorrow morning at ten o'clock."

"Your Honor, we can't build a proper gallows that fast," Marshal Drew said.

"How proper does it have to be?" Frewen said. "All we need is something that will elevate him from the ground far enough to get the job done. I'm sure there are tree limbs, beams, pylons, appendages, bracings, or stanchions extant in this town that could serve the purpose. Find one."

"Yes, sir."

"This court is adjourned."

"Come along, Clem," Marshal Drew said, reaching down to take Clem by the arm.

"Wait a minute! What about all them protests and things? Ain't we goin' to wait to see what happens with them?"

"The judge has sentenced you to hang tomorrow, and that is exactly what you are going to do," Marshal Drew said.

"It ain't right," Clem said. Then, as he was led out of the saloon, he shouted back over his shoulder. "It ain't right, damn you all to hell!"

Chapter Seventeen

In jail that night, Clem's sleep, what little there was, was filled with dreams.

His feet were dangling over the back of the wagon as his ma and pa drove down to the Current River for the all day preaching. All of the neighbors were gathered there, sitting on blankets listening to a traveling preacher as he walked back and forth in front of them, preaching about the fires of hell and stabbing his finger into the air to emphasize his points. Then it came time for the baptism and dozens lined up to go down to the water.

"No, I ain't goin' to go down to the crick and let you dunk me in the water."

"You have to be baptized if you want to be saved," the preacher said.

"I don't want to be saved."

"But you must. You must give your soul to the Lord."

"I ain't a-goin' to do it."

"Then you will burn in hell!" the good rever-

end said, pointing a long, thin, bony finger at Clem.

Clem shouted out loud, and waking with a start, sat straight up on the cot.

"Are you all right in there?" the deputy called back.

"What time is it?"

"It's one-thirty."

"I've got nine and a half hours left," Clem said.

The deputy came to the jail cell and looked in. There had been two other prisoners in jail when they brought Clem in, but both were in for being drunk and disturbing the peace only, so Marshal Drew let them go. He didn't want any other prisoners around while he was holding Clem.

"You want something? A cup of coffee, maybe?" the deputy asked.

"Coffee? What about whiskey? You got 'ny whiskey?"

"Sorry. I can't give you any whiskey. Coffee will have to do."

"All right, give me a cup of coffee then."

The deputy walked back to the front of the jail, poured a cup of coffee from the blue metal pot that set on top of the pot-bellied stove, then brought it back to Clem.

"Thanks," Clem said.

"Do you want something to read? I've got

234

a couple of books here."

"I ain't never learnt how to read," Clem said.

"All right," the deputy said. "If you want any more coffee, just let me know."

"Hey, Deputy," Clem called.

The deputy turned.

"Can you read?"

"Yes."

"Have you ever read anything about hell?"

"Yes, I've read about it."

"Do you think it's real?

"Yes, I believe it's real."

"I'm goin' there, aren't I? I'm goin' to hell."

"You probably are."

"Well I don't care," Clem said with forced bravado. "I've got lots of friends there. We'll have us a grand time."

As the deputy went back to the desk out front, Clem returned to sit on the cot. He thought of Sam Logan and his other friends in the Yellow Kerchief Gang. He wondered if any of them would show up for his hanging. He wished they would. He wouldn't give them away or anything. He would just like to see one friendly face in the crowd.

At the end of Sussex Street stood a tall cottonwood tree. Approximately twelve feet from the ground was a large limb that ran at almost a perfect right angle to the tree trunk and extended out for several feet. Marshal Drew and two members of the city council, upon close examination and consideration, decided that the tree would suffice for the hanging. As soon as the decision was made, Charley Keith, the town painter, made a sign that was nailed to the trunk of the tree.

On This Tree
At 10:00 A.M.
Will Be Hung the Murderer
Clem No Last Name

By nine-thirty that morning, nearly all the residents of Sussex were gathered around the tree, awaiting the event. A couple of entrepreneurs were taking advantage of the gathering by peddling homemade candy and cookies. Mr. Dysart, the photographer, had his camera and tripod, and he had already set it up at three different locations, trying to find the most revealing angle.

There was some excitement when a buckboard was brought out and positioned under the tree, then a rope was thrown over the limb. One end of the rope was tied to the limb; the other end was tied in a hangman's noose.

The Reverend D.L. Mullins had been asked to provide some comfort to the condemned, so he was present as well. But never since he had become a man of the cloth had he seen a gathering this large, and he decided he could not turn his back on this opportunity. He climbed up onto the back of a buckboard and began preaching.

"Brothers and sisters, this is a somber occasion. We are gathered here to hurl the soul of a sinner into the abyss of eternity. And while we watch as this sinner is cast into hell, it is time for us to examine ourselves to see if . . ."

"Hey! We didn't come here to hear no preachin'!" someone shouted from the crowd. "If we want to hear preachin' we'll go to church. We come here to see that murderin' son of a bitch get his neck stretched!"

There was a smattering of nervous laughter in the crowd.

"Oh but you must hear me, my friends," the preacher said. "For the words you hear me say today could keep your souls from eternal torment."

Although the preacher continued his sermon, there were few, if any, who were listening, and fewer still who were actually paying attention to him. Matt and Frewen had come to the hanging, as well as Morrison, Frewen's foreman, and several of his cowboys, especially Jeff and all those who had been particular friends with Burt. Although there were quite a few women and children in the audience, neither Clara, Jennie, nor Winnie had come, Frewen having specifically asked them to stay away.

"I would like to think that this is one of the men who killed Graham, Bates, Emmitt and Cooter," one of the cowboys said.

"Yes, and Snead and Coleman too," Frewen said.

"That's funny," Marshal Drew said, looking around the crowd.

"What is funny?" Frewen asked.

"I see a lot of Thistledown cowboys here, but I don't see Reed, or Mr. Teasdale. You'd think they would have an interest in this. They've got as much to lose from the rustlers as anyone else."

"Hmm, you're right," Frewen said. "I don't know why William isn't here. I'm sure he knows about it."

"Maybe he just doesn't want to watch a hanging," Marshal Drew said. "It isn't everyone's cup of tea."

"It's not something I particularly want to watch, either," Frewen said. "But my hope is that seeing a rustler die by hanging will have a sobering effect on the others."

"Here the son of a bitch comes!" someone shouted.

"How do you feel, Clem? You ready to hang?" another called out.

Clem's appearance not only ended the impromptu sermon, it also halted all conversation. As Clem was led from the jail, he was wearing the same clothes he had been wearing when Matt brought him in, a collarless blue shirt and gray trousers held up with suspenders. The only difference was that he was not wearing the yellow kerchief now, the thought being that having it around his neck might interfere with the hanging. Clem's legs weren't hobbled, but his hands were handcuffed behind his back. He squirted out a stream of tobacco juice just as he reached the buckboard.

Earlier that morning a carpenter built a set of steps that would allow him to climb easily onto the buckboard, but when he reached them, he hesitated.

"Get on up there, Clem," Marshal Drew said. "You got no one but your own self to blame for bein' here, so why don't you show us you can die like a man?"

Clem glared at the marshal. "Maybe you'd like to show me how it's done," he suggested.

"Come on, Clem," Marshal Drew said, less harshly this time. "Hangin' is bad enough. I don't figure you want to turn it into a spectacle, do you?"

"Seems like it is too late for that," Clem replied. "Looks to me like we're already givin' the folks a show."

Clem climbed the temporary steps up onto the buckboard and Marshal Drew went up right behind him. Drew moved Clem until he was positioned under the noose, then he slipped it down over Clem's head. Clem winced as he felt the rope against his neck.

From his elevated position, Clem could look down on everyone, and he stared into all the faces of the spectators, glaring at them defiantly.

The clergyman who had been preaching fire from that very buckboard now stepped up to Clem.

"Do you want to repent?" he asked.

"What have I got to repent for?"

"Why, you have killed, sir."

Clem looked out over the faces of the crowd. "Yeah? Well, what do you think you people are about to do?"

"There is a difference. We have a God-given right to execute murderers," the preacher said.

"Do you now? And the folks here? Do they have a God-given right to watch me hang?"

"I beg of you, sir, if you wish to be saved, think now, of our Lord and Savior, hanging on the cross."

"Saved? You mean if I think about Jesus hanging on the cross I won't be hung?"

"I am speaking of the salvation of your eternal soul."

"I don't give a damn about my eternal soul. It's the here and now that I'm thinkin' about."

"You are goin' to meet God with heresy in your heart and blasphemy on your lips? You'll spend an eternity in hell for that!"

"Yeah, well, thanks a lot for the words, preacher," Clem said sarcastically. "They've been just real comfortin'."

The preacher, red-faced with anger, turned toward Marshall Drew. "I wash my hands of this lost soul," he said.

"Yeah, didn't Pontius Pilate do the same thing?" someone called up to the preacher.

"Good Lord in Heaven, what have I just done?" the preacher asked. He walked quickly off the buckboard cum scaffold. Marshal Drew followed him down. Now the only ones left on the buckboard were Clem, who was standing there with the noose around his neck, and the driver, who was sitting in the seat. The driver of the buckboard had not turned around during the entire time, but remained stoically seated, holding the reins of a team of horses.

"Any last words, Clem?" Marshal Drew called back up from the ground. There was a hushed expectation over crowd.

"Daggett," Clem said.

"What?"

"That's my last name. Daggett. Tell the undertaker to put it on my tombstone. I don't want to spend eternity in that hole, and folks not know who I am."

"All right, Mr. Daggett, I'll do that," Marshal Drew said.

"D-A-G-G-E-T-T. That's how you spell it."

"Look, when you're jerked off the back of the buckboard, don't hunch up your shoulders," Marshal Drew said. "If you don't fight it, it'll be over quicker."

"How am I going to stop myself from hunching up my shoulders?"

"I don't know, but if you can keep from doing it, it'll be better for you."

"Don't I get a hood?"

"I forgot to have one made. But I can tie a bandanna around your eyes if you want me to. That'll keep you from seeing what's going on."

"No, that's all right." He looked out over the crowd. "I want the ladies and the kiddies to be able to see my eyes pop out." He cackled an insane laugh, and some of the children cried out and buried their faces in their mothers' skirts.

Someone handed Marshal Drew a whip, and he raised it up, then popped it loudly over the heads of the team of horses. They dashed forward, pulling the buckboard out from under Clem. He fell, and the limb sagged under the sudden weight.

There were oohs and aahs from the crowd as Clem swung back and forth, pendulum-like, in a long, sweeping arc.

CHAPTER EIGHTEEN

On the day following the hanging, William Teasdale and his wife Margaret were dinner guests of Moreton and Clara Frewen. Jennie Churchill and her son Winston were also there, as was Lily Langtry.

The purpose of the dinner was twofold: one, to welcome Jennie and her son to America, and another, to say good-bye to Lily, who would be leaving the next morning by stagecoach on her way to Medicine Bow, where she would catch a train to San Francisco.

"It is nice when we all get together like this," Margaret said. "It is as if we are re-creating a bit of England here, in this desolate and Godforsaken American West."

"Oh, Margaret, do you really feel that way?" Clara asked. "Because I love it here."

"Of course you do, dear. You and your sister are both Americans, after all."

"I'm not an American," Lily said. "And I

like the American West as well."

"If you dislike it so, why do you stay here?" Jennie asked.

"Because my husband has chosen to live here," Margaret said. "Though God knows why."

"I'll tell you why," Teasdale said. "Thistledown is larger than the largest estate in England. The opportunity here is limitless."

"It would be," Frewen said, "if it were not for Sam Logan and the Yellow Kerchief Gang. But I am beginning to have hope that Mr. Jensen may take care of that problem for us."

"Do you really think that one man, even a hired killer, working alone against fifteen members of the Yellow Kerchief gang can succeed?"

"I wouldn't call Mr. Jensen a hired killer," Frewen said.

"Oh? And what would you call him? He has been here for a few weeks only, and already three men are dead because of him."

"Only two," Frewen said. "I take full responsibility for hanging Mr. Daggett."

"Yes, and I wish I had had the opportunity to have gotten to you before you did that. I fear, Moreton, that you overstepped your authority to declare that a magistrate that you hold in England would give you power to act as a judge here."

"Since the deed is done it is, at this point, a mere technicality," Frewen said. "If I need an American appointment, I can easily get one."

"Perhaps so, but that doesn't change the situation with regard to Matt Jensen. He is a man who lives in that dark world that decent people, such as we, will never know. He is an evil man."

"I don't think he is an evil man at all," Jennie said. "He met Winnie and me at the depot and escorted us here to Frewen Castle. He was a perfect gentleman, all the way."

"And I must say that when I met him the first day he arrived, he was very much a gentlemen," Lily said.

"Don't let that gentlemanly façade fool you," Teasdale said. "Matt Jensen is very much a killer. I have it on good authority that he killed four men within one month before he came here."

"If that is the case, then why is he not in jail?" Frewen asked.

"Three of the men he killed were wanted murderers. The fourth, I understand, was attempting to rob him."

"Then what you are telling me is that all the killings were justifiable."

"No, what I'm telling you is, he is a man who dispenses his own justice. Civilized people don't take the law into their own hands."

"As long as the people he is killing are the same people who have been killing my employees, then I can find no fault with him," Frewen said.

"What about you, Winnie?" Teasdale asked. "I imagine young boys like you could be easily persuaded by such things as a fast draw and a straight shot."

Winnie had been listening to the conversation in rapt attention. "Drawing quickly and shooting accurately are not the most important things," Winnie said. "The most important thing is to always be on the side of right. So I believe that, no matter how many Mr. Jensen has killed, he has been on the side of right, and fighting against evil. And that makes him a good man."

"That is most astute of you, young man," Frewen said.

"That's what Mr. Jensen told me, and I haven't forgotten it," Winnie said.

"Nor should you," Frewen said. "I am afraid there will always be a struggle of good versus evil. And we must always strive to be on the side of good."

"Enough talk about killing," Clara said.

"Let's do find a more pleasant subject of discussion, shall we? Winnie, what about you? Now that you have been here for a few days, what do you think of America?"

"Oh, I find it a most delightful place," Winnie said. "Sometimes it is like being at sea, one can look all the way to the edge of the world. If Papa were American and Mama British, instead of the other way around, why, I might live here and be a cowboy."

"Not necessarily so," Clara said. "Moreton is British and I am American, yet here we are and here we live."

"You want to be a cowboy, do you?" Teasdale asked.

"Yes, sir. I've read about cowboys. They are knights of the range."

Teasdale chuckled. "You might not think that after a spring roundup when they have gone for a month or more without a bath, or even a change of clothes. Dirtier creatures you have never seen."

"I don't feel that way," Frewen said. "I have found the men who work for me to be honorable, loyal, even noble men. Some of them have died defending the ranch. What more could you ask of any man?"

"More than likely they weren't defending the ranch as much as they were defending themselves," Teasdale said. "The cowboys who were killed on the island, those who were killed at the Taney Creek line shack, and the young man who was just killed, Burt Rawlings, were all fighting for their own lives."

"Lives that had been put in peril because they were employed by me. I have nothing but admiration for them," Frewen said.

"You know, Moreton, that could be your problem," Teasdale said.

"What are you talking about?"

"You are too easy on your cowboys. You seem to be suffering higher losses to the rustlers than anyone else. How do you know that your cowboys aren't the ones who are stealing from you?"

"Because as I mentioned earlier, seven of them have already died defending the ranch. No, we all know who the culprit is here. It is Sam Logan and his band of cutthroats."

"Well, I can't deny that," Teasdale said. "It certainly seems as if the Yellow Kerchief Gang is having their way with the rest of us. The wonder is that the law has made no effort to stop them, or to bring them to justice."

"The law? Hurrumph!" Frewen said, making a scoffing sound deep in his throat. "There is no law in Johnson County except for whatever law we can provide for our-selves. That is why I hired Matt Jensen, and that is why I assumed the role of judge in the recent court case. Only if we show these brigands that we mean business will we ever have peace here."

"Well, there is no need for me to reiterate my disagreement with you, so I'll just let it go at that," Teasdale said.

Teasdale looked over at young Winston Churchill, who had been following the conversation with concentrated attention.

"I'll just bet this young man would go after Sam Logan and the Yellow Kerchief Gang all by himself, if you would let him," Teasdale said.

"Sir, I would like to think that I am not without courage, but neither am I without good sense," Winnie replied. "I have no wish to encounter these outlaws."

"A wise decision," Teasdale said. "But tell me, what does a young man like you do out here, so far away from your own home and friends?"

"I like it here," Winnie said. "But I would like it even more if I had a horse."

"A horse?" Jennie said. "Heavens, Winnie, what would you do with a horse?"

"Why, I would ride him, Mama. I would ride him all over Uncle Moreton's ranch."

250

"And what would you do, as you rode all over the ranch?" Frewen asked.

"That is easy. I would punch cattle," Winnie insisted.

"Punch cattle?" Jennie said.

"Yes, don't you remember, Mama? Mr. Jensen told us that is what cowboys do."

"Yes, I do remember. But Winnie, I'm sure your father has a higher and more noble future planned for you than to punch cattle," Jennie said. "Besides, I would not like to see you on a horse," Jennie said.

"Why not?" Winnie asked.

"Because, dear, you have never even been on the back of a horse, and I'm afraid you might fall off."

The others laughed and Winnie, with cheeks burning in embarrassment, looked down at the floor.

"May I be excused now, Mama?" he asked.

"Certainly, dear."

"What a well-mannered boy," Lily said. "You must be very proud of him."

"I am," Jennie said.

"But you don't have much confidence in him," Teasdale said.

"Oh, but I do — within reason. And since he has never ridden a horse before, I do not think it unreasonable for me to be concerned should he suddenly decide to do so."

"You might have been a bit too harsh on him," Lily suggested.

Jennie looked toward Lily as if to convey her resentment over Lily commenting about her relationship with her son, but she checked any retort, then ameliorated her expression with a smile.

"Perhaps I was," she agreed. "But Winnie is such a headstrong boy and almost totally without fear. I feel that I must provide the cautionary restraint that he lacks."

"So, Miss Langtry, you will be leaving tomorrow?" Teasdale asked.

"Yes, I am going to San Francisco."

"I would think that you would stay in New York, where there are enough people to make the theater profitable."

"My tour through the West has been profitable in more ways than money," Lily said. "And New York has become so cumbersome for me now. If I go for a stroll in the park and stop for a moment to admire the flowers, people run after me in droves. If I venture out for a little shopping it is particularly hazardous, for the instant I enter an establishment to make a purchase, news spreads that I am there. A crowd then gathers by the front door so as to make a normal exit impossible and the proprietor is forced to escort me out the back door."

"Such is the price of fame," Frewen said. "But tell me, Lily, would you give it up and become a seamstress or a store clerk?"

"Never in a million years!" Lily replied, and everyone laughed. "I suppose, now that I think about it, there is as much pleasure as there is discomfort in fame."

Moreton and Clara Frewen took Lily Langtry to the stage depot the next morning to see her off. Clara waited in the carriage as Frewen walked from the carriage to the stage office with Lily. Their driver took Lily's suitcase to the waiting coach and stood watching as it was loaded into the boot.

"Really, Moreton, if you expect anyone to visit you, you must see to it that a railroad is built closer to Sussex than Medicine Bow. That is such a beastly trip by coach," Lily said.

"I'll see what I can do," Frewen replied.

Lily looked back at the carriage and, with a big smile, waved at Clara. "Of course, Clara might have something to say about that. I'm not sure she enjoys my visits all that much." She spoke through her smile, hardly moving her lips.

"You are a beautiful woman, Lily. And all

women are threatened by beautiful women."

"Nonsense. Clara and Jennie are both for more beautiful than I."

"Consider this. I was surrounded by beautiful women this past week. Other men should be so lucky," Frewen said.

"Miss Langtry," Ed, the driver, said. "We'll be getting underway soon as you get aboard."

"I'll be right there," Lily said. Lily extended her hand and Frewen took it, shook it briefly, then with a nod toward the driver, returned to the carriage.

"I enjoyed her visit more than I thought I would," Clara said.

"I'm glad," Frewen replied. "I know that she thinks the world of you."

"Hiyaaaah!" Ed shouted, popping his whip over the head of the six-horse team. The horses started forward and with yet a second pop of his whip, Ed started the team into a rapid trot.

Out at Thistledown Ranch, a rider dismounted, reached into his saddle boot and pulled out his rifle. Neither Winchester nor Henry, this was a Sharps .50 caliber with a thirty-four-inch barrel and a double-set trigger. He carried the rifle in his right hand, hanging low as he started toward the front door of the house.

"Hold it, Mister, where do you think you are going?" Reed called.

When the man looked back toward him, Reed gasped. The man had some sort of skin condition that made his face beet red. In addition, the skin was so tightly stretched that it gave one the impression that he was staring at a red skull. He had very thin lips, and his eyes were more yellow than brown. Not since he was a child, and attended church and Sunday school at the insistence of his mother, had Reed ever given any thought to Satan. But if Satan had suddenly appeared in front of him, Reed was sure he would look exactly like this man.

"Is this the Thistledown ranch?" the man asked.

"Yeah, that's what it says on the gate. Who are you?"

"My name is Silva. Carlos Silva, and I have come to offer my services to Mr. Teasdale," the man said, his voice a sibilant sigh.

"What sort of services would that be, Mr. Silva?"

"Whatever service Mr. Teasdale might want," Silva said, emphasizing his statement with a slight lift of the rifle he was holding.

"There is a lady in the house," Reed said. "Mr. Teasdale never discusses business around her." He pointed to the stable. "Suppose you wait over there. I'll go get Mr. Teasdale and bring him to you."

Silva nodded, but said nothing. He walked over to the stable and leaned back against the unpainted and sun-bleached wall as he waited. A few minutes later Reed returned with Teasdale.

"I'm William Teasdale," Teasdale said. "I understand you wanted to speak with me?"

"I've heard that you want someone killed," Silva said.

"What? What would make you say such a thing?"

"Perhaps I have made a mistake," Silva said. "I'll just be on my way then." He started toward his horse.

"Wait!" Teasdale called after him.

Silva stopped, but he didn't turn around.

"Where did you hear something like that?"

"I heard it from Kyle Houston."

"Houston is dead," Teasdale said.

"Yes. He was stupid. And so were you to hire him."

"Hold on there!" Reed said. "You don't come on Thistledown and call Mr. Teasdale stupid!"

Silva gave Reed only the barest glance, then he turned his attention back to Teasdale.

"I am expensive," he said. "But, unlike Houston, I will deliver."

"Are you faster than Houston was?"

"I'm not fast at all," Silva said.

"Then how do you intend to — uh — do the job?" Teasdale asked.

"With this." This time Silva lifted the rifle high enough that Teasdale got a good look at it.

"That's a most unusual-looking rifle," he said. "Two triggers? Why two triggers when it has but one barrel?"

"One trigger sets the other, taking up all the slack so that it fires with the lightest of finger pressure," Silva said. "Would you like to see a demonstration?"

"Yes."

Silva took a dime from his pocket and handed it to Reed, then he pointed to a fence post that was at least one hundred yards away. "Get yourself a piece of cord and tie this coin to that fence post," he said.

Reed laughed. "Are you serious? You won't even be able to see it from here, let alone hit it."

"If I miss, I'll ride away with no further attempt to sell my services," Silva said. He looked at Teasdale. "But if I hit it, you will hire me to kill Jensen. And my price is five thousand dollars."

Teasdale was silent for a moment.

"Do I shoot or not?"

Teasdale held up his finger. "One shot," he said. "No excuses if you miss."

Silva nodded.

"Go put the dime up, Mr. Reed," Teasdale said.

As Reed started toward the distant fence post, Silva walked back over to his horse. Reaching down into his saddlebag, he removed something long and black, then he returned. It wasn't until then that Teasdale saw that it was a telescopic sight.

Teasdale put the scope on, made a few adjustments, then waited until Reed returned.

"I got it tied on," Reed said. "Can you see it? It's about six inches below the top of the post."

"I can see it," Teasdale said. "But barely."

Silva loaded the huge bullet into the breach, then, cocking the rifle, he raised it to his shoulder, set one trigger, then bent his head down to look through the sight. He held it for about three seconds before he pulled the trigger.

The resultant boom of the heavy-caliber round rolled out over the yard, startling the horses in the stable and corral so that several of them whinnied while others began galloping around. The other ranch hands on the place, those who weren't actually out on the range, began to appear from various locations, the cook shack, the machine shop, the barn, and the carpentry shop, drawn by the loud explosion.

"What happened?"

"What was that?"

"Mr. Teasdale, is ever'thing all right?"

"Everything is fine," Teasdale called back with a dismissive wave of the hand. "Mr. Reed, go retrieve the dime," he said.

"Oh, there won't be any dime," Silva said.

"If there is no dime, how will I know if you hit it?"

"You'll know," Silva said. "Mr. Reed," he called. "Do you have a pocket knife?"

"I do."

"You will need it to retrieve what is left of the dime," Silva said.

By now the other hands, having figured out what was going on, came to stand near Teasdale and Silva. They watched with interest as Reed took out his knife and began digging around in the fence post. A moment later he returned, holding his right hand palm up, fist closed.

"Is that the dime?" Teasdale asked.

"Some of it," Reed said. He opened his hand to show nothing but slivers of silver.

"Son of a bitch!" one of the hands said. "Are you telling me that he hit a dime on that post from here?"

"That's what he done, all right," Reed said.

"Very well, Mr. Silva, the job is yours, with one caveat," Teasdale said. "You get nothing until the job is completed."

Silva held out his hand. "A dime," he said.

"I beg your pardon?"

"I would like you to replace the dime."

Teasdale laughed. "All right," he said, sticking his hand in his pocket. When he pulled it out, he was holding a silver dollar. "I don't have a dime, but it was worth a dollar to see the show."

"Thank you," Silva said, taking the dollar. He started toward his horse.

"Where are you going?" Reed called.

"To do the job I was hired to do," Silva replied.

CHAPTER NINETEEN

Matt was with a group of cowboys who had been rounding up cattle, and though he hadn't been hired as a cowboy, he did lend a hand here and there when it was required. He awakened just before dawn, rolled out of his blankets, pulled on his boots, then sat staring into the fire. Although he was an early riser, he was not the first one up. Tibby Ware, the black cook, had been up for an hour, and now he stood in the light of his lantern at the lowered tailgate of his wagon, rolling out biscuits for breakfast. He had already made coffee, and the aroma permeated the encampment area.

Just beyond the bubble of light created by the cook's lantern and the campfire, the cows that had already been rounded up stood in the quiet darkness, watched over by a single night rider. Matt walked over to the large blue coffeepot which was suspended over an open fire.

"Mr. Ware, may I have a cup of coffee?" he asked, knowing that the cook was supreme when it came to the allocation of food.

"Indeed you may, sir, indeed you may," Ware answered. "I've already taken off the first batch of biscuits, if you would like one. And there's butter and honey here."

"Thank you, Mr. Ware," Matt answered. He poured himself a cup of coffee, then held it out in a salute toward the cook. "This will do me for now."

"All right. I'll get back to my cookin' then," Ware said. "But if you need 'nything, just ask."

"I appreciate it."

Matt took a swallow of his coffee as he stared down into the fire, watching the flames curl around a piece of glowing wood. That was when he heard three shots being fired — the signal that had been arranged in the event cattle rustlers were spotted.

Tossing his coffee aside, Matt hurried toward the rope corral where he saddled Spirit as quickly as he could. Then, mounting, he galloped away from the small encampment even as the others were just beginning to stir in their bedrolls.

"Where's he goin' so fast?" one of the cowboys asked.

"Didn't you hear them three shots bein' fired? Poke must be in trouble," another said.

Matt heard the shooting then, not a signal this time, but several rounds being fired in a pattern that suggested trouble. He rode hard toward the sound of the guns, in the direction of the muzzle flashes which were lighting up the predawn darkness.

When he arrived, he saw Poke lying on the ground behind his dead horse, being assailed by at least four men. Snaking his rifle from its saddle sheath, Matt raised it to his shoulder and fired, knocking one of the riders from his saddle. Jacking another round into the rifle, he fired again, taking down a second man. The remaining two rustlers turned and galloped away.

Putting his rifle back in the saddle sheath, Matt pulled his pistol and walked out into the gray shadows of early dawn to check on the men he had shot. He found them both dead.

By now the rest of the outfit arrived, carrying weapons and ready to do battle.

"We don't need you," Poke said. "Me 'n Mr. Jensen done took care of 'em all by ourselves."

"Yeah, I'm sure you were a big help," one of the cowboys said, and the others laughed.

"Yeah? Well the sons of bitches kilt my horse, is what they done."

"It wasn't your horse, it was Mr. Frewen's horse."

"Maybe, but he's the one I'd been usin'. He was a good horse, too."

"And Poke kept them from getting any of the cattle," Matt said.

"Yeah," Poke replied with a big grin on his face. "I kept 'em from taking any of the cows."

"We're just teasing you, Poke. I think you done real good out here," another cowboy said.

Carlos Silva was sitting in a back corner table at The Lion and The Crown Saloon. The first day he came into the saloon, Lucy started toward him, but stopped when she saw his face. For a moment she felt as if the devil himself had come for her because of the life she was living, and, terrified, she turned and moved as far away from him as she could. And though she no longer believed he was the devil, she still avoided him.

Lucy was not the only one who avoided any contact with Silva. Neither Rose nor any of the other girls would have anything to do with him. But it wasn't just the women who avoided him. The men who were regular customers also tended to give him a wide berth. There was about him a "scent of sulfur," the bartender, Harry Moore, suggested when he talked about the strange and silent red-faced man who had come every night now, for a week.

He ordered the same thing every night. Two mugs of beer, a plate of pickled pigs' feet, and a boiled egg. Almost immediately there was speculation about who he was, and what he was doing here. He didn't wear a gun, so nobody thought he was particularly dangerous — though his looks were enough to frighten all but the most confident person.

Silva had come to The Lion and The Crown every day waiting for his "subject" to show up. He had no intention of confronting Matt Jensen, so there would not be a shoot-out in the way of Kyle Houston. Carlos Silva had killed seventeen men, though not one of the killings had been the result of a face-to-face confrontation. That wasn't the way Silva worked. He operated from afar, killing every one of his victims from a distance of from five hundred to one thousand yards.

But despite his long-distance killing, before he shot anyone, he wanted to — no, he had a compulsion to — see them up close. He wanted to see them breathing, eating, drinking, laughing, and talking with others. He wanted to experience some of their life before he took it from them. He intended to kill Matt Jensen, just as he had promised. But he wanted to get a close look at him first, and Reed had told him that from time to time Jensen frequented this particular saloon.

Silva had heard stories about Matt Jensen, he had even seen dime novels that were written about him. Matt Jensen was a famous man, certainly far more noted than anyone Silva had ever killed before. Because of the way Silva worked, most people had never even heard of him. But after this job, after killing Matt Jensen, Silva had an idea that he would be well known. He would become famous for killing a famous man.

On his fifth consecutive day of coming to The Lion and The Crown Saloon, four men came into the saloon, laughing and talking. Silva listened.

"Harry, four beers."

"Yes, sir, Mr. Morrison," the bartender replied. "What brings you to town? We don't often see you in the middle of the week like this."

"We brought two more Yellow Kerchiefs into the undertaker," Morrison said. "That's four of them gone now. I'm telling you the truth, Matt Jensen is like a one-man army."

Upon hearing Matt Jensen's name, Silva began to pay very close attention to the four men. Was Jensen among them?

His question was answered a moment later when Marshal Drew stepped into the saloon.

"Mr. Jensen?" the marshal called.

One of the four men turned toward the marshal. He was a tall man, with broad shoulders and narrow hips. There was a holstered pistol on his right hip, and the way he wore it told Silva that the stories he had heard about Jensen were probably not exaggerated.

"Yes, Marshal?"

"One of the men you brought in was Clyde Beamer. There's a two hundred fifty dollar reward out on him, so if you'll stop by my office I'll issue a voucher that you can cash at the bank."

"All right, thanks," Matt said.

"And here I was about to buy the first round," Morrison said. "Drink up, boys, this round will be on Matt Jensen. With the reward he's got comin', he can buy all the drinks for the rest of the night."

Matt chuckled, then pulled out the money. "All right," he said. "I wouldn't want it to get around that I'm cheap."

Silva studied Jensen over the next several minutes, observing how the others around him seemed to defer to him. He was obviously very popular and well respected. He was a handsome man who appealed to the women, Silva could tell that by the way the bargirls reacted to him and the way he reacted to them, laughing and joking with them, and treating them with respect, despite their occupation. It was clear that Matt Jensen was everything that Silva was not. And soon he would be dead.

As Silva anticipated killing him, he felt a charge of excitement course through his body. He had never been with a woman, had no interest in women, but he had heard it described what a man felt like when he was with one.

Silva was feeling that now.

It was always like this — he would see his subject up close, see him talking, laughing, living, knowing what his subject did not know, that soon he would be dead. Silva's heart began beating faster, and he closed his eyes and clenched his fist to bring himself under control.

Two days after Matt had killed the two would-be rustlers, William Teasdale arrived at Frewen Castle, driving a carriage to which was tied a horse.

"What is this?" Frewen asked, coming down off the porch to meet him.

"It's a horse for the boy," Teasdale said. "You can't have a boy out here without a horse."

"You didn't have to do that, William," Frewen said.

"I know I didn't have to," Teasdale said. "But it is something I wanted to do. He can ride it as long as he is here. When he goes back to England, I'll send someone over for the horse."

"Yes, but you heard his mother. She doesn't want him riding."

"Moreton, the boy needs a mediator and advocate. I am sure that if Lord Randolph were here, he would be on the boy's side. You are just going to have to be his surrogate father while he is here. Be strong. Stand up to Lady Churchill."

"By damn you are right," Frewen agreed. "And what a wonderful thing for you to do, William, to bring a horse for Winnie to ride. Just a minute, I'll get him out here."

A few minutes later, Winnie, with a broad smile spreading across his face, was standing on the front porch looking at the bay Arabian horse.

"That has to be the most magnificent horse in the entire world," Winnie said.

"Well, young man, he is yours for as long as you are here."

"Can I ride him right now?"

"Of course you can ride him. That's why I brought him to you," Teasdale said.

Winnie walked out to the horse, then, seeing how high the stirrup was from the ground, was a bit confused as how best to mount him.

"Lead the horse over to the steps," Frewen suggested. "That will be the easiest way to get on, until you learn how."

Winnie led the horse over the steps, then using the steps, climbed into the saddle. Frewen handed him the reins.

"Winnie! What are you doing?" Jennie asked, coming out onto the front porch at that moment.

"I am going horseback riding," Winnie replied.

"To what end?"

"Just to be riding."

"What a waste of time."

"Mama, no hour of life spent in a saddle is a waste of time," Winnie said.

"You say that as if you have hours in the saddle."

"I admit that this will be my first hour,

but some day I will have many hours on the back of a horse. And, years from now, when I am old and gray, I can look back on this and say, 'This was my finest hour.' "

"No, I don't think you should go riding. Please, get down now," Jennie said.

"Jennie, let the boy ride. I promise you, there is not one American boy in the entire West who is Winnie's age who is not riding with proficiency," Frewen said.

"Proficiency," Jennie said. "You have just made my point, Moreton. How can Winnie ride with knowledge and skill when he has no experience?"

"And how does one gain experience, Jennie? One gains experience by involving themselves in an activity that leads to proficiency. Let the boy ride, I beg of you," Frewen pleaded.

"Please, Mama?" Churchill added.

The expression on Jennie's face indicated clearly that this was not something she favored, but her objections were overcome by the combined efforts of Winnie and Frewen.

"All right," she said reluctantly, finally giving in.

"Thank you, Mama!" Winnie said. "Thank you so much!"

"Please, Winston, do be careful," Jennie

said. "Don't do anything foolish."

"Don't worry, Lady Churchill," Teasdale said. "I had my foreman pick out the most gentle horse in our stable."

"That was very nice of you, Sir William," Jennie said, though the tone of her voice and the expression on her face indicated that she wished he had not made a horse available for her son.

"Mr. Morrison, suppose you ride out with him this first time," Frewen suggested.

"All right," Morrison said. "Tell you what, young man, come along with me and watch me saddle my horse. If you are going to ride, that's something you'll need to know."

Winnie followed Morrison into the stable, where the foreman picked up a saddle and took it over to the stall where he kept his own horse. He put the saddle over the wall of the stall, then picked up a brush and stepped up to the horse and began brushing its back.

"The first thing you want to do is brush your horse's back and make sure you remove any dirt or grit that might be under the saddle. Also you want to be certain that all the hair is flat. If you don't, it could cause the horse to chafe under the saddle. And always check for sores or wounds before you put the saddle on. You got that?"

"Yes, sir," Winnie replied.

"Good. Now, you'll start with the saddle blanket. You want to put the blanket forward, over the withers, then pull it back into place. That keeps the hair flat beneath the saddle. Oh, and make sure the blanket is even on both sides."

Morrison demonstrated by putting the saddle blanket on the horse.

"Now, before you put on the saddle, hook the stirrups over the horn. That way, they won't hit the horse as you put the saddle on him. And when you put the saddle on, lift it high enough that it doesn't hit the horse or push the saddle blanket out of position. Put it slightly forward, then move it back in to position, and put it on gently."

Again Morrison showed what he was talking about by actually doing it.

"Now all you have to do is tighten the cinch. You want it tight enough, but not too tight, otherwise the horse will be uncomfortable. Leave enough room that you can get your fingers between the cinch and the horse."

All the time he was talking, Morrison was demonstrating and now his horse was saddled and ready to go.

With his horse saddled, Morrison walked over to Winnie's horse and removed the saddle and blanket.

"Now, you do it," he said.

"I didn't ask Sir William what this horse was named," Winnie said as he went about saddling the animal, repeating step by step the procedure Morrison had showed him.

"I doubt that he has a name," Morrison said. "I'm sure he just came from the remuda."

"Then I intend to name him," Winnie said.

"I'm sure he will like that. What are you going to name him?"

"He is such a noble-looking horse that he needs a noble name," Winnie said. "I think I shall call him Tudor Monarch."

Morrison laughed. "That's quite a name," he said.

When the horse was saddled, Winnie gave the animal a pat on the withers.

"Get mounted, and we'll take a ride," Morrison said.

Winnie started to lead the horse back to the porch.

"Where are you going?"

"Over to the step so I can get on the horse."

"What if you had to dismount while you were out on the trail? How would you get back on then?" Morrison asked.

"I don't know."

"Let me show you."

Morrison pulled the left stirrup down far enough for Winnie to put his foot in it. Putting his left foot in the stirrup, then throwing his right leg over the horse, he was able to get into the saddle.

"Now, reach down and pull up on this adjustment strap until the left stirrup is even with the other one," Morrison suggested.

Winnie did so, then a huge smile came across his face. "Oh, what a wonderful thing. I am a cowboy," he said. "I am truly a cowboy."

CHAPTER TWENTY

Carlos Silva had the perfect spot for his ambush. He was on top of a two-hundred-foot-high butte with a perfect view of the big log house called Frewen Castle. Anyone leaving the house or either one of the bunkhouses to go out onto the range where Frewen's cattle were would have to pass right under this butte. He had come here before dawn, and now as the rising sun turned the Powder River into a gleaming stream of gold, he was able to observe the activity at the ranch. He saw the cook step out of the cook shack and toss out a pan of water. He watched cowboys going to and coming from the four outhouses that were lined up behind the two bunkhouses. He observed for nearly an hour as the ranch hands went into the cookhouse for their breakfast, then came out and started about their daily duties.

Then he saw Matt Jensen. Jensen stepped

out of the cookhouse, still holding a biscuit. He ate the last of it just before he went into the stable, and a few minutes later Jensen led his horse out, mounted, then rode off. He was coming this way, and would pass right under the butte.

The first thing Silva had done when the sun rose this morning was to establish his range and field of fire. He located a boulder that was about waist-high, and he aimed at it to get the range. He figured it at just under five hundred yards, and he set his telescopic sight accordingly.

As Jensen started toward him, Silva picked up some sand and dropped it to measure the windage. Now he waited as Jensen came riding slowly up the road. Then, just before he reached the boulder that Silva had established as his firing point, he raised the rifle to his shoulder. Peering through the scope, he placed the crosshairs so that the center point was just in front of Jensen's ear; then he moved forward about two inches, all the lead he required at the rate Jensen was moving. He adjusted the set trigger, then moved his finger back to the firing trigger. All he had to do now was just touch it. He felt the rush.

A wasp landed on Spirit's neck, and Matt

leaned forward to brush it away. As he did so he felt the concussion of the bullet taking off his hat. Had he not leaned forward at that exact moment, the bullet would have gone through his head instead of his hat. An instant later he heard the boom, much louder than any ordinary gunshot.

Because the gunshot was so loud, Matt knew that it wasn't a repeating rifle. It had to be a buffalo gun, which meant that the shooter would have to reload before he could shoot a second time. Matt slapped his legs against Spirit, and the horse burst forth like a cannon shot. As he was galloping away, Matt turned to look back up on the top of the Butte and saw that the shooter, confident that he was out of range of any return fire, was standing upright, leisurely reloading his rifle.

Matt continued to gallop away, opening distance between himself and the shooter.

"Damn!" Silva said out loud. "How did the son of a bitch know exactly when to duck?"

With his rifle reloaded, Silva raised it to his shoulders and sighted a second time. By now the range had opened up to at least half a mile. Silva had made shots this far before, so he was confident he could do it again. He set the trigger, then touched it, the recoil rocking him back.

This bullet passed so close to Matt that for brief second the concussion of its passing made him think he had actually been hit. Again he heard the roar of the rifle, followed by the rolling echo as it bounced off the distant hills. Obviously distance wasn't enough protection from this shooter, so Matt pulled his rifle out, dismounted, then sent Spirit out of the way. He figured he had about eight seconds before the next shot, and he used the time to run across the road where he was able to squat behind a boulder. He wanted to go all the way over to the edge of the butte, but if he did so, he would be exposed for too long a time, so the rock would have to do for now.

Unfortunately, the boulder wasn't very large, and it was all he could do to get behind it. A third shot knocked off a chip of rock as large as an apple, and the chip struck Matt in his right shoulder. The impact felt like someone had hit him with a hammer and he felt a tingling all the way down his right arm to the tips of his fingers. But that gave him another eight-second opening, and he improved his position, this time actually making it to a coulee that reached back into the very butte on which he had spotted the shooter. Once there, he started climbing.

Silva saw him running from behind the boulder, and if his rifle had been loaded, he would have gotten him. He had to admit that Jensen was pretty smart, figuring out just how much time he had between the shots. But he also knew that Jensen couldn't stay there as long as Silva could stay here. Silva had enough water and jerky to stay for two days if he had to. Silva saw that Jensen was carrying a rifle with him. He was too far away to see what kind of rifle it was, but he imagined it was either a Winchester or a Henry. It didn't matter; neither model could come close to this one in range. He was in the perfect standoff position. Jensen would be in kill range long before he could get close enough to use his own rifle.

Silva pulled out a piece of cloth, opened it up, and selected a piece of jerky. He took a bite of it, then returned it to the cloth and put the cloth back in his pocket. He chewed the jerky for a moment, then he took a swallow of water from his canteen, and wondered where Jensen was.

Matt climbed the butte. Then, staying just below the crest, he worked his way around behind where he thought the shooter was.

Carefully, he moved up almost to the top, got down on his hands and knees and crawled the rest of the way up. Once there, he raised up to look over the edge.

He saw Silva about two hundred yards away.

Matt pulled his pistol and shot it in the air, just to get the shooter's attention. The shooter spun toward Matt, then raised his rifle. The shooter was good, Matt knew that. But he also knew that someone who prided himself on his marksmanship would not hurry his shot. Matt did hurry his shot, firing, cocking the rifle and firing again, the second shot following so quickly on the first that it joined with the echo of the first shot.

Matt saw the shooter react to being hit. He fired, but because he had been hit just as he was pulling the trigger, his shot went wild. He dropped his rifle, then slapped his hand over his wound. He walked forward in a few staggering steps, then fell to his knees. Dropping his own rifle, Matt pulled his pistol and hurried across the flat top of the butte to the man he had just shot.

By the time he got there, the shooter had fallen forward on his stomach. Kneeling beside him, Matt turned him over. He was still alive, but barely so, and he was gasping audibly for breath.

"Who are you?" Matt asked.

"Silva. Carlos Silva."

"Why were you shooting at me, Silva?"

"It's what I do for a living," Silva said. He tried to laugh, a coughing, wheezing kind of laugh, and as he did so, blood bubbled from his mouth. Ironically, his face was so red that the blood wasn't immediately noticeable.

"You won't be doing it anymore," Matt said.

Silva didn't hear him, because Silva was dead.

"Just before he died, he told me his name was Carlos Silva," Matt said to Marshal Drew. "Have you ever heard of him?"

"No, I don't think I have," the marshal replied. "At least, not before a few days ago. But I understand he has been been hanging out in The Lion and The Crown for a while. You say he started shooting at you for no reason?"

"Yeah, and from a long way off, with a special rifle."

"What kind of rifle?"

"It's out there, stuck down his saddle holster," Matt said, making a motion toward the street with his thumb. "A fifty caliber, with a scope."

"Fifty caliber?" Marshal Drew whistled. "Now that would do a job on a man."

"It would," Matt said.

"Are you going to take him down to Welsh, or shall I?"

"I'll take him," Matt said.

Marshal Drew chuckled. "You know, you have given him more business this month than he has had for the previous six months."

"As long as the business I give him isn't me," Matt said with a smile.

"Yeah, I know what you mean."

"Another one for me, Mr. Jensen?" Welsh asked. He looked at the body. "My word, what did you do to his face? Why is it so red? By now the blood has usually drained out and they are almost white, but his face is still as red as a beet."

"I don't know," Matt said. "Marshal Drew said it was always like that."

"I suppose I can cover it with powder and paint or . . ." Welsh started, then he stopped and shook his head. "No," he said. He smiled. "I'm going to leave it just as it is."

Matt left the body with Welsh, then walked down to The Lion and The Crown to have a beer. He started to pay for it, but Harry pushed the money back.

"The ladies are buying your beer," he said.

"What? Why?"

"Word has already gotten around that you shot Carlos Silva."

"That was fast. I just brought him in half an hour ago."

"Yes, but enough people saw him thrown over his horse that they knew what happened. For about a week, he came in here every day, and sat right back there in that corner, scaring the ladies and my customers. I say good riddance."

"What have you got to eat here?" Matt asked.

"Ham, beans, cornbread," Harry said.

"Sounds good."

Matt found a table and began playing solitaire as he waited for his food. A few minutes later, one of the bargirls brought it to him and when he reached into his pocket to pay, she held out her hand.

"No," she said. "The other girls and I want to pay for your meal."

"Well, that's very nice of you," Matt said. "I thank you."

"Hey!" someone shouted, stepping into the saloon then. "Wait until you see what Welsh has standing tied to a board in front of his place now."

"We know," Harry said. "It's Carlos Silva."

"No it ain't."

"What do you mean, it isn't? Who is it, if it isn't Silva?"

"It's the devil his ownself," the man said. "I'm serious, come look!"

Matt knew they were probably talking about Silva's red skin, so he stayed to eat his meal while nearly everyone else in the saloon hurried down to see for themselves. A few minutes later one of the customers came back and stepped up to the bar. "Give me a whiskey, Harry, a strong one. Mickey is right. Welsh does have the devil standing up down there."

"Don't be silly, Carl," Harry said, pouring the drink and handing it to him. "It's just Silva."

"The hell it is. It's the devil hisself, I tell you." Carl put a coin down on the bar. "I'll have another one. Otherwise, I'll be seeing the devil in my nightmares tonight."

The three bargirls had left when most of the customers did, and when they came back, two of them were comforting the third.

"What is it?" Harry asked. "What's wrong with Rose?"

"She fainted when she saw the devil."

"What the hell are you talking about? Has everyone gone crazy? I'm going to go see for myself," Harry said, taking the towel down from his shoulder and starting toward the front door.

Finished with his meal now, Matt left with Harry, retracing the steps he had taken earlier when he came straight to the saloon from Welsh's Undertaking Parlor.

There was a large crowd gathered around in front of the place, more people than Matt would have thought were even in town. He had to admit that Silva was strange-looking, but his looks hardly seemed to justify a crowd this large.

Then, when he got there, he saw what had caught everyone's attention.

Silva was strapped to a board, just as some of the other outlaws had been. His face was shining red, and his yellow eyes were open. The skin was so tightly drawn across his face that it looked like a red skull, but Welsh had taken the illusion a little further. Although Silva was clean-shaven, Welsh had pasted a small triangular beard to his chin. And, on top of his head, sticking up through his hair, was a pair of red horns.

Matt had to admit that what he was looking at resembled the most bizarre artist's rendition of Satan that he had ever seen. He could understand why people might think he was the devil.

■ ■ ■ ■

"Silva's dead," Reed said.

"What?" Teasdale replied. "How do you know?"

"Because Welsh has him tied to a board in front of his place," Reed answered. "Not only that, he's got the son of a bitch made up to look just like the devil. I tell you the truth, it was enough to give me the willies."

"Jensen killed him?"

"That's what they are saying."

"How many lives does that bloody bastard have, anyway?" Teasdale asked, angrily. "I have hired two men who were supposedly the best in their business to take care of him, and neither one was able to do the job."

"And don't forget the stagecoach holdup that Logan arranged," Reed said.

"Yeah, that too."

"Since Jensen came on the scene, Logan has not been able to take one cow from Frewen," Reed said.

"You think I don't know that?"

"I'm sure you did. I was just commenting, is all."

"We've got to get rid of that bloody bastard before he makes a mess of everything," Teasdale said.

"I've got an idea, if you are willing to go along with it," Reed said.

"What would that be?"

"I'd say you offer a reward to anyone who takes care of him. That way we won't have to find anyone — the word will get out and there will be enough people willing to collect on the money that they'll find us."

"Hmm," Teasdale said, stroking his chin. "You know, Reed, that might not be a bad idea."

"The only thing is — it has to be a high enough reward to get people interested in it," Reed said.

"I've been told that Frewen has paid Matt Jensen five thousand dollars to regulate for him. I think it would be poetic justice if the reward on Jensen's head would also be five thousand dollars. That is, if you think that would be high enough. And the beauty, of course, is I won't have to pay it until after the job is done."

Reed grinned broadly. "Mr. Teasdale, a reward that large will have half the gunmen in the West coming after him. There will be someone after him constantly — and what will make it even better is — he won't know when someone is going to turn up next, who it will be, or where they will be coming from."

"How do we announce such a thing?" Teasdale asked. "It isn't exactly as if we can go to the constabularies and get reward posters circulated."

"You don't worry about that," Reed said. "Once a few people get wind of this, it will spread like wildfire. We'll have people from Texas to California coming up here to collect."

"One more thing," Teasdale said. "It can't be known that I am the one putting out the reward. This can't be traced back to me. If it is, it would ruin everything."

"I'll take care of that."

"No, you can't put out the reward either. You are working for me. If it is traced back to you, that would be the same thing as tracing it to me."

"I didn't mean I would take care of it by being the one to post the reward. All we have to do is have Sam Logan post the reward for us. That will not only keep it from coming back to you — Logan also knows people who know people, and that will get the word out."

"Yeah, that's a good idea," Teasdale said. "Go see him, tell him what we need."

CHAPTER TWENTY-ONE

From the *Sussex Standard:*

War with Cattle Rustlers

For the last month there has been a war conducted of good versus evil. The good resides in the person of Matt Jensen, a regulator hired by Mr. Moreton Frewen. The representative of evil is Sam Logan and the group of cattle rustlers who call themselves the Yellow Kerchief Gang.

This paper is pleased to report that good seems to be triumphant over evil, for no less than six cattle rustlers have thus far been dispatched to the nether world that awaits those who ply their reprehensible occupation at the cost of lives and property of decent folk.

That Matt Jensen's one man war against the malevolent forces arrayed against our cattlemen and their brave young cowboys has been successful is evidenced by the reduced number of cows rustled since his arrival. Not one cow has been stolen. This newspaper says hurrah for the likes of Matt Jensen, and warns the evildoers that their days of iniquity in Johnson County are numbered.

Sam Logan read the article, then handed it back to Reed. "All right, I read it," he said with a growl. "Why did you show it to me? Do you think I have to read in the newspaper what a pain in the ass Jensen has been?"

"I showed it to you because I want you to see how important it is that we get rid of the son of a bitch," Reed said.

"Yeah, well, we've tried three times. And it hasn't worked any time, besides which my cousin got hisself kilt and so did Silva. Except I don't give a shit about Silva, that back-shootin' bastard. He's good riddance as far as I'm concerned."

"Yes, well, now we have another plan," Reed said.

"What is that?"

"We aren't going to try and hire anyone in particular. We're just goin' to put out a five thousand dollar reward on his head. And we will pay it to anyone who kills him, no matter who it is."

"Yeah," Logan said. "Yeah, that might work. Only thing is, how are you going to get the word out?" Logan picked up the newspaper. "It ain't like you can put an ad in the newspaper. And you probably ain't goin' to be able to get anyone to print up posters on it either."

"I know. We thought maybe you could get the word out."

"Why me?"

"Several reasons," Reed replied. "Number one, your business is being hurt by Jensen more than Mr. Teasdale's business is. You are the one he is after. And you have a network of contacts that will allow you to get the word out. Mr. Teasdale, on the other hand, can't let it be known that he is behind the reward."

"All right," Logan said. "I'll put the word out. But I want a thousand dollars for doing it."

"Why would you want a thousand dollars? Hell, like I said, you are the one Jensen is looking for. I would think you would be happy to have Teasdale put up the money for a reward that might just save your life," Reed said.

Logan smiled. "Let's just say it is my handling fee," he said.

"I don't know if he will go along with it," Reed said.

"You can talk him into it."

"Why should I? It's not my neck that's on the line here. Jensen isn't looking for me."

"Well, wouldn't you like to have a handling fee?"

"Me?"

"Yeah. Say, five hundred dollars? You get an extra thousand dollars for me to spread the word and handle the reward, and there's five hundred dollars in it for you," Logan said.

Reed smiled. "I like the way you think, Sam Logan."

Jake Scarns was in the Buffalo Gals Saloon in Buffalo when he saw Moe Greer come into the bar. Scarns and Greer had spent some time together in the Colorado State Prison. When Greer saw Scarns, he stopped at the bar, bought a bottle and took it and two glasses over to the table where Scarns was sitting with one of the girls from the saloon.

"Beat it," Greer said to the bargirl.

"Wait a minute, cowboy, you can't just run me off like that. Scarns, are you going to let him talk to me like that?"

"Yeah," Scarns said. "What do you mean by running her off? I was enjoyin' her company."

Greer gave the girl five dollars. "My pard 'n I have some talkin' to do," he said. "You can come back later."

The girl took the money with a big smile.

"Well, honey, if you put that way, I'll be glad to go," she said. She ran her hand through Scarns's hair. "When you are ready for me to come back, you just whistle."

"All right," Scarns said.

As the girl was leaving, Greer poured two glasses of whiskey and slid one over to Scarns.

"What's all this about?" Scarns asked.

"Five thousand dollars," Greer said.

Scarns tossed the entire drink down, then he slid the glass out as Greer refilled it.

"All right, I'm interested."

"Have you ever heard of a man named Matt Jensen?" Greer asked.

"I saw him once, down in Colorado," Scarns said.

"Would you recognize him on sight?"

"Yeah, why?"

"Would he recognize you?"

"No, I don't see why he would. Like I said, I saw him once, but I never actually met him. What's this about, Moe?"

"Someone I know is willing to pay five thousand dollars to have Matt Jensen killed."

"Ha! You're talking about Sam Logan, ain't you?"

"How do you know?"

"Hell, it's been in the paper, how Sam Logan had a good thing going until this fella Jensen showed up."

"All right, yes, I am talking about Sam Logan," Greer said. "So, are you interested?"

Scarns got his whiskey glass refilled and tossed it down before he answered.

"Yeah," he said. "For five thousand dollars I'll kill the son of a bitch in front of the county sheriff."

Two days after the meeting between Greer and Scarns, Matt was in The Lion and The Crown. He had just finished one beer and asked Harry for another when he saw, by the reflection of the mirror behind the glass shelf full of bottles, that someone was rising from a table behind him and pulling his gun.

Instantly, Matt drew his own pistol and whirled toward the man. When that man saw how quickly Matt had drawn, he held his hands up, letting the pistol dangle from its trigger guard.

"Who are you?" Matt asked.

The man didn't answer and Matt cocked his pistol, the double click of the sear engaging the cylinder making a loud sound in the now silent room. "I asked who you are."

"Scarns! Jake Scarns!" he said. "Don't shoot, Jensen. Don't shoot!"

"Why the hell shouldn't I?" Matt replied. "You were about to back-shoot me, weren't you?"

"My God, Mister, you're not real, you know that? What does it take to kill you?"

"I don't know," Matt said. "How much are you getting paid?"

Matt just took a chance on asking that question. It was something he suspected, but not anything he knew for sure.

"Five thousand dollars."

"Looks like you're going to have to give the money back."

"I ain't got it. Nobody's got it yet. It's the reward for killin' you. I ain't goin' to be the only one tryin'."

"Who has put up the reward?"

"You're askin' too damn many questions," Scarns said.

"Who else is coming after me?" Matt asked. "Are there others?"

"Hell, with that much money on your

head, there's prob'ly a dozen or so. I don't know who else."

"I tell you what," Matt said. "For the time being, I'm going to park you in the jail."

"What do you mean? You ain't got no authority to put me in jail. You ain't carryin' a badge."

"Yeah, I am," Matt said. "I'm carrying a badge for the Union Pacific Railroad."

"Are you crazy? There ain't no railroad up here."

"Have you ever ridden on a train?" Matt asked.

"What? Yeah, of course I've been on a train. So what?"

"If you've ever been on a train, that means you've used the railroad. And that's all the authority I need. Let me have your gun."

"You know what I think?" Scarns asked. "I think you're just sayin' that. There ain't no way your badge can mean anything just 'cause I've been on a train. You can't take me to jail 'cause I ain't done nothin', and you got no authority over me."

"Give me your gun," Matt repeated.

"All right, if you say so." Scarns smiled then, slowly, turned the pistol around so that the butt was pointing toward Matt.

"But you be careful with your gun," Scarns said. "I've done give up, and this

297

here saloon is full of witnesses who'll swear I was handin' you my gun. You shoot me now, you'll hang."

"All right, Scarns," Matt said. He let the hammer down, then lowered his pistol. "I'm going to park you in jail, and that's where you are going to stay until I find out who is paying you. And if there are any others after me, you are more than likely going to have company."

"You ain't scarin' me none, Jensen. I won't be in jail long. I didn't do nothin'. I might've wanted to, but I didn't. And you can't keep a man in jail for wantin' to do somethin'."

Matt reached for Scarns's gun, but Scarns suddenly executed a border roll. Matt wasn't often caught by surprise, but this time he was, not only because Scarns had the audacity to try such a thing, but because he was so good at it.

Because Matt had let the hammer down and his pistol and lowered it, he had to raise the gun back into line while at the same time cocking it. The quiet room was suddenly shattered with the roar of two pistols shooting at almost the same time. The others in the saloon were even more surprised than Matt had been, and though a few of them yelled and dove for cover, it was too late because the action had already begun. Gray gunsmoke billowed out from the two pistols, spreading into a cloud that momentarily obscured the results of the unexpected shoot-out. From their various positions around the saloon, everyone looked toward the bar where the action had taken place, waiting until the smoke cleared enough for them to see.

Gradually the smoke began to roll away, and as it did, everyone could see Scarns still standing there with a broad smile on his face. He took one step toward Matt, then the smile left his face and his eyes glazed over. With a groan he pitched forward, his gun clattering to the floor.

Matt was ready to fire again if need be, but a second shot wasn't necessary. He stood in place for a moment, looking down at Scarns before he finally holstered his pistol.

"Did you see that?" someone asked.

His question wasn't answered, because everyone in the saloon had seen it.

There were shouts from outside, then the sound of people running. Several came into the saloon and stood under the rising cloud of gunsmoke to stare down at the dead man on the floor. One of those who ran into the saloon was Marshal Drew.

"Marshal, it wasn't Jensen's fault," Harry said quickly. "Ever'one in here will tell you that this fella on the floor, Scarns he said his name was, started it all."

"Yeah," Marshal Drew said with a resigned sigh. "They have all been like that. Matt, you are a good man, I'll attest to that. But I swear, the grim reaper must just hover over you."

"Another one?" Teasdale said. "Are you telling me that Jensen killed another one?"

"Yeah, someone who was trying to collect the reward," Reed said.

"How do you know he was trying to collect the reward?"

"Because he said it out loud, and everyone in the saloon heard him," Reed said.

"My God, that's not good," Teasdale said, growing pale.

"He didn't say who offered the reward," Reed said. "And of course he wouldn't know anyway, because he thought the reward would be coming from Sam Logan. And anyone else who might try and collect is going to think the same thing."

"Yes," Teasdale said. "Yes, I suppose that is right, isn't it?"

"And, look at it this way," Reed said. "Jensen isn't dead, that's true, but you aren't out any money yet, either. And you won't be until someone actually gets the job done."

"That leaves a question hanging though, doesn't it?" Teasdale said.

"What question is that?"

"Is there nobody that can kill that bloody bastard?"

CHAPTER TWENTY-TWO

In the town of Curtis Wells, about twenty miles east of Sussex, Pete Carter, Tim Hodge, and Ben Decker were in the Back Lot Saloon.

"Five thousand dollars," Carter said. "That's how much the reward is to take care of Jensen."

"Five thousand dollars? We was only going to get a hunnert dollars apiece," Hodge complained. "Who's givin' this reward, anyway?"

"From what I hear, it is Sam Logan."

"Sam Logan? He don't have that much money," Decker said.

"How do you know he don't? He's been runnin' a pretty good operation in Johnson County for near 'bout a year, now. Hell, there ain't no tellin' how much money he's got," Carter said.

"What I'm wonderin' is why he would be willin' to give out so much money as a reward for killin' Jensen, when he was only goin' to give us a hunnert dollars apiece," Hodge said.

"Well, think about it," Carter said. "From what I hear, Jensen is playing hell with Logan's operation. He's already killed half a dozen of his men, and if you had somethin' good goin', and there was a chance that some son of a bitch was goin' to mess it up for you, wouldn't you want to get rid of him?"

"Yeah, I guess, but, it don't seem fair that he would be offering all that money to someone else, and not to us."

"Who said it ain't to us?" Carter asked.

"What do you mean?"

"It's a reward," Carter said. "It will be paid to anyone takes care of Jensen. All we got to do is get to him first, and the money is ours."

"How do we do that?" Decker asked. "We already run into him once, and it didn't work out all that well, if you remember."

"No, we didn't run into him. He ran into us," Carter said. "This time we will do it different."

Matt was having his lunch at The Lion and The Crown when he saw Carter, Hodge, and Decker come into the saloon. He recognized them right away and wondered what they were doing there. Then when they started toward him, he knew that their presence was no mere accident.

"Well, Mr. Jensen, it looks like we meet again," Carter said.

"I didn't think you boys would show up in Sussex," Matt said.

"Oh, I'm sure you didn't," Carter said.

"Tell me, Jensen," Decker said. "Did you really think you could steal our guns and get away with it?"

"I didn't steal them, I just held on to them for a while. If you want them back, all you have to do is go see Marshal Drew."

"Nah, we don't want them back," Hodge said. "We got us new guns."

"Do you, now?"

Matt took a swallow of his beer, then put the mug on the table. He dropped his hands in his lap.

"You boys do seem to have something on your mind," Matt said. "And I'm just betting it would be the reward money."

Carter smiled. "You know about the reward, do you?"

"Yes. Evidently a couple of men have already tried for it."

"Yeah? Where are they now?"

"Oh, the town gave them choice lots down

304

in the cemetery."

"We've talked enough, Carter," Hodge said. "I say let's just go ahead and kill him now."

"You're goin' to do it, are you Hodge?" Carter asked.

"Yeah, I'm going to do it," Hodge answered. "He don't look all that tough to me. Last time he was standin' behind us, if you remember. This time we are face to face, and I say let's do it, get our money, and be done with it."

Hodge moved his hand down to hover just over his own gun. "What about it, Mr. bigshot gunfighter? You want to settle this now?"

By now, all the rest of the conversation in The Lion and The Crown had ceased, and everyone turned to see if this was going to progress any further.

"That's pretty brave of you — what did your friend call you? Hodge?"

"Yeah, the name is Hodge, Tim Hodge. What about it, Mr. Matt Jensen, Mr. bigtime gun fighter? I'm gettin' pretty tired of jawin'. I say that you either go for your gun now, or get plumb on out of the county with your tail tucked down between your legs."

"You are challenging me to a gunfight, are you, Mr. Hodge?"

"Yeah, that's what I'm doing. I'm challenging you to a gunfight."

"That's not really fair now, is it?" Matt said. "I mean with me sitting down, and you standing up. It's sort of hard to make a quick draw from a sitting position. Are you going to allow me to stand up first?"

A broad, mocking smile spread across Hodge's face. "Well now, what do you think, boys?" he asked. "Should I give this famous gunfighter a chance and let him stand up? Or should I just kill him where he sits for being so stupid as to let himself get caught in this predicament?"

Matt made no move toward his own gun, but he did smile up at Hodge and his smile was even colder and more frightening than Hodge's smile.

"You aren't going to let me stand, are you, Hodge?"

"No, I ain't."

"I didn't think so. And this isn't the first time some coward challenged me while I was sitting down. So," Matt continued. "You might say that I was ready for it. You see, I already have my gun out, and I am pointing it at you, right now."

"What the hell are you talking about?" Hodge asked. "Hell, your gun ain't out. I can see your gun in that fancy holster, plain as day!"

"Oh, I'm glad you noticed. That is a nice holster, isn't it? I had that made, especially for me, down in El Paso."

"Mister, you ain't makin' no sense at all. What gun do you have pointed at me?"

Matt brought his hand up from under the table. His fingers were wrapped around a small pistol.

"Well, now, that would be this gun, Mr. Hodge," Matt said. "It is a Derringer, two barrels, forty-one caliber. It doesn't have that much range, but hell, how far are you from me, anyway? Six feet? Ten feet? They say that's about how far Lincoln was from John Wilkes Booth when he killed him with this same kind of weapon."

Hodge stood his ground for a moment longer, his eyes narrowing, a muscle in his cheek twitching, and sweat breaking out on his forehead.

"That — that — where did that gun come from?"

"Oh, I can't give away all my secrets now, can I, Mr. Hodge?"

"Ha! Looks to me like you have a problem," Hodge said.

"And what problem would that be?" Matt asked.

"You can't count."

"Why would you say that?"

Hodge smiled. "You've only got two barrels on that gun, and there are three of us."

Matt looked down at his pistol, then at the three men. "Damn if you aren't right, Hodge. There are three of you, and I have only two barrels."

"Which means," Hodge said, his confident smile growing broader, "That you can't kill all three of us."

"You're right again. I can't get all three of you," Matt said. "So here's what I'm going to do. Since you seem to be the only one smart enough to have figured that out, I'm going to let you live, but I'm going to kill the other two."

"What?" Carter shouted. "The hell you say!"

"I tell you what," Matt said. He cocked the pistol. "Why don't I just shoot them now and get it over with? I believe I can kill both of them before you can kill me. Shall we try it?"

"No!" Carter said. He pulled his pistol and pointed it at Hodge. "Hodge, you put that gun away, now! You think I'm going to let him shoot us, just so you can shoot him?"

"He's bluffing," Hodge said. "He can't kill all three of us."

"I ain't worried about all three of us, you

dumb son of a bitch!" Carter said. "I'm only worried about me. Get your hand away from your gun, now, or I'll blow your damn head off myself!"

Hodge moved his hand away.

"Good move, Mr. Hodge," Matt said. He turned the pistol toward Carter. "Now, you are making me nervous. I would appreciate it very much if you would put your gun back in its holster."

"All right, all right, I'm doing it," Carter said, holstering his pistol. "Come on," he said to the other two. "Let's go."

The three men left the saloon, but Matt was reasonably sure that he hadn't seen the last of them. He finished his lunch and then went outside. He had just stepped down from the boardwalk when the first shot came. It hit the support post right beside him. Then, even as he was locating the shooter, who was just behind a watering trough on the opposite side of the street just in front of the feed and seed store, there was a second, then a third shot. All three shots came from different locations.

Matt darted into the space between the saloon and the leather goods store that was adjacent to The Lion and The Crown. With his gun in hand, he backed up against the wall of the leather goods store, then looked back into the street. He wasn't the only one who had been stirred into action, because the street, which had been crowded with pedestrians a moment earlier, was emptying quickly as everyone hurried to get out of the line of fire.

So far he only knew the location of one of the shooters, that being the one behind the watering trough across the street. That there were two more convinced him that these had to be the same three men who had braced him in the saloon earlier.

At the far end of the street, Gordon Prouty, unaware of the drama being played out before him, came into town driving a wagon. The right rear wheel was squeaking badly, and he knew he was going to have to pack the thing with grease.

As the wagon continued on into town, everyone was aware of its presence, from the squeaking axle to the sound of the wheels rolling on the hard dirt, to the rattle of chains, tongue, and doubletree, to the clopping of the horses' hooves. It drew the attention of all, and they worried about Mr. Prouty for fear he might get caught in the crossfire. For the moment, though, there was no crossfire as the attention of everyone, even the shooters, was on the wagon.

Matt used the distraction of the wagon to

run back to the alley. A ladder was attached to the rear of the leather goods store and, holstering his pistol, Matt climbed to the top. Then, bending down at the waist so not to be silhouetted against the sky, Matt ran to the front of the building and stood behind the false front. Looking around the edge of the false front, he saw that the wagon had passed all the way through town and was now at the far end of the street and turning into the lumberyard.

Matt had hoped that from this vantage point he might be able to see the shooter behind the watering trough, but he couldn't. In fact, he wasn't even sure the shooter was still behind the trough.

"Where'd he go?" Matt heard somebody shout. "Hodge? Decker? Either one of you see 'im? You have any idea where he went?"

The call came from the roof of the apothecary which was just across the street from Matt. Matt stepped out from behind the false front.

"Are you looking for me?" he called.

"There he is!"

Matt recognized the one on the roof of the apothecary as Carter. And Carter, even as he was shouting to the others, took a shot at Matt and missed. Matt shot back and didn't miss. Carter fell from the roof of the drugstore, landing on the boardwalk that passed in front of the store. He hit so hard that he actually broke some of the planking.

Decker and Hodge both shot at Matt, and though both of them missed, they came close enough to cause him to drop back down behind the false front for both cover and concealment. This time he saw where both shots came from. One of the shots confirmed his belief that one of the shooters was still behind a watering trough. The other came from just inside the front door of the Chinese laundry.

Hurrying to the rear of the building, Matt climbed down the ladder, then ran several buildings up the street. Moving up through the gap between Sikes' Hardware Store and the lumberyard, Matt looked back down the street. He saw Hodge peering out from the front of the laundry, and Decker rising up to look over the watering trough. Both men were focusing their attention on the false front of the leather goods store. That was where they last saw him, and that was where they believed him still to be.

Taking advantage of the fact that they were focusing on where he wasn't, Matt managed to dart across the street, unseen by either of his adversaries. Moving between two buildings, Matt was now able to move down the alley on the opposite side of the street from where he had been. Reaching the back of the Chinese laundry, he saw two Chinese men and three women standing out back with terrified expressions on their faces. When they saw him, they became even more frightened, but he held his fingers to his lips, then, by motions, let them know that he was a friend.

Matt started to open the back door, but one of the men shook his head, then signaled that he should enter another way. Following him, Matt was shown a small half-door on the side of the building. Smiling and nodding, the Chinese man pointed, indicating he should go into the building that way.

Matt did as he was directed, though he didn't know why until he got inside. Then he saw that this way enabled him to be behind a freestanding shelf, out of sight of Hodge. Had he come in through the back door as he had planned, Hodge would have seen him the moment he opened the door.

"Decker!" Hodge called. "Decker! Do you see him?"

"No!" Decker's voice came back.

Matt stepped out from behind the shelf.

"Drop your gun, Hodge," Matt said.

"Son of a bitch! How'd you get in here?"

Hodge's cry fell somewhere between surprise, anger, and fear.

"Drop it!" Matt called again.

"The hell I will!"

Hodge fired at Matt, the bullet flying past Matt's ear. Matt returned fire and Hodge, now with a bullethole in his chest, was propelled backward through the front door, back out into the street. He fired two more times, almost in reflexive action, both bullets going into the dirt. He fell flat on his back.

"Hodge, what happened?" Decker shouted, rising up from his position behind the water trough.

"I happened," Matt said, stepping out through the front door of the laundry.

"You!" Decker shouted. Lifting his pistol he began shooting. His shooting was so wild and erratic that Matt wasn't in any danger, but he knew that innocent people in the town were, so he fired back, once.

One shot was all it took.

With the shooting stopped, and the gunsmoke of the several discharges drifted away, the townspeople gradually began reappearing. Some gathered in front of the apothecary around Carter's body, which was lying in, and not on, the boardwalk. Others were collected in front of the Chinese laundry, staring down at Hodge. Still more stood congregated at the feed and seed store, looking down at Hodge.

Marshal Drew checked all three bodies, then came over to talk to Matt, who was leaning against a hitching rail with his arms folded across his chest, just looking out at the people. Marshal Drew was unable to discern any expression of excitement, fear, or anger. There was absolutely nothing to indicate that he had just been in peril, or that he had just killed three men. From the expression on Matt's face, he might have been observing the commerce of a normal day.

"I heard what happened between you and these three men back in The Lion and The Crown," Marshal Drew said. "You gave them every opportunity to walk away from it, and they didn't. These are the same three who tried to hold up the stagecoach, aren't they?"

Matt nodded.

"They must have been pissed that you broke it up."

"I don't think so."

"What do you mean?"

"I don't think revenge had anything to do with it. In fact, I don't think they were even trying to rob the stagecoach."

"Really? Then what the hell were they planning?"

"I think they were there to kill me," Matt said. "And when it didn't work that day, they came back."

"For the reward?"

"Yes."

"There will be more coming after you, won't there?"

"There will be until I can get to the source of the reward."

"Sam Logan?"

"I suppose so," Matt replied.

"What do you mean, you suppose? Everyone says it is Logan."

"Over the years I've learned to trust nothing that I hear and only half of what I see," Matt said.

CHAPTER TWENTY-THREE

Over the several days since young Winston Churchill had been given access to a horse, he spent at least four hours a day in the saddle. He gained confidence and poise, but he also learned the meaning of the term saddle sore. However, he neither complained nor even mentioned it, bearing up stoically in order to continue with this, his newfound passion.

By now, Winnie had become not only a familiar sight around the ranch, but a favorite of the cowboys as well. He joined them as they attended to their regular duties, such as seeing that the cattle were moved around the ranch to water and grazing areas, mending the fences, even branding when necessary. He was invited to eat in the cookhouse with the other cowboys, and he became a regular at mealtimes, learning not only to eat but to relish the cowboy fare of biscuits, beans, fried steak, and especially apple pie. And though he was used to drinking tea, he was teaching himself to drink strong, black coffee.

"They call it grub," he explained to his mother. "And it is quite tasty."

"Heavens," Jennie said. "How can anyone eat something that is called grub?"

"You can eat it if you are a cowboy," Winnie said.

"I see," Jennie said with a smile. "And you are a cowboy now, are you?"

"Yes."

"What makes you a cowboy?"

"Mama, I have given blood, toil, tears and sweat on the range. I believe that makes me a cowboy."

Jennie leaned down and kissed Winnie on the forehead.

"I certainly won't question that," she said.

Believing that the time had come to put his plan into operation, Teasdale rode out to Logan's headquarters at Nine Mile Creek. Following the ritual which would let the lookouts recognize him from some distance, he rode up the coulee until he reached the shack. Word had already reached Logan that Teasdale was on his way in, so he was waiting out front.

"If you're here to complain that I ain't

318

brought you no more cows from the Frewen ranch, I already know that I haven't," Logan said. "And there ain't likely to be any more either, till we get rid of that bastard Jensen."

"That's why I'm here," Teasdale said. "I think I know how to get rid of him."

"Yeah? Well you're going to have to let me in on it, 'cause I sure as hell ain't figured out a way, yet. We've got a five thousand dollar reward out on him. Six men have tried to kill him and all six are pushin' up daisies."

"Mr. Jensen appears to be a man of extraordinary acumen, reflexes, and nerve," Teasdale said.

"If you mean he's harder to kill than cockroaches, I agree."

"I do have a plan in mind, though," Teasdale said. "It isn't one that I wanted to use, but I believe it may be our best chance. Indeed, it may be our only chance."

"What is it?" Logan asked.

"Frewen's sister-in-law and nephew are here, visiting from England. The nephew is a ten-year-old boy, the son of Lord Randolph Churchill. His name is Winston. If Winston were to be abducted . . ."

"To be what?" Logan asked.

"Taken," Teasdale explained. "We could

319

set up a scenario whereby . . ."

"Look, you're goin' to have to talk English to me. What the hell is a scenario?"

Teasdale sighed. "What I am trying to say is this. The boy goes riding just about every day, and he is getting bolder and bolder, which means he is going farther and farther from the house. If you would send a couple of men out to abdu— to grab him — and bring him here, we could lure Jensen into a situation that would allow us to take care of him once and for all."

"What you are saying is, you want us to use the boy as bait, and set a trap for Jensen," Logan said. "Is that it?"

"Yes, that is exactly what I am saying."

"Then why didn't you say so in the first place, instead of all this other blather — scenarios and that sort of thing?"

"Never mind," Teasdale said. "The point is, you know exactly what I am talking about."

"All right, where will the boy be?"

"I can't tell you that, because I don't know, exactly. All I know is that he is doing a lot of riding, all over the ranch. I think there will be several opportunities to find him out on his own, and when you do, all you have to do is take him."

"What if he don't want to be took?"

"It is obvious that he will not want to be taken," Teasdale said. "But he is a ten-year-old boy, so I expect you to be able to deal with it. But, and this is very important," he said, holding up a finger to emphasize his point. "I don't want the boy hurt. If he is hurt, he will be useless to us as bait."

"All right," Logan said. "If he is wandering around out there on his own, like you say he is, we ought not to have no trouble in snatching him. But what do we do after we get him?"

"Get a message to Moreton Frewen, telling him that you have the boy, and that you will only release him to Matt Jensen."

Over the last several days of riding on his uncle's ranch, Winnie was beginning to be able to find his way around. He discovered that it was very easy to navigate by positioning particular peaks and rock formations. But as a final fallback, he knew that the Powder River ran right behind Frewen Castle, so he could never get lost as long as he followed the waterways. Going out, he would keep the Powder River to his right. If he rode off on an exploration, he knew that he only had to reverse his course and return to the river, then he could follow it back. Today, he planned to be out for most of the day, and he had prepared for it by bringing a lunch prepared for him by the ranch cook. It consisted of a biscuit, fried chicken, and a piece of cake. Reaching the junction of the Powder River and William's Creek, he turned northwest to follow the creek for a little way before he dismounted to eat his lunch. From there, he had a magnificent view of the Big Horn Mountains to the west and the Black Hills to the east. To the south lay the Powder River Basin, several hundred thousand acres of rich and well-watered grassland that made Johnson County ideal for raising cattle.

The thing that made this area good for cattle also made it good for game, and he could see deer, bighorn sheep, elk and antelope wandering around the area. Finishing his biscuit and chicken, he picked up the cake. The cook had wrapped it in a piece of cloth to keep it moist.

While sitting there eating his cake, Winnie listened to the babbling of William's Creek as it made its way another quarter of a mile to empty into the Powder River. He had never been anywhere that he considered more exciting or beautiful than this ranch. He thought about the journal his teacher had asked him to keep and realized that it had been a long time since he had posted anything in it. It was just that there had been so much going on that he had not taken the time to get around to it, but he had brought it with him today, and he took his journal and a pencil from his saddlebag and began to write.

When one thinks of the American cowboy one might think it to be a romantic thing, a man on horseback in the open plains, surrounded by purple mountains highlighted by a golden sunset. I know that was my idea when first we arrived here. But in the time I have been here, I have learned that it is not as I thought it was.

I still consider the American cowboy to be a noble person, but now I realize that the nobility is in the work that he is required to do. The work is most arduous and the cowboys who come back to eat their "grub" in the cookhouse in the evening are tired from a long day of moving cattle from one spot to another, mending fences, pulling cows from quicksand, and chasing down the calves that wander off. They do this sometimes with a kerchief tied over their noses to combat the dust, or with their hats pulled down low to stop the rain, and while freezing in the cold winter blasts, or sweating in the almost unbearable heat of summer.

I don't say that they do this without complaint, for the cookhouse is filled with complaints of the day, but they are complaints without rancor. In fact, complaining is the cowboy's way of communicating, for they are delivered in a manner that is designed to elicit more laughter than sympathy.

I have come to believe . . .

That was as far he got when he looked up and saw three riders approaching him. Thinking they were some of his uncle's cowboys, he waited until they got very close. Only then did he realize that he had never seen any of them before, not even in the cookhouse at meals.

"Hello, boy," one of the riders said.

"Hello, sir," Winnie replied, trying not to show his nervousness over this unexpected meeting. He closed his journal, then lay it down under a rock to keep the pages from blowing.

"Would your name be Winston Churchill?"

"It is, indeed," Winnie answered with a relieved smile. If they knew his name, then surely they would mean no harm to him.

One of the riders approached very close.

"That's a nice-looking horse," the rider said. "Is it yours?"

"It is a loan from Sir William," Winnie said. "But he has been given to me to use while I'm here, so I have named him. I call him Tudor Monarch."

"That's a pretty high-falutin name," one of the riders said. That same rider reached out and took the reins of Winnie's horse.

"Excuse me, sir, but why did you take the reins of my horse?"

"Winston, get mounted. We're going to take a little ride together."

"I'd rather not take a ride with you, if it is all the same to you," Winnie said. "I have my ride planned for the day. It is necessary that I do that so that Uncle Moreton and Mama will always know where I am."

"Don't worry about that. We'll tell them where you are."

The other two riders came up very close, and Winnie knew that he was in great danger.

"Am I being abducted?" he asked.

"If that means are you being snatched up, the answer is yeah, that's what we are doing."

"To what end?" Winnie asked.

"To what end?" The rider that was holding the reins to Tudor Monarch chuckled.

"Did you hear that, Grant? He wants to know to what end. Ain't he about the damnedest talkin' boy you ever been around?"

"I'll tell you to what end," Grant said. "There's a group of us that wants your uncle to do somethin' for us, and we figure he will do it if he knows that's the only way he'll see you alive again."

"What is it you wish done?" Winnie asked.

"We want him to send Matt Jensen to come fetch you," Grant said. "Do you think your uncle will do somethin' like that?"

"I don't really know Uncle Moreton all that well, so I can't tell you with honesty whether he will or will not do what you ask."

"You better hope that he will do it, boy," one of the other riders said. "Because if he don't, we'll send you back to him, belly-down, on this horse."

Donnie Lewis was looking for strays when suddenly three men rode out of a coulee with guns drawn and pointed at him. All three were wearing yellow kerchiefs.

"Whoa!" Lewis said, throwing his hands up. "What do you want? I ain't got no money and I ain't herdin' no cows!"

"We want you to do something for us," one of the riders said. "We want you to deliver a note to Moreton Frewen."

"What kind of note?"

"Why should it matter to you what kind of note?" the rider asked. "The only thing that should matter to you is this. If you deliver it you live, if you don't you die."

"Now, tell me, cowboy, what is it to be?" one of the other men asked.

"I'll deliver the note," Lewis said.

"Yeah, I thought you might." The rider handed him a folded piece of paper. "How fast is that horse?" he asked.

"I beg your pardon?" Lewis asked.

"How fast is that horse?" the rider repeated. "Do you think he is fast enough to get you out of rifle range in a minute?"

"I — I don't know."

The rider pulled his rifle and cocked it. "You better hope he is. 'Cause in one minute I'm going to take a shot at you. So I suggest you get goin' now."

Lewis jerked his horse around, then slapped his legs against the side of the horse, urging him into a gallop. He leaned forward, not only to urge the horse to a faster pace, but also to present a smaller target in case the man actually did shoot at him.

A minute passed, and there was no bullet. Either the man didn't shoot at him, or

Lewis was far enough away now that if he did shoot, the bullet was far wide of its mark.

Forty-five minutes later, Lewis showed the note to Myron Morrison, thinking it might be better to go show it to the foreman first. Morrison read the note, then with compressed lips and narrowed eyes, looked back up at Lewis.

"Where did you get this?" he asked.

"Three men come up on me," Lewis said. "It was them that give this here note to me, tellin' me that if I didn't deliver it, they was goin' to shoot me. As soon as they let me go, I hightailed it out of there. They said give it to Mr. Frewen, but I figured maybe it would be better if you done it."

"Thanks a lot," Morrison said, sarcastically.

"I mean, you don't mind bein' the one to show it to 'im, do you? Bein' as you are foreman and all."

"All right," Morrison said. "I'll take the note to him."

Morrison walked from the bunkhouse across the yard to the huge log edifice. When he pulled the doorbell chain, Benjamin answered.

"Yes, Mr. Morrison?" Benjamin asked in

his stiff, upper tone British voice.

"I have a note here that Mr. Frewen needs to see."

"Lord Moreton is in the drawing room at the moment; if you would like, I can deliver the note to him," Benjamin said.

"I'd like nothing more in this world than for you to give this note to him," Morrison said. "But I don't think it is something you are going to want to do."

"Oh, heavens," Benjamin said. "Very good, sir. If you would come this way?"

Frewen was in the drawing room looking at the latest figures that he was preparing to send to his business partners back in England. The figures were not good. The Powder River Cattle Company was operating at a severe deficit.

"Lord Moreton?" Benjamin called from just outside the door to the drawing room.

"Whatever it is, Benjamin, let it wait, please," Frewen said. "I need to get this report ready to go. Though God knows I wish I didn't have to."

"Mr. Frewen, I expect you had better take time for this," Morrison called in through the door. "It's pretty important."

"All right," Frewen said. He pushed the book of numbers to one side, then turned toward his foreman. "What is it? What do you have for me?"

Morrison handed the note to Frewen. "Donnie Lewis brought it in a few minutes ago. He said that he ran across three men and they gave it to him."

With an anxious feeling, Frewen unfolded the note.

Frewen —
We've got the boy. If you want to see him alive again, send Jensen to junction of Nine Mile Creek and the Powder River at ten o'clock tomorrow morning. He must be alone. If we see anyone with him, we will kill the boy. If he does not show up we will kill the boy.

"God in Heaven," Frewen said. "Do you think anyone would actually be so low as to kill a boy?"

"Yeah, I think they would," Morrison said.

Frewen read the note again, then let out a loud sigh of frustration. "I don't understand. Why do they want Mr. Jensen to come to Nine Mile Creek?"

"It's pretty obvious," Morrison said. "They want him there so they can kill him."

"Oh, my!" Frewen said. "Then I am being asked to choose between the life of my nephew and the life of Mr. Jensen."

"Yes, sir, I'd say that's about it," Morrison said.

Frewen leaned back and pinched the bridge of his nose. "I — I don't know where to go with this," he said.

CHAPTER TWENTY-FOUR

When Matt went into the parlor of Frewen Castle, he saw Jennie crying and Carla trying to comfort her. Morrison was standing near the fireplace while Frewen was sitting in a big leather chair with his head leaning forward, his forehead resting on his fist.

"What's wrong?" Matt asked.

Frewen held the note out toward Matt.

"Read this," he said.

As Matt took the piece of paper from Frewen, he looked over at the crying women, and wondering what it was about, he read the note.

After he read it, he handed it back.

"What do you make of that?" Frewen asked.

"We don't have any choice, Mr. Frewen," Matt said. "I have to go."

Matt walked over to where Jennie and Clara were sitting together on a leather sofa. "Don't worry," he said. "I will find Winnie for you."

"Oh, Matt," Jennie said. Standing, she embraced him, pulling him hard against her. Matt could feel her tears against his cheeks. "Please, Matt, please bring Winston back safely to me."

"I will," Matt said. "I promise you, I will."

"Matt, you do know that they are using the boy for bait, don't you? They are setting you up to be killed." Frewen said.

"It won't be the first time a trap has ever been set for me," Matt said.

"I'm sure it isn't. But this one — I mean, to use young Winnie as they are doing is so — diabolical," Frewen said.

"I'll grant you that it is," Matt said. "But they have made a big mistake."

"How is that?" Frewen asked.

"They've given away their hand."

"I'm the one that is at fault here," Frewen said. "I let him, indeed I encouraged him, to feel free to ride anywhere on the ranch. It just never dawned on me that he would be in any danger. I mean, what would they want with him? If something happens to my nephew because of me, I will never forgive myself."

"I am going to find him, Mr. Frewen. I am going to find him and I am going to bring him home safely."

"Do you think you can do that?" Frewen asked. "Tell me the truth, now. I don't want you saying just what you think will make me feel better. I want to know if you really think you can do it."

"Yes, he can," Jennie said. "I know Mr. Jensen. And I am convinced that he will be able to find and rescue Winnie."

When they brought Winnie to the little house, they put him over in the corner next to the fireplace. He had seen some of the line shacks during the last several days of his rides around the ranch, and this was just like a line shack, though perhaps a little larger than most he had seen. It couldn't actually be a line shack though, because it was at the head of a long, deep ravine, or coulee, as he had heard the cowboys call such things.

There were at least six men in the shack, all wearing yellow kerchiefs. And though the men who had abducted him had not been wearing yellow kerchiefs at the time, they had since put them on. This gave them a sense of camaraderie and belonging, as if they were soldiers in an army. Four of the men were playing cards. One of the four, a man without a beard, but with a long, bushy, dark black mustache, had identified himself as Sam Logan. Logan, Winnie knew from the conversations he had overheard, was the head of the gang of rustlers who had been stealing cattle from his uncle. One of the men was cooking, while the sixth was sitting on a bunk, cleaning his gun.

Winnie was frightened, but he was also curious about such men as these, and he watched and listened.

"Hey, kid," one of the card players said. "I hear you are from England. Is that right?"

"That is correct," Winnie said.

"Ha," the questioner said. " 'That is correct,' he said. You reckon all kids from England talk like that?"

"It ain't just the kids. You've heard Teasdale talkin', ain't you? Always so prim and proper."

Suddenly, and unexpectedly, Logan hit the man who had just spoken with a wicked backhanded slap. The blow left the man's lip bleeding.

"What the hell did you do that for?" he asked, and taking off his yellow scarf, he used the corner of it to dab against the cut on his lip.

"Because you've got a big mouth, Poindexter. And you don't know when to shut up," Logan said.

"What did I say? All I said was . . ."

Logan glared at him, and Poindexter suddenly realized what he had done.

"Oh," he said. "I'm sorry. I didn't mean nothin' by it. I won't say anythin' else."

"Yes, that's probably the wisest thing for you to do," Logan said. He threw down his cards. "Deal me out. Clayton?"

"Yeah?" Clayton replied. Clayton was the one who had been doing the cooking.

"How much longer till we can get some grub?"

"These beans is all done, and I'm takin' off some pan cornbread now," he said.

Logan stepped over to the stove, got a bowl of beans and broke off a piece of cornbread. Getting a spoon, he carried the bowl with him and stepped over to squat down beside Winnie.

"Boy, you been listenin' to what we was talkin' about?" he asked, as he took a spoonful of the beans.

"No, sir, I'm sorry, I wasn't listening. Should I have been? I'm too frightened. I suppose I have just been wondering what was going to happen to me."

"Nothin' is going to happen to you if ever'one does what they are supposed to do," Logan said. He broke off a piece of cornbread and dropped it in his bowl, then scooped it up along with some beans. "Uh-hmm. These beans ain't bad. Clayton used to cook for a big ranch, now he cooks for us, and he makes a lot more now than he used to." Logan turned to call toward Clayton. "That's right, ain't it Clayton? You're makin' a lot more now than you used to?"

"A lot more," Clayton said.

"You hungry? You want somethin' to eat?"

"No, sir," Winnie said. "I had a rather good lunch before your three men came to get me. Besides, I am too frightened to eat, now."

"You're scared, huh?"

"Yes, sir, very much."

"Well, I've got to hand it to you, kid. You ain't showin' it much."

"I have been taught to keep a stiff upper lip."

"A stiff upper lip?" Logan said. He chuckled and ran his finger across his mustache. "What does that mean? I've never heard that used before."

"It is a British idiom," Winnie explained. "It means to remain undaunted in the face of danger and adversity. It is best expressed in a poem by Alfred, Lord Tennyson. Would you like to hear it?"

"Yeah, let me hear it."

Winnie began to say the poem as if presenting it in a class of declamation.

> " 'Forward, the Light Brigade!'
> Was there a man dismay'd?
> Not tho' the soldier knew
> Some one had blunder'd:
> Theirs not to make reply,
> Theirs not to reason why,
> Theirs but to do and die,
> Into the valley of Death
> Rode the six hundred."

"What is that about? What do you mean, the 'valley of death'?"

"It refers to a regiment of British cavalry led by Lord Cardigan against the Russians during the Crimean War. There were six hundred who started the charge, and nearly half of them were killed," Winnie said.

"I'll be damned," Logan said. "And you think that was good, do you?"

"I do not think it is good that so many were killed," Winnie said. "But I think the fact that they showed honor, courage, and kept a stiff upper lip is to be admired."

"And I think they were crazy. If I had been there, you had better believe that I wouldn't have done anything so crazy."

"What would you have done?"

"I would have run away," Logan said.

"You would do so at the expense of your honor?" Winnie asked.

"Ha! Honor? Kid, I'm a rustler and a murderer. To me, the only honor is in staying alive."

"I see."

"The only place there is honor is in poems and stories and such," Logan continued. "Honor ain't nothin' real."

"Oh, but I believe it is, sir," Winnie said.

"Do you know anyone with honor?"

"Oh, indeed I do, sir. Mr. Jensen is a man of honor and courage."

Logan chuckled. "Well, we will see just how much honor and courage Jensen has, won't we? Do you think he will try to rescue you?"

Winnie gasped. "That's why you are holding me here, isn't it? You are using me as bait."

"You're a smart kid, ain't you? But don't worry. Once we draw him into the trap, we'll let you go."

Logan left Winnie and went back to talk to the others.

"Jensen will show up at the point tomorrow at ten o'clock. Only we are going to be there by nine — no, make it eight."

"Hell, that's two hours early," Poindexter said. "Why do we need to be there so early?"

"In case he gets anxious and comes early, I want us to already be there," Logan said.

No one came to talk to Winnie for the rest of the day. He stayed over in the corner next to the fireplace and listened carefully to their conversation to see if there was anything he could learn that might be used to his advantage. He studied the layout of the shack in order to try and determine a way of escaping. There were only two windows high on the walls at each end, one over a double bunk bed, the other over the stove. The only other way out was the single door in the front of the building.

That night Winnie accepted the offer of a bowl of cold beans.

"Now, boy, let me tell you how this is going to work," Logan said. "One of us is going to be awake all night long. We'll be keeping an eye on you, so don't get any idea about tryin' to escape, because it ain't goin' to happen. You understand that?"

"Yes, sir," Winnie replied.

When it got dark enough, the men lit a lantern and set it on the table so they could see to play cards. Winnie stretched out on the floor and went to sleep.

He had no idea how long he had been asleep when he woke up. It was still dark and the lantern, though still burning, had been turned down very low so that the room, though illuminated, was barely so. The air was rent with the snoring of the sleeping men, and Winnie sat up to have a look around.

Perhaps this was his opportunity to escape!

Getting on his feet as quietly as he could, he started toward the door. That was when he saw someone sitting in a chair right beside the door.

Winnie's spirits fell when he saw that; then he remembered that Logan had told him that he was going to keep someone awake all night long so they could keep an eye on him. Winnie recognized him. It was Clayton, the cook.

But as Winnie continued to stare at him for a long moment, he saw that Clayton didn't seem to be moving.

Winnie took a step toward him, walking as quietly as he could.

Clayton had not noticed him, and Winnie felt a surge of hope and excitement when he realized that, like the others, Clayton was asleep!

Moving quietly, and scarcely daring to breathe, Winnie crossed the floor and stepped up to the door. The problem now was whether or not he could open the door without it squeaking.

Reaching up with a nervous hand, Winnie turned the door handle, then pulled it open.

It didn't make a sound.

Stepping outside, Winnie pulled the door shut. If he was lucky, he could be a considerable distance away before anyone noticed that he was gone. Looking back toward the door to make certain Clayton didn't notice his absence and suddenly jerk the door open, he stepped down from the porch.

"Where are you goin', boy?" a man's voice asked.

Gasping, and with his heart leaping to his throat, Winnie turned around to see Poindexter standing in front of him. Before he could react, Poindexter reached out to grab him.

"Well, now," Poindexter said. "It's a good thing I came outside to take a piss, ain't it? Otherwise you might have wandered off somewhere and got yourself lost. You don't want to get lost up here, boy. There's wolves and bears about."

Still holding him by the arm, Poindexter pushed Winnie back into the line shack.

"Hey!" he shouted, his shout loud enough to wake everyone.

"What?"

"What are you shouting for?"

"What's going on?"

"I just thought you fellas might like to know that the boy here was escaping. Seems to me like we was supposed to be keeping an eye on him."

"Clayton, you the one s'posed to be watchin' him now, ain't you?" Logan challenged.

"I — I must have dozed off," Clayton said. "I'm sorry, I didn't see the boy leave."

"If this was the army you'd be stood up against a post an' shot for fallin' asleep on guard duty," Logan said.

"I said I'm sorry. I don't lie aroun' all day like you boys. I cook, an' that means I'm on my feet most of the day."

"All right, here is the way it is going to be," Logan said. "If the boy escapes again, I'll kill whoever is supposed to be watching out for him." He looked at Winnie. "Did you hear that, boy? If you escape again, you will be responsible for someone getting killed. And then when we find you — and we will find you — I'll kill you as well. Now, get back over in that corner and stay there."

Winnie complied with Logan's order without comment.

CHAPTER TWENTY-FIVE

At the junction of Nine Mile Creek and the Powder River, Matt tied Spirit off so he couldn't be seen. Then he climbed up onto a precipice that afforded him enough elevation to be able to see for a long way in either direction, or at least as far as he could see in the darkness. It was three A.M., and he had come in the middle of the night so he would be there far in advance of the time set by the note. It was his intention to see whoever Logan was going to send to meet him.

From here, he could see back down the Powder River and up the small creek, both streams reflecting silver in the moonlight. Sitting down, he leaned back against a Ponderosa pine and waited. Overhead, the wind stirred the pine needles and moved the branches in a quiet whisper. It was a pleasant sound, and the air was soft and cool; and if his mission had not been critical, one that could mean life or death for a young boy, he could enjoy this moment.

From the time Matt left what he now thought of as his "apprenticeship" with Smoke Jensen, he had never settled down in any one place. He knew that Smoke enjoyed his ranch, loved his wife Sally, and was comfortable as a stable businessman.

Matt had been tempted a few times to follow his mentor's example and find a good woman with whom he could settle down. The closest any woman had ever come to filling that role was Kitty Wellington. Kitty had been one of the other orphans in the Soda Creek Home for Wayward Boys and Girls. A few years ago he had heard from her. A widow, she had inherited a horse ranch from her husband, and when she got into trouble, she sent for Matt. Sitting here now in the middle of the night, listening to the whisper of the wind in the trees, gave him the opportunity to think of his time with her.

The wind whispered as it came off the sails, and the sun created a million dancing diamonds on the surface of Lake Michigan. Matt and Kitty were seated on the afterdeck of the yacht, eating the meal the chef of the yacht had prepared for them. The yacht was about a mile off shore and from there, they had a great view of the city of Chicago. A passenger train was racing south along the lake shore.

"Where do you think that train is going?" Kitty asked.

"I don't know," Matt answered. "New Orleans, maybe?"

"Oh, wouldn't you like to go to New Orleans?"

"Some day, perhaps," Matt said. "But not today. I'm enjoying where I am right now."

"So am I," Kitty said. "I have had such a wonderful time in Chicago that I don't even want to go back. I hate to say this, but I could almost be convinced to sell the ranch."

"And do what?" Matt asked.

"The same thing you do," Kitty said. "Just wander around."

Matt shook his head. "No, Kitty, you don't want to do that."

"Why not?"

"Didn't you say Tyrone, Prew, Crack, Jake and the others at the ranch were your family?"

Kitty was silent for a long moment. "Yes," she finally replied. "Yes, I did say that, didn't I?"

"Besides, you don't want to quit now. The army not only bought all your horses, they told you they would buy as many as you could provide."

"Did you hear them say that it was the finest bunch of horses they had bought all year?" Kitty asked, proudly.

"Yes, I did hear that," Matt said. "And now, without the pressure of paying off a loan, the money you got from selling your horses to the army, and the guarantee they gave you for future contracts, you could just enjoy your ranch and your horses."

"Do you think you could?" Kitty asked.

"Do I think I could what?"

"Enjoy my ranch, my horses, and me?" Kitty said.

"Kitty, I —"

"No," Kitty said, holding up her hand and interrupting Matt in mid-sentence. She smiled at him. "Don't answer that, Matt. Let me keep my dream."

"Let you keep your dream? Oh, I don't know. I'm not so sure about that," Matt said, smiling.

"What do you mean, you aren't so sure?"

"Kitty, you have just proven to me that your dreams seem to have a way of coming true."[1]

And of course there was Jennie Churchill. In the years since Matt had become an adult, he had had his experiences with

[1] *Snake River Slaughter*

women — some, like Kitty Wellington, came close to winning his heart — but most were women who did nothing more than provide him with pleasurable interludes.

He knew that he could have such an interlude with Jennie — she had all but told him that. But though it might seem to some that Matt lived a life without parameters, facing death with equanimity, enjoying the pleasures of women when the opportunity presented itself, he was a man of strong moral character. And that moral character said that he would keep inviolate the sanctity of marriage. But he knew that wasn't the only reason he would not have anything to do with Jennie. There was something about the boy, Winston Churchill, that reminded Matt of himself. And he would do nothing to tarnish the image the boy had of him.

The next morning Teasdale arrived at Frewen Castle. When Benjamin showed him in to the parlor, he saw Frewen, Clara, and Jennie all with worried looks on their faces.

"William, have you heard?" Frewen asked.

"Yes," Teasdale said. "That's why I have come to wait with you."

"That is very nice of you," Frewen said.

Teasdale went over to the sofa where Jennie was sitting. "Mrs. Churchill, I'm so sorry this has happened. And now I feel guilty about it."

"Why should you feel guilty?" Jennie asked.

"Because I made a horse available for the boy," Teasdale said. "And if hadn't been out riding by himself, he would have never been abducted."

"Oh, don't be silly," Jennie said. "I've never seen Winnie happier than he has been these last several days, riding all over creation. If you hadn't given him a horse to ride, I'm sure Moreton would have."

"Benjamin," Clara called.

"Yes, madam?"

"Would you please bring tea for everyone?"

"Yes, ma'am," Benjamin said.

"I must say, you are taking this better than I would have thought," Frewen said.

"Matt told me he would bring Winnie home safely," Jennie said. "And I believe him."

"Does he have any leads?"

"Only what the note said," Frewen replied. Walking over to his desk, he picked the note up, then brought it to Teasdale who sat down to read it.

"It says they want him there by ten o'clock," Teasdale said. "It's probably about

349

time for him to leave, don't you think?"

Frewen chuckled. "He's already there."

"What?" Teasdale answered in surprise.

"He said he wanted to be there when they arrived, so he left in the middle of the night."

"But isn't that rather foolish of him?" Teasdale asked.

"Foolish? How?"

"They asked him to be there at ten o'clock, not in the middle of the night. Aren't you afraid that if they feel they have been double-crossed that they might do harm to the boy?"

"I don't feel that way at all," Frewen said. "I think they wanted him there at ten o'clock because they planned to ambush him. This whole thing was merely to set a trap for Mr. Jensen. I'm sure you have heard that someone has posted a five thousand dollar reward, payable to anyone who can kill him."

"Yes, the story is all over the valley," Teasdale said. "And from what I understand, there have already been several who have tried, unsuccessfully, to collect the reward."

"To their sorrow," Frewen said. "So far six men have tried, and six men have died."

Benjamin returned with the tea and for the next few moments the four sat around the parlor, sipping their tea in silence.

"Tell me truthfully, Moreton," Teasdale said. "Considering everything that has happened, are you not having second thoughts about this ranching venture of yours?"

"I will confess that this entire enterprise has been much more difficult than I ever would have imagined, and I have tried to explain this to my backers. If the spring rains fail, grazing on the upper range is nonexistent. We've had two bitter winters. And when we do manage to get our cattle through the winter and drought, the herd has to be driven for five hundred miles before they can be shipped to Chicago. And then, on top of all that, I've had my herd decimated by this despicable Sam Logan character."

"There is a way that you can avoid all this," Teasdale said. "My offer to buy you out still goes."

"I appreciate that, William, I really do," Frewen said. "But there is no way I am going to turn my back on this now. I just can't face the humiliation."

"Humiliation? Moreton, you have had six of your cowboys killed, you have had nearly a third of your herd stolen, and now your nephew is in great peril. Humiliation is the absolute last thing that you should worry about."

"Maybe humiliation was a bit too strong a word," Frewen said. "I suppose the word I should use is pride. I have too much pride to quit now."

"Moreton, I'm sure you are familiar with the saying: 'Pride goeth before a fall.' "

"More specifically, Proverbs sixteen, verse eighteen, 'Pride goeth before destruction, and a haughty spirit before a fall,' " Frewen said. "Yes, I have considered that, believe me."

"I have to hand it to you, Moreton, to stick it out the way you have."

"I've been lucky to have a friend like you, William," Frewen said. "Not only because I need a reminder of England now and then, but also because you have faced the same hardships I have, and you have stood up to them better. You are not only a friend, you are an inspiration."

Teasdale cleared his throat. "Yes, well, uh, I suppose I had better get back to Thistle-down. I just wanted to come over and let you know that I am thinking about you and the boy. Please feel free to call upon me if there is anything you need."

"Thank you," Frewen said.

Teasdale went back to the ladies, and bowing before each of them, lifted their hands to his lips.

"You are a very brave woman, Lady Churchill," Teasdale said. "I do hope everything turns out well for you."

"Thank you, Sir William."

As Teasdale drove the buggy back to his ranch, he considered what Frewen had told him about Matt Jensen going to Nine Mile Creek in the middle of the night. He had not anticipated anything like that, and he was sure that Logan hadn't, either. This would be a change in plans. Could Logan deal with it?

Surely he could. Jensen was only one man. One man against six.

Teasdale brightened as he thought about that, and he hurried the horse into a trot. He needed to get back to Thistledown to plan the next move after they got rid of Jensen.

CHAPTER TWENTY-SIX

It was a little before nine o'clock in the morning when Matt heard them coming. Lying flat on the rock and sliding back so as not to be seen, he watched them approach.

"Poole, you get up there and keep a lookout. When you see him comin', give us a signal."

The one called Poole started up the side of the bluff and Matt knew that he would be coming to this very rock, so he slipped down from the rock and started down, so that as Poole was climbing up, Matt was climbing down.

"Hey, Greer?" Poole called back.

"Yeah?"

"What's the reward on killin' Jensen?"

"Logan says Teasdale has offered five thousand dollars to anyone who can kill Jensen."

"Does that go for us, too?"

"Sure, I don't see why not."

"Ha! And what do we get from him for each cow we steal? Five dollars? We'd have to steal a thousand cows to make that kind of money. He must really want him dead."

"Yeah. So tell me, are we goin' to shoot the son of a bitch here? Or are we goin' take him back to the cabin?"

"Logan wants us to bring him back to the cabin," Greer said.

"Yeah, you know why he wants us to bring him back. That's because if we take him into Logan before we kill him, it would be a six-way split. But if we kill him here, it will only be a three-way split."

"You want Logan mad at you, do you? I don't know about you, but Logan ain't the kind of man I want to cross. He said bring him back to the cabin, and that's just exactly what we're goin' to do."

"Hey, Poole," Bragg called up. "Do you see him comin'?"

"Nah," Poole shouted back. "I don't see nothin'."

"Hell, if he's goin' to get here at ten o'clock, you ought to see him by now. No doubt he'll be followin' the river. Look again."

"I did look again," Poole said. "I ain't seen 'im."

"Damn," Greer said in a conversational voice to Bragg. "What if he don't come?"

"I don't know. We'll kill the boy, I reckon."

"Yeah, I guess so. You'd think he would come, though."

"Really? Think about this. He has to know that if he comes here, he's comin' to get hisself kilt. Now let me ask you. Would you do that? Would you trade your life for the boy's life?"

"Hell no," Greer said. "But Jensen is different."

"Different how?"

"I don't know, different how. Just different. What time is it?"

Bragg took out his pocketwatch and looked at it. "It's ten o'clock," he said.

"And I'm right on time," Matt said, stepping out of the tree line.

"What? What the hell?" Bragg said. "Greer!"

"Yeah, I see him," Greer said.

Matt was standing not more than thirty feet away from Greer and Bragg. And while the two Yellow Kerchief Gang men had their pistols in their holsters, Matt had his gun in his hand, leveled at them.

"Where did you come from?" Greer said.

"It ain't a question of where, it's a question of when," Bragg said. "You didn't just get here, did you?"

"Your friend is smarter than he looks," Matt said. "I got here early. Very early. Call Poole down."

"Poole?" Greer called.

"Yeah?" Poole's voice floated back down.

"Come down here."

"What for? I ain't seen nothing yet."

"He's already here," Greer said.

"What? What do you mean?"

"I mean he is already here, standing right in front of us. Come on down."

Matt moved a bit deeper into the tree line and watched as Poole stepped out to the edge of the flat rock where Matt had spent the last several hours. Poole had his pistol in his hand, and he was looking down toward Greer and Bragg.

"What do you mean he's standing in front of you? I don't see him," Poole said.

Matt stepped out of the tree line so Poole could see him. "I'm right here," Matt said. "Why don't you come on down and join the party?"

"The hell I will!" Poole said. Raising his pistol he aimed and fired at Matt. The bullet clipped a few pine needles off a branch that was but an inch away from Matt.

When he saw that Poole was about to shoot at him, Matt raised his own pistol and fired simultaneously. Matt saw the puff of dust and a little mist of blood where his bullet hit the middle of Poole's chest. Poole dropped his pistol, staggered a few steps forward, then pitched off the rock, doing a half turn on the way down so that he landed flat on his back.

Bragg made the calculation that with Matt's attention diverted by Poole, he wouldn't be able to respond quickly enough if he drew on him. The calculation was wrong. Even as he was drawing his gun, Matt turned toward him with his pistol blazing.

If Greer had given a thought to drawing on Matt, he abandoned it quickly and put his arms up in the air.

"I ain't goin' for my gun! I ain't goin' for my gun!" he shouted.

Having heard the shooting, Logan, Poindexter, and Clayton came out of the cabin. Logan and Poindexter had pistols in their hands, Clayton was holding a double-barrel shotgun.

"What the hell was that shootin' about?" Logan asked. "I told them I wanted them to bring him here."

"Logan, look!" Poindexter said. "Someone is comin' up the path."

"There's only two of 'em," Logan said. "Wait, that's Greer. Ha! Lookie there, boys! Greer's got the drop on 'im! Good man, Greer, good man!" Logan shouted.

As the two riders approached the house, Matt was riding in front with his hands in the air. Greer was behind him, holding a pistol.

"What happened?" Logan asked. "Where's Poole and Bragg?"

Suddenly Greer turned his horse and bolted.

"Shoot 'im! It's a trick!" Greer shouted. "I ain't got no bullets in this gun!"

Clayton raised his shotgun, but before he could fire, Matt drew his pistol and shot, taking Clayton first because he believed the shotgun presented the most danger.

Before Matt could turn his pistol on Logan and Poindexter, they darted back into the cabin and slammed the door.

"We've got the boy in here!" Logan called. "And if you don't throw down your gun and put your hands up, we're goin' to . . ."

"Logan! Where's the boy?" Matt heard Poindexter shout. "He ain't here!"

"What do you mean he ain't here? We just left him."

Matt smiled. "Good boy, Winnie!" he called. "Wherever you are, just stay there

359

until I tell you to come out."

"You was supposed to watch him!" Matt heard one of them say.

A full-sized man couldn't have done it, and probably not even a small man. But Winnie had gone into the fireplace, then climbed up into the chimney. It had originally been his intention to escape through the chimney, but except for the very base of it, the chimney was much too narrow. Winnie had his feet on one side and his hands on the other, wedged in position and hanging on for dear life.

"What the hell! Where is he?" Logan shouted in anger and frustration.

"How the hell am I supposed to know?" Poindexter replied.

"Logan," Winnie heard Matt call. "Do you remember what you did to four of Frewen's cowboys? Do you remember when you set fire to the shack and burned them out?"

"I don't know what you are talking about!" Logan replied.

"Well, that's too bad," Matt said. "Because I'm about to give you a taste of your own medicine. I'm going to set fire to the cabin. You can either come out, or you can stay in there and burn to death. And frankly, I hope you stay in there."

If Matt Jensen actually did set fire to the cabin, Winnie knew that he would be trapped in here. Should he call out?

No, he decided. Right now Matt Jensen had the advantage over Logan and Poindexter. But if Logan and Poindexter had him, his advantage would be lost. If he surrendered now, he would not be killed in a fire, but Matt Jensen would certainly be killed. And after they killed Matt, Winnie was fairly certain he would be killed as well. On the other hand, Jensen might yet be able to save both of them.

Winnie decided to stay where he was.

Outside the cabin, Matt began gathering up some dead limbs and dry pine needles. When he got them together, he piled them up on the front porch, then struck a match to them. The dry pine needles flamed up as quickly as if they had been soaked in coal oil. The dried wood of the cabin caught easily, and within less than a minute the fire was leaping up to the porch roof.

"You'd better make up your minds pretty quick!" Matt called. "This whole thing will burn down in just a couple of minutes. Come out slow, with no guns and your hands up!"

Suddenly the front door opened and

Logan and Poindexter came out, not slow and unarmed as Matt had demanded, but running, shouting and firing their pistols. Matt took both of them down with two quick shots.

"Winnie!" he called. "Winnie! Are you here, hiding somewhere? It's all right, they're dead!"

Matt heard coughing, and looking toward the front door he saw Winnie running through it, waving his arms to keep the smoke away.

"Winnie!" Matt shouted, and he darted through the flames that were already licking at the front porch, scooped Winnie up, then ran back out into the open area with him.

"Winnie, are you all right? I'm sorry, I didn't know you were in there!"

"I'm all right," Winnie said, coughing a few more times.

Winnie was covered with black soot from head to toe.

"What the hell? Are you sure? How did you get so black?"

"I hid in the chimney of the fireplace," Winnie said.

"Like Santa Claus?" Matt teased.

"Mama has told me that in America Father Christmas comes down the chimney, but I have seen drawings of Santa Claus and

362

from what I saw in the chimney, I don't think that is true."

Matt laughed, then wrapped his arms around Winnie and pulled him to him. That was when he saw Greer raising a rifle, aiming at them.

"Get down!" Matt shouted, shoving Winnie forcefully to the ground. Matt dropped to one knee just as Greer fired, and he heard the bullet snap as it popped just over his head. Matt returned fire and Greer fell back.

A couple of hours later, after stopping at the river to allow Winnie to clean up and also to retrieve his journal, the two of them rode through the front gate of Frewen Castle.

"Winnie!" Jennie screamed in joy, running from the porch with her arms outstretched. "Winnie, oh, thank God you are safe!"

"And thank Mr. Jensen," Winnie said.

CHAPTER TWENTY-SEVEN

Jennie was in the kitchen with Clara and the cook, supervising a very special welcome-home dinner for Winnie: his favorite roast beef with Yorkshire pudding. Winnie was sitting on the front porch with Frewen and Matt. Matt had been invited for the welcome-home dinner.

"I don't know what happened to Tudor Monarch," Matt said. "I didn't see him when we left."

"Well, I wouldn't worry about him," Frewen said. "Horses are pretty smart. He hasn't turned up here, but I expect he has gone back to Thistledown. I'm surprised though, that William hasn't said anything about it."

"Uncle, that reminds me," Winnie said. "I overheard a strange thing while I was being held captive."

"What is that?"

"One of the outlaws, Mr. Poindexter,

made a strange comment. He said, 'You've heard Teasdale talking haven't you? Always so prim and proper.' And he said it in a way that led me to believe that it wasn't just something that had overheard, but something that occurred in an actual conversation with Sir William. And then, after he said that, Mr. Logan struck him in the face. When Mr. Poindexter asked him why he hit him, Mr. Logan said, 'Because you've got a big mouth, Poindexter.'

"Later, Mr. Logan asked me if I had overheard them, and though I had, I pretended as I had not because it seemed important to him that I not have heard. I found that very strange."

"Winnie, what are you suggesting?" Frewen asked. "Are you suggesting that Sir William was in league with Sam Logan? That is impossible. He is my closest friend. He is a fellow Englishman."

"So was Guy Fawkes," Matt said.

"You know of Guy Fawkes?" Frewen said. "I am impressed. But it isn't the same thing."

"I think it is," Matt said. "I wasn't going to say anything yet, but since Winnie brought it up, I'll mention it now. When Greer, Bragg, and Poole arrived to meet me, they were talking about the five thousand dollar reward that was put out on me."

"Yes, well it has been no secret that there was a reward posted for you," Frewen said. "Everyone knows about that."

"Yes, and everyone, including me, assumed that the reward had been posted by Sam Logan. But that isn't true. It was posted by William Teasdale."

"Oh, my God," Frewen said. Putting his elbow on his knee, he bent his head forward and pinched the bridge of his nose. "I should have seen this," he said. "William and his repeated offers to buy me out — at much less than the ranch is worth — is all part of the pattern, isn't it?"

"Yes, it is. And I'm glad you understand," Matt said. "I was afraid I might not be able to convince you."

"No, I'm convinced," Frewen said, shaking his head. "And what Winnie said makes sense now, as well. Logan would not have wanted him to overhear something that would implicate William."

"What are you going to do now, Uncle Moreton?" Winnie asked.

"I must confront him," Frewen said. "He must not be allowed to think that he can get away with it."

"There is no need for you to do that," Matt said.

"I don't agree. He must be confronted," Frewen said.

"Oh, I'm not saying he doesn't need to be confronted. I'm just saying you don't need to do it. I'm going to."

Frewen held up his hand. "That isn't necessary, Matt. You stopped the Yellow Kerchief gang, you stopped the rustling. You have fully lived up to your bargain, and earned every cent I paid you."

"This one is for me," Matt said. "William Teasdale put a five thousand dollar reward out for me. I take something like that very personal, so I will be calling on him, personally."

At the side of the house, but back behind the porch where he couldn't be seen, Myron Morrison stood in the shadows, listening to the conversation. When he had heard all he needed to hear, he went to the stable, saddled his horse, and started to ride away.

"Hey, Mr. Morrison, where you going?" Ian called out to him. "If you're going into town, wait a minute and me 'n Johnny will ride in with you."

"I'm not going to town," Morrison said. "I've got something to take care of."

Johnny came out of the bunkhouse then, still wiping away the residue of shaving cream. "Where's Morrison goin'?" he asked.

"I don't know, he just said that he had somethin' to take care of."

"Ah, he ain't no fun anyway," Johnny said. "Ain't it good that Jensen found the boy and brought him back safe?"

"Yeah, but that ain't all he did. He took out the whole Yellow Kerchief gang, all by hisself."

"Damn, you remember when me 'n you tried to stand him up when he was first comin' in?" Johnny asked.

"Yeah," Ian answered. "I'm sure glad we didn't try nothin'."

"We woulda been dumb to try."

"Dumb and dead," Ian said. "But if you recall, Johnny, you had a notion there, didn't you?"

"Yeah," Johnny admitted sheepishly. "I had a notion."

Once he reached Thistledown, Morrison rode through the gate unchallenged. Then, dismounting, he walked up to the front door and pulled the bell cord. Teasdale himself answered the door.

"You took quite a risk, coming here like this, didn't you?" Teasdale asked. "I thought we were going to keep our meetings secret."

"I suppose I did, but it is a risk that needs

to be taken," Morrison said. "We need to talk. I suppose you know that Sam Logan is dead."

"No, I didn't know that," Teasdale responded with a gasp of surprise.

"And he isn't the only one who is dead. Jensen wiped out Logan's entire gang. Every one of them."

"I'll be damned," Teasdale said. "Who is this man? Is there no way to stop him?"

"You had better hope there is," Morrison said.

"Why, what do you mean?"

"He knows about you."

"He knows what about me?"

"He knows everything about you. He knows that you were the one backing Logan. He also knows that you are the one who put the reward out on him."

"Bloody hell," Teasdale said. "How does he know that?"

"He overheard some of Logan's men talking. Now he's coming for you," Morrison said.

"What?" This time Teasdale's gasp was a ragged expression of terror. "What do you mean? Coming where? When?"

"Today."

"I've got to get out of here," Teasdale said.

"No, you don't. That won't do you a bit

of good. He would just come after you."

"My God, my God, what can I do, what can I do?" Teasdale asked, now verging on the edge of raw panic.

"How many cowboys do you have working for you?"

"Twenty-two," Williams said.

"How many of them do you trust? I mean absolutely trust?"

"I — I don't know. I'd have to find out from Reed."

"I'd say no more than ten," Reed said when the same question was put to him.

"Do you know which ten?" Morrison asked.

"Yes, of course."

"Send the others away," Morrison said. "The rest of us will establish a defensive position, and when Jensen shows up, we will take care of him once and for all."

"What about Frewen?" Teasdale asked.

"Without Jensen, Frewen is weak. My guess is, once Jensen is dead, and he knows he is dead, he will be anxious to sell out."

"Good."

"Just don't forget the arrangement we have," Morrison said. "One quarter of his ranch comes to me."

"I made the deal and I'm sticking with

it," Teasdale said. "One quarter to you, and one quarter to Reed."

"You got 'ny ideas about how to set up this defensive position you were talkin' about?" Reed asked.

"I was a major during the war," Teasdale said. "I have set many defensive positions."

"Yeah, well, I was in the war too," Reed said.

"There's a difference," Morrison said.

"What's the difference?"

"My side won."

Before Matt left the bunkhouse, he loaded his rifle, then his pistol, plus three extra cylinders. With seven rounds in his rifle and a total of twenty-four accessible rounds for his pistol, he was ready to take on whatever Teasdale might have ready for him.

As he was tightening the cinch on Spirit, Frewen came out of the house to talk to him.

"Are you sure you want to do this alone?" Frewen asked. "I could ask Mr. Morrison to get some men together to go with you."

"They would just get in the way," Matt said. "And I don't want to get any more of your men killed. You've lost enough."

"That's the truth," Frewen said. "Besides which, I don't know where Mr. Morrison is.

Some of the boys tell me he rode into town, which I think is quite strange. It is not like him to just disappear, especially at a time as critical as this."

"Matt?" Jennie called, coming out onto the front porch. "Matt, where are you going?"

"I need to take care of some business," Matt said.

"Dangerous business?"

Matt swung into the saddle, then looked down at Frewen. Frewen reached up his hand, and Matt took it.

"I would say God go with you," Frewen said. "But I expect this is going to be more of the devil's work than God's."

"I expect so," Matt replied. He touched the brim of his hat and gave a slight head nod to Jennie, then he rode off.

"Oh," Jennie said as Matt rode out through the gate. "I'm afraid he might be killed."

"There will be some killing done," Frewen said. "Of that, I've no doubt. But I have a feeling that Mr. Jensen will come through this just fine."

CHAPTER TWENTY-EIGHT

"I want a lookout posted in the loft of the barn at all times," Morrison said. "And I want another one on top of the barn and the top of the machine shed. Also, get somebody up on top of the silo."

Morrison was standing on the plaza at Thistledown, giving orders to Reed.

"Who the hell are you to be givin' the orders here?" Reed asked. "I'm foreman of this ranch."

"And I own it," Teasdale said. "You will do what Mr. Morrison says."

"All right, all right," Reed said. He looked at Teasdale. "Just so long as you don't back out on our deal after this is all over."

"I assure you, once this is all over, all obligations and commitments I have made will be satisfied. Now in the meantime, we need to defend against this man Jensen. So please do whatever Mr. Morrison tells you to do."

"What about the rifle pits? How are they coming?" Morrison asked.

"Why are you doin' all this, anyhow?" Reed asked. "We ain't gettin' ready to fight off no army."

"Oh but we are, friend, believe me we are," Morrison said. "Matt Jensen is a one-man army."

"You act like you are afraid of him," Reed said.

"I *am* afraid of him. You would be too, if you had any sense. Look at the people you've sent against him. Kyle Houston? He was supposed to be faster than lightning. Carlos Silva? He could kill a man from a mile distant, they say. Jake Scarns? How far did he get? They had their try at him, but he killed all three of them. And that was before he killed Sam Logan and every member of the Yellow Kerchief Gang. You're damn right, I'm afraid of him. Now, get busy and do what I told you to do."

"All right, all right," Reed said. "I'll get the lookouts all posted like you said, and I'll get men in the rifle pits. How about a cannon or two and maybe a Gatling gun? Would you like them as well?"

"Damn right, if I thought we had some," Morrison said.

"You keep talking about Jensen like this

and you are going to scare everyone to death," Teasdale said.

"I want everyone to be scared of him," Morrison said.

"How good is he, anyway?"

"You have to ask? Six men have tried to kill him, and all six died."

"Those could have all been flukes," Teasdale said. "I mean you have the ranch laid out like a battlefield in the Franco-Prussian War. Only it isn't the Prussians, it's Matt Jensen. He is only one man."

"What's your point?" Morrison asked.

"My point is, when you have a good battle plan, and I think you have laid this out brilliantly; when you have the advantage of surprise, and we certainly have that; and when you have superior numbers and fire power, then it is simply a matter of execution."

"Execution, yeah," Morrison said. "But whose?"

It was mid-afternoon and the sun was midway down in the western sky. The men were suffering from the heat and they slapped at flies and gnats and squinted into the unrelenting glare of bright sunlight as they waited. The longer they waited, the more nervous and irritable they became.

"Where is he?" one of the men asked. "I

thought Morrison said he was comin'."

"Maybe he ain't comin' at all."

"Hell, I'm not going to hang around here all day swattin' flies and waving at gnats for nothin'."

"You ain' doin' it for nothin'. You're gettin' a hundred dollars to hang around here all day. Don't you think that's worth swattin' a few flies?"

"Yeah. And when you think about it, I'd rather swat flies than be gettin' shot at. I don't care if the son of a bitch comes or not."

Matt knew that a long afternoon of waiting would just increase the tension. That was one of the reasons he hadn't actually made his presence known. Right now he was on a hill about two hundred yards away from the big house, and he had been there since just after morning. He knew when it was lunchtime, because from where he was positioned, he could smell meat and potatoes cooking. His stomach growled in protest. All he had to satisfy his own hunger was a piece of jerky and a couple of swallows of water.

After his meager meal, Matt lay flat on his stomach, then looked through his binoculars at the activity below. He had known that he would find Teasdale and Reed and a few of his cowboys here, but he was a little surprised by how many there were.

That isn't what surprised him the most, though. What surprised him the most was seeing Myron Morrison, Frewen's trusted foreman, standing side by side with Teasdale and Reed, pointing to various places on the ranch.

"Why, you traitorous son of a bitch," Matt said under his breath.

Then he smiled. Morrison was pointing out every defensive position to Teasdale, and in so doing, was pointing them out to Matt as well.

Though he was surprised at the number of defenders, he wasn't surprised by the preparations they had made for him. If Morrison laid them out, they had to be good. Matt knew of Morrison's military background.

Matt was able to make a careful survey of every defensive position that had been established. There were four rifle pits just inside the main gate, each pit containing two men, with each man in the pits having an overlapping field of fire. The overlapping field of fire meant that there was no way to approach from the front without coming under fire from more than one of the defenders.

In addition to the rifle pits, Matt picked five more strategic positions. There was a man on the roof of the machine shed, one on top of the barn, and another one in the hayloft. There was also a man on top of the silo.

Morrison and Reed didn't appear to have any specific defensive positions, but were free to move about as needed. Teasdale went back into the house and would probably stay there when the shooting started. He didn't know whether Mrs. Teasdale was in the house or not, but he assumed that she was, and he didn't want to hurt her. Morrison's military acumen was apparent in the way he had deployed the defenses. He could stop an army in its tracks.

Matt smiled. But he wasn't an army, he was one man. And he was pretty sure that one man, sneaking through the cracks, could get through. At least, he was gambling on that.

As the sun dipped lower in the west, Matt decided to try and improve his position. There was another protected spot off to his left, a little ridge line that protruded, like a finger, pointing right at the big house. The end of the finger was a hundred yards closer to the house than he was now, and from there Matt would be able to see more clearly what was going on. But if he was going to do it he would have to do it now, before it got too dark to see. Reaching that vantage point, however, meant he would have to cross an exposed area that was about fifty yards wide.

Matt moved back down off the rock and walked over to his horse. Since he had gotten into position, his horse had enjoyed a fairly relaxed afternoon cropping grass, drinking water, and depositing horse apples. Matt figured Spirit should be well rested now, and that was good, because he was going to call upon him to run the gauntlet.

"You ready, Spirit?" Matt asked, patting the horse on its neck. "I hope so, because when we go, you're going to have to give me all you've got."

Gripping his pistol, Matt put his foot in the stirrup and lifted himself up. But he didn't get in the saddle. Instead, he remained bent over, hidden behind his horse. Once he had his balance and a good hold, he urged the animal across the open area. Spirit broke out into the clearing at a full gallop.

"Here he comes!" someone shouted.

"What do you mean? That's just a horse, there ain't nobody ridin' it!"

"The hell there ain't! There the son of a

bitch is, hangin' on to the other side!" someone else yelled.

Knowing now that he had been spotted, Matt raised up and fired just across the saddle.

The men in the rifle pits, the one on the roof of the machine shed, and the one on top of the silo began shooting, but Spirit was at full gallop, and Matt was mostly out of sight. Also his appearance had been sudden and unexpected, so no one was shooting accurately. Even after Matt had made it all the way across and was completely out of their line of fire, they kept up their shooting until, finally, Morrison shouted at them to stop.

"Stop, stop! What the hell are you shooting at? Cease fire! Quit shooting! You're just wasting ammunition!"

The firing fell silent.

"Where'd he go?"

"Was he hit?"

"Does anyone see him?"

"How about everyone just keep your mouth shut and your eyes open!" Morrison ordered.

Matt was in a good, secure position now. No one could take a shot at him without exposing themselves, and he was close enough to observe everything. He knew he wasn't going to be able to improve his position until after it got dark. But with the sun already a blood-red disk low on the western horizon, darkness wasn't too far away.

Before it was too dark to see, Matt made a careful examination of the big house. Once, he saw Teasdale peering anxiously through the downstairs window.

It was about an hour after dark when Matt got an unexpected break. A few of Teasdale's men who had spent the day searching the range for him were now coming back. Not realizing there were riding into any danger, they continued on into the compound without identifying themselves. The men who were nearest the front gate were already so nervous that they were jumping at every shadow. They had completely forgotten about those who were out on the range and were totally surprised to see a large body of men ride up on them.

"Son of a bitch! Look at that!" one of the men shouted. "What the hell? Nobody said nothin' about Jensen havin' a whole army with him!"

A rifle shot rang out from one of the pits, and it was returned by the approaching horsemen, who thought they were being fired at by Matt Jensen. Their return shot was answered by another and by another still, until soon the entire valley was alive with the lightning of muzzle flashes, and the thunder of rifle and pistol fire.

Matt realized at once what was happening, and he decided to take advantage of the opportunity that had just presented itself. As the guns banged and crashed around him, he sneaked out of his hiding position. He mounted, then rode north for a couple hundred yards, out of the line of fire. He had no intention of getting shot accidentally when none of them had been able to shoot him by design.

From his new position, the thump and rattle of gunfire was much quieter, but still ongoing. Matt looked back toward the battle and could see the flashes of light from each gunshot.

The first thing he had to do was get down to the house unobserved and without risking a stray bullet, and that was easier said than done. As the shooting continued, Matt began to make a wide circle, staying at least a quarter of a mile from the big house until finally he was around behind it. Just as he got into position, the men recognized that they had been shooting at each other, and with curses and shouts, the firing finally stopped.

"How many have been hit?" someone shouted.

"Parker's been kilt!"

"Damn!"

"Smitty is dead too."

A further inventory turned up four killed and two wounded.

"Son of bitch, we done this to ourselves," someone shouted in frustration. "You know damn well Jensen is out there somewhere laughin' his ass off at us."

"Where did he go?" one of those who had been out looking for Matt asked.

"Last time we seen him, he was just to the end of that ridge yonder, but I'll bet you he ain't there no more."

"Then where is he?"

"You want my thinkin'? He left. He seen there was too many of us."

"I wouldn't take no bets on that," another said. "I got me a strong feelin' he's still out there, just waitin' to see more dumb things we can do."

CHAPTER TWENTY-NINE

As the men were shouting at each other, Matt used the noise to cover any sound, and the darkness to cover any visual contact, as he moved through the shadows past the smokehouse where the aroma of the cured meat reminded him that he had eaten nothing but a few pieces of jerky all day. He saw an outside door that led to the cellar. He was sure it would be locked, but when he tried it, he discovered to his surprised satisfaction that he could lift it open.

Matt closed the door behind him, then went down the steep stairway, feeling his way step by step. He had never been in such dark before. He literally could not see his hand when he held it three inches in front of his face. When he reached the bottom, he held his arm out in front of him and began moving it back and forth, using it to feel his way across the dirt floor until he encountered a support post. He took out a match and struck it against the post. In the flare of the match, he saw a stack of candles on a shelf and he got to them, managing to light one just before his match went out.

Now, in the golden bubble of light, he could see, and he made a closer examination of the cellar. He saw several jars of canned food, tools, rope, a furnace, and a coal bin. And he saw a set of steps going up. He used the candle to get him over to the steps, then he blew it out.

Matt moved up the stairs, one at a time, treading softly on each one until he reached the top. This door, too, was unlocked, and Matt opened it. He found himself on a small landing, with four more steps going up in the opposite direction.

When he got to the top, there was a bit of ambient light coming from a room to the left, and improving his position to where he could look inside, he saw Teasdale, Morrison, and Reed together in the parlor. Morrison and Reed were both standing at the window, looking outside. Teasdale was sitting in a big leather armchair.

"I can't believe the dumb bastards shot each other up like that," Reed said.

"Why not? Stonewall Jackson was killed by his own men," Morrison replied. "Things like that happen."

"What do we do now?" Reed asked.

"If they don't get so nervous that they start shootin' each other again, we'll just wait out the night. Right now, in the dark, he has the advantage. But when it gets light, he will be exposed, and it'll be our turn again."

"Where do you think he is now?" Reed asked.

"It doesn't matter. We know that he isn't here, and we know that his objective is Teasdale. Right now, we have the upper hand." Morrison turned away from the window, stretched and yawned, then walked over toward a sofa.

"Where are you going? What are you doing?"

"I'm going to take a nap," Morrison said. He looked up at the big grandfather clock. "It's two o'clock. Wake me at four, then you can get a couple hours."

Looking around, Matt saw that he was in a small anteroom that was just off the parlor. He decided that this must be Teasdale's office. There was a closet at the back of the room, and when Matt opened it and checked inside, he was able to determine that it was wide enough that he could move into one end and be completely out of sight. He decided that if Morrison could take a nap, he could, too. He would sleep until morning.

Matt always did have an internal clock. He could tell himself what time he wanted to awaken and do so within two or three minutes of that time. He opened his eyes just before the clock chimed six. He could see a thin line of light coming under the closet door. Moving to the door, he stood there for a moment listening, then slowly and quietly opened it and stepped out into Teasdale's office.

It was full daylight outside.

Matt retraced the steps to the parlor. Reed was asleep on the sofa, Teasdale was asleep in the big leather chair, and Morrison was looking through the window.

"Morrison, you should be ashamed of yourself," Matt said.

"What the hell!" Morrison shouted spinning around. Morrison's pistol was in his holster. He saw that Matt's gun was in his hand. "Where did you come from?"

"What is it? What is going on?" Teasdale asked, waking up groggily. Seeing Matt Jensen standing in his parlor, gun in hand, shocked him almost into insensibility.

"How? How did you get through everyone?" Teasdale asked.

"It was easy," Matt said. "While they were shooting each other, I just came on into your house. I spent the night in your office. That is a very nice office. You had a very good thing going here, Teasdale. It's a shame you couldn't have been satisfied with what you had. You had to try and break Mr. Frewen by sending Logan and his outlaws out to steal his cattle."

"I didn't do that," Teasdale said.

"Don't lie to me, Teasdale," Matt said with an irritable tone to his voice. "I don't like it when people lie to me. I know damn well you have been working with Logan, and I have his journal to prove it."

"What? What are you talking about? What journal?"

"Ahh, I see you didn't know about his journal, did you? He wrote it all down, everything, dates, how many cattle he stole, how much money you gave him for each head. What was it? Five dollars a head, I think his journal says."

Matt was running a bluff. There was no journal; he was merely using the information he had overheard in the conversation between Pool, Greer, and Bragg.

"What fool would keep a journal like that?" Teasdale asked in anger, and Matt knew that his bluff had worked.

"What I don't understand is how you could do something like that to a fellow countryman — someone who is supposed to be your friend," Matt said.

"Frewen is an incompetent idiot," Teasdale replied with a scoff. "He has lost thousands and thousands of dollars for his investors. Once they find out what I have done, they will thank me."

"And will they thank you for murdering so many of Mr. Frewen's men? How many was it? Six?"

"I had nothing to do with anyone getting killed," Teasdale said.

"What about Kyle Houston? Carlos Silva? Jake Scarnes? What about Carter, Hodge, and Decker? Did you have nothing to do with them being killed?"

"What are you talking about? You killed those men!" Teasdale said.

"Because you offered them money to kill me. You are the one who set it in motion, Teasdale."

"You can't hold me responsible for that."

"I can, and I do. By my count, Teasdale, no fewer than twenty-two men have died because of your greed and ambition. And that isn't counting how many were killed last night when your own men started shooting at each other. You are a mass murderer, Teasdale. You have killed more men that Billy the Kid."

"You — you are crazy!" Teasdale said. "No court will believe that!"

"No court will believe it? No court? You don't understand, do you? I *am* the court. I am the prosecutor, I am the jury, I am the judge, and I am the executioner. I find you guilty as charged, and I sentence you to death."

Matt cocked his pistol, raised it, and aimed it at Teasdale's head.

"No! God no!" Teasdale cried. He dropped down to his knees and held his hands up as if praying. "I beg of you. Don't kill me! Don't kill me! I didn't know so many people were going to be killed. I thought Frewen would give up and go home."

"William!" a woman's voice said. Margaret Teasdale had just appeared in the door that opened onto the hall from the parlor. "You did that? You are the cause of all those men being killed? You are the cause of Moreton Frewen's troubles?"

"You don't understand, Margaret," Teasdale said. "I did it for you. I did it all for you."

"For me? You did it for me? How *dare* you say that?" Margaret said. "Clara is the best friend I have in this world. How can I ever face her again?"

"Stand up, Teasdale," Matt said.

"No, please, no."

"Stand up, William! Stand up and face him like a man, for God's sake!" Margaret said.

Teasdale got up, and when he did, it was obvious to all in the room that he had wet his pants. He began shaking uncontrollably.

Matt eased the hammer down, then lowered his pistol. "The killing ends now," he said. "How many men do you have outside?"

"I had seventeen, counting the men who were out on the range looking for you. But four were killed, last night, and five were wounded. There are eight left."

"Reed, go outside and call them in. I want them disarmed and standing out front. All eight of them."

Reed left to carry out Matt's instructions. Teasdale walked over to the wall, then leaned against it, shaking and whimpering.

"What happens to me?" Morrison asked.

"You are the biggest disappointment of all, Morrison," Matt said. "Frewen trusted you completely. The boy looked up to you. All of your men respected you. Benedict Arnold has nothing on you."

Morrison looked down in shame.

"Don't ever show your face at the ranch again. Leave, now."

"I've got some things back at the ranch, I'll have to go back . . ."

"No. No going back. Leave now."

"Come, Teasdale," Matt said, motioning toward the front door with his pistol. When they stepped out onto the porch, Reed and the eight remaining men had gathered out front. Reed saw Morrison mounting his horse.

"Hey, Morrison, where are you going?" Reed called.

Morrison didn't reply. Instead, he urged his horse into a rapid trot through the gate and up the road, riding quickly away from Thistledown.

"Men," Matt said. "There is no job for you here. There is no money for you here. My advice to you is to leave."

"Where are we supposed to go?" one of the men asked.

"I don't care where you go," Matt said. "But I'll tell you this. If I ever see any of you again, I'll shoot you on sight."

The eight men looked at each for a moment, then they broke into a run toward the stable. Less than three minutes later, all of them were mounted, and leaving at a gallop.

"Those men are riding my horses," Teasdale said.

"You don't have any horses," Matt said. "Reed, get the dead and the wounded onto a wagon and get them in town. What I told the men goes for you as well. I don't ever want to see you around here again."

With the business taken care of, Matt motioned for Teasdale to go back inside. Margaret was sitting on a chair in the corner of the room, weeping silently. Teasdale started toward her, but she turned away from him.

"No!" she said. "Stay away from me! You disgust me!"

Matt picked up the phone and called Marshal Drew.

"Marshal? Matt Jensen. Come out to Thistledown, I've got a prisoner for you. That's right, Thistledown. Your prisoner is William Teasdale."

Epilogue

Number 10 Downing Street, London
June 23, 1944

"Mr. Prime Minister?" An RAF colonel said, sticking his head into the cabinet room where Winston Churchill and General Eisenhower were still in conversation. "We have the strike report on the American attack at Peenemünde."

"Yes, yes, let us hear it," Churchill said. "This is where the Boche are launching their bloody buzzbombs," he said to Eisenhower, even though Eisenhower had already been thoroughly briefed.

"Three hundred seventy-seven B-17s bombed the launch site at Peenemünde, the experimental headquarters at Zinnowitz, and the marshalling yards at Straslund. Three B-17s were lost and sixty-four badly damaged. There were two hundred ninety-seven escort fighters, consisting of P-38 Lightnings and p-51 Mustangs. Three of the Mustangs were shot down. The launch pad near *Werke Süd* was a complete loss."

"Thank you, General," Churchill said. "And my prayer for the American boys who carried out the raid," he added to Eisenhower after the RAF colonel left.

Churchill refreshed his drink, then he held up the bottle of Tennessee mash for Eisenhower.

"Recharge your glass, General?"

"No, I'm fine, thank you," Eisenhower said. "I would like to hear the rest of your story, though. What happened to Teasdale and Frewen?"

"Teasdale was tried and found guilty of receiving stolen property. He should have been tried for murder, but they didn't think they could make the case. He didn't serve one day in prison; instead he was deported back to England where he was disgraced and ostracized by his peers. Three years after he returned, his wife found him one morning, slumped over his desk with a bullet in his brain. He committed suicide. Margaret, I am glad to say, remarried, and lived comfortably until she died, about six years ago.

"Frewen drove all his cattle a thousand miles north to Alberta where he sold out. Then, for the next thirty years, he traveled the world, investing in inventions, disinfectants, forests, poets, artists, and gold, silver, and coal mines. He never succeeded at any venture he tried, though he never quite went bankrupt. Late in life, he actually became a member of Parliament, and I am happy to say that I was the first one to welcome him. I loved that old man, despite his faults and foibles."

"And Morrison?"

"Believe it or not, Morrison and I corresponded for a while. And he and Uncle Moreton even reconciled. He was a sheriff's deputy down in Texas the last time I heard from him."

"Reed?"

"Less than six months later, Reed was killed in an aborted bank robbery."

"You don't have to tell me what happened to the boy," Eisenhower said. "I know where he wound up."

Churchill chuckled. "I never heard again from some of the cowboys I met — Jeff Singleton, for example, or Tibby Ware, or any of the others. I'm sure they never thought I would amount to anything — and indeed, whether I have or have not will be for history to decide. But I do wonder, sometimes, if they have ever made the connection between the Prime Minister of

Great Britain and the boy who used to eat 'grub' with them."

"You don't have to tell me anything more about Matt Jensen, either," Eisenhower said. "I have read enough books about that gentleman to know what a stalwart and heroic career he had."

Churchill held up his finger. "General, I have something I would like to give you."

"Oh?"

"I have kept it for lo, these many years. But because it is truly American in origin, by rights, it should belong to an American. And not just any American, but to one who is worthy. Wait here for a moment."

Churchill left the cabinet room for fully a minute while Eisenhower lit a cigarette, wondering what this was all about. When Churchill returned, he was holding a small silver box.

"This is for you," he said, handing the box to Eisenhower.

Eisenhower looked at the box in curiosity.

"Not the box — what is inside," Churchill said.

Eisenhower opened the box and saw inside a single bullet. He removed the bullet, then held it out to look at it, his curiosity still not satisfied.

"It is a bullet," Eisenhower said.

Churchill chuckled. "Yes. But not just any bullet. This, my dear General, is a forty-four caliber bullet that Matt Jensen personally removed from the cylinder of his pistol. He gave it to me as a keepsake. But now, on behalf of a grateful nation for what you have done for us, I take tremendous pleasure in giving to you."

"Mr. Prime Minister, I don't know what to say," Eisenhower said. "I appreciate this, very much."

"I thought you might," Churchill said. "Us 'cowboys' are simpatico that way. Oh, there is one way I would let you get rid of it, though," he added.

"How is that?"

"If you could find a Colt .44 pistol and use it to personally put a bullet in Hitler's head."

Churchill laughed, and Eisenhower laughed with him.

In the car on the way back to 20 Grosvenor Square, Eisenhower opened his hand and looked at the bullet Churchill had given him. The thought that Matt Jensen had personally held this bullet, and now he was holding it, gave him a sense of connection to one of the heroes he had read about.

"Kaye?"

"Yes, General?" his driver replied.

"Next time you order a batch of Westerns for me, see what you can find about Matt Jensen."

ABOUT THE AUTHORS

William W. Johnstone is the *USA Today* and *New York Times* bestselling author of over 220 books, including *The First Mountain Man, The Last Mountain Man, Blood Bond, Eagles, A Town Called Fury, Savage Texas, Matt Jensen: The Last Mountain Man, The Family Jensen, Sidewinders, The Last Gunfighter,* and the stand-alone thrillers *Vengeance Is Mine, Invasion USA, Border War, Remember the Alamo, Jackknife* and *Home Invasion.* Visit his website at www .williamjohnstone.net or by email at dogcia2006@aol.com.

Being the all around assistant, typist, researcher, and fact checker to one of the most popular western authors of all time, **J.A. Johnstone** learned from the master, Uncle William W. Johnstone.

Bill, as he preferred to be called, began tutoring J.A. at an early age. After-school hours were often spent retyping manuscripts or researching his massive American Western History library as well as the more modern wars and conflicts. J.A. worked hard — and learned.

"Every day with Bill was an adventure story in itself. Bill taught me all he could about the art of storytelling and creating believable characters. *'Keep the historical facts accurate,'* he would say. *'Remember the readers, and as your grandfather once told me, I am telling you now: be the best J.A. Johnstone you can be.'* "